THE
Drummer's
HEART

THE Drummer's HEART

NEW YORK TIMES BESTSELLING AUTHOR
PENELOPE WARD

First Edition
Copyright © 2024
By Penelope Ward

This book is a work of fiction. All names, characters, locations, and incidents are products of the author's imagination. Any resemblance to actual persons, things living or dead, locales, or events is entirely coincidental.

Editing: Jessica Royer Ocken
Proofreading and Formatting: Elaine York, Allusion Publishing
www.allusionpublishing.com
Proofreading: Julia Griffis
Cover Photography: © Wander Aguiar Photography
Cover Model: Jerrin Strenge
Cover Design: Letitia Hasser, RBA Designs

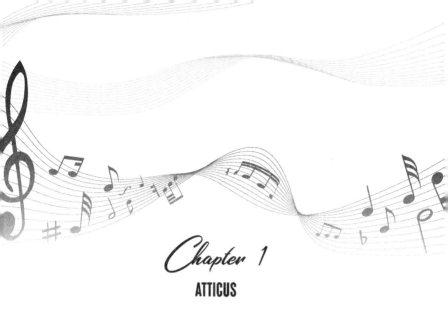

Chapter 1

ATTICUS

I couldn't remember the last time my heart had raced like this. The palpitations had started the moment my ex had lit up my phone earlier, and they had only gotten worse since we'd spoken.

Nicole.

The woman I'd never get over.

The woman whose name my bandmates couldn't even utter—it would set me back for hours.

Nicole had called to say she needed to talk to me about something after she got off work today and wanted me to set aside some time. So I'd abruptly left my friend's house for my hotel. I'd been staying in Shady Hills, Missouri, for a few days, where our band's frontman, Tristan Daltrey, had a second home. As the drummer for Delirious Jones, I often followed my bandmates around even when we weren't working. Tristan and Ronan Barber, our bass player, were pretty much my emotional support animals after the toughest few years of my life. They were my best friends and like brothers to me; but right now, as I waited for this phone call? I needed to be alone. During the call, it was very possible I'd punch a hole in the wall. Didn't want that to happen at Tristan's house in front of everyone.

The numbers on the digital clock next to my hotel-room bed kept changing. With each second, my legs bounced faster as I sat on the edge of the mattress. In the three years since Nicole and I had split, she had never called me. I couldn't help but imagine the worst.

Is she getting married?

Is she pregnant?

The suspense was killing me.

I flinched when the phone finally rang. As my screen lit up, I took a deep breath. Her number was still programmed into my phone as *Wife.*

Wife Calling.

I'd never had the heart to change it.

I answered the call and cleared my throat. "Hey, Nicole."

"Hi." She paused. "It's been a while—well, I mean, other than earlier today."

"Yeah, I know what you mean." I exhaled. "I was surprised to hear from you. Wasn't sure I'd ever hear from you again."

"I get it. Um..." She paused.

"What's going on?"

"It's Mimi."

My stomach sank. *Her grandmother.* "Did something happen?"

"Not yet, but she's not doing well."

Relieved that Mimi was at least still among the living, I let out a long breath. "I'm very sorry to hear that. What specifically is the issue?"

"Well, she's bedbound now, can't do anything for herself anymore. One of her legs is stuck in a weird position, and she can't move it. This all happened very quickly over the past few months."

Guilt came over me. There was no excuse for not having visited Nicole's grandmother these past few years, no matter how tense things had been. She was like *my* grandmother. Who the hell doesn't visit their grandmother for three whole years?

"I'm sorry," I repeated. "That's why we need to talk? To let me know about Mimi?"

"Partially."

"Okay..." I stood from the bed, beginning to pace and pulling on my hair.

"I sort of... I never told Mimi..." Nicole hesitated.

I stopped pacing. "Never told her what?"

"That you and I got a divorce."

"What?" My eyes went wide. "She doesn't know we're not together anymore?"

"I know that's bad. It's just that... She loved you—*loves* you—so much. And I never wanted to disappoint her. I told everyone else in my family not to say anything to her, and they've stuck to their word."

I shook my head in disbelief. "She thinks we're still married?"

"Yes."

I raised my voice. "She hasn't wondered why I haven't come around in three damn years?"

"She thinks your schedule hasn't allowed it. I've been making excuses all this time."

Now I felt even worse. "Who's taking care of her right now?" I scratched my head. "Does she need money?"

"That's not why I'm reaching out," Nicole assured me. "She has plenty of savings for now and round-the-clock home care."

"What made you call me now and not, say, a month ago?" My chest tightened. "Do you think she's close to..." I swallowed. "The end?"

"She reached out and asked if both of us would come stay with her. If ever I was going to tell her the truth about us, now is *not* the time. She's in such a fragile state. I could make another excuse for why you're not around, but I feel guilty. This could be the last chance you have to see her. I decided I needed to put aside my pride and at least ask if—"

"You want me to visit her...with you?"

"Sort of. Her live-in aide is going away for two weeks. Mimi asked if you and I would mind staying during that time—not only to visit her, but to help take care of her."

My mouth dropped open as the reality of this proposal hit me.

"I know it's a lot to ask. I—"

"Let me get this straight. You want me to *pretend* we're still married for two whole weeks while we're taking care of Mimi?"

She sighed. "I know it sounds crazy. You don't have to say yes."

"Sure. Right," I quipped. "I could say no and then live with that guilt for the rest of my life." As much as my head was spinning, I knew my answer. It was a no brainer. "When do you need me there?"

"Really?"

"When do you need me?" I repeated.

"Next week. I know it's short notice."

I paced again. "Well, the timing is kind of good, actually. The band is on break. So I can swing it."

"It means a lot that you're willing to do this for me. Given...everything."

Everything.

There were many things that word encompassed, things that made me sick to my stomach just thinking about them. And now that I was about to face Nicole again, I would also have to face *everything*.

"I'm doing it for her, not for you," I clarified.

Maybe that sounded harsh, but I needed to protect myself. The alternative would be unbearable.

"Understood." She paused. "I'll be arriving in New Jersey a week from today—just need to tie up some loose ends at the salon. Not sure if you can plan to arrive around the same time."

"I'll book something after we get off the phone."

"Depending on the timing, we can say you were traveling in from a show, so you had to meet me there. You know, she'll wonder why we don't arrive together."

"Yeah. What difference does it make what we say, though? The whole thing will be one big lie."

A tense silence settled over the line. "I figured maybe you wouldn't mind seeing your family while you were back in Monksville."

I sighed. "I was actually planning to go back during this break. So this is not the worst thing in the world."

"Not the worst thing in the world, aside from having to spend time with me, right?"

Was that supposed to be funny? Little did Nicole realize that spending time with her brought me just as much excitement as it did dread. And that was *exactly* the problem. This was why I'd never gotten over her. No matter the pain we'd been through, she would always be the one, even if half the time it hurt to think about her.

Rather than respond to her last comment, I simply said, "I'll be there. Anything else?"

"No." She sighed. "Thank you again."

"Yeah," I murmured.

After we hung up, I sat on the bed and put my head in my hands. Two weeks with Nicole, pretending to still be married. It would be a miracle if I survived it.

～

Later that night, there was a knock on my hotel room door.

I opened it to find Ronan looking miffed.

He held up his hands. "What the hell, man?" He brushed past me into my room.

Shit. I'd been so consumed by Nicole's phone call, I'd forgotten to return to Tristan and Emily's for the party they were throwing to celebrate the release of our album, *The Rocker's Muse.* Their backyard barbecue must've been over by now.

"I'm sorry. I just wasn't in the mood to celebrate," I told him.

He flopped onto the bed, causing the mattress to bounce. "Well? What did Nicole want? I've been dying to know. Couldn't stop thinking about it all day."

I explained the phone call.

He blew out a breath. "Well, I'm relieved."

"Why is that?"

"I'd been assuming the worst and thought I was gonna have to keep you from killing someone tonight or stop you from jumping off the nearest bridge."

"What did you think she was going to tell me?" I didn't really want to hear the answer.

"I thought maybe she was getting married—or worse, that she was pregnant with that dude's baby."

The mere thought of that made me sweat. I might punch a hole in the hotel wall after all. I couldn't admit that both of those scenarios had already crossed my mind. "Don't repeat that again," I warned him.

"Come on." He smirked. "You must have been thinking something like that."

I shook my head. "I didn't know what to think. I'd come up with every scenario imaginable going into that phone call. I'm still sick to my damn stomach. Haven't even eaten all day."

"So, how exactly do you *pretend* to still be married to someone you can't even bear to think about because it upsets you so much?"

I stared out the window to the dark parking lot below. "I guess I'm gonna have to put on my acting hat."

It wouldn't be the first time I'd had to *pretend*. After all, for the past few years, I'd done nothing but throw myself into women, pretending to want the rockstar lifestyle just to stay sane. Everyone thought I was a manwhore by nature and that I loved sleeping around, but in reality, I'd never been more miserable, never felt more alone. I'd been pretending to be someone I wasn't for a long time now. I wasn't proud of some of the things I'd done since my divorce. But being someone else was a hell of a lot easier than being Atticus without Nicole.

Ronan grimaced. "She's not gonna bring him around, is she?"

My fists tightened. "Not if she cares about his life..."

Ronan stood and placed his hand on my shoulder. "You need me to come out to Monksville with you?"

"Why would I need that?"

He cracked his knuckles. "For moral support. And for backup, in case we need to kick some ass."

Although it was tempting, I wasn't a freaking baby. I could do this. "I'll be fine."

Ronan looked skeptical. "Well, just say the word, and I'll be on a plane."

I nodded. I knew he meant that. Ronan was the most loyal friend I could ask for. Tristan had my back as well, but now that he had Emily in his life, he didn't have as much time. It had felt like Ronan and me against the world lately, two single jackasses with nothing better to do than to be there for each other.

Ronan's phone rang, interrupting my thoughts. I watched as he answered.

His eyes widened. "No way! Congratulations, man. Holy crap." He covered the phone with his hand and turned to me. "Tristan and Emily are engaged!"

My mouth dropped. "Wow. Congratulations."

I knew Tristan had bought a ring and had been waiting for the perfect moment to propose to his girlfriend. But I wasn't expecting it to happen today.

"You didn't tell us you were gonna do that tonight," Ronan told him. After a few seconds, he turned to me again. "He says he didn't trust us to not act all weird and give it away."

"You're the one who would've messed it up, and you know it," I teased.

Ronan shrugged and returned to the phone. "Okay, maybe I would've gotten a little excited. Better that you didn't say anything."

Ronan kept giving me the play-by-play as he got info from Tristan. "He did it after everyone left the barbecue."

Smiling, I nodded, feeling happy for my friend, even if my own life was in shambles.

As Ronan continued to talk to Tristan, my mind wandered. It felt like forever since I'd experienced the kind of joy Tristan had right now. But it also seemed like just yesterday that I'd put a ring on Nicole's finger, that we'd gotten married and planned a life together. The reminder of everything I'd lost stung. Especially after talking to Nicole today.

Now I'd have to face my past in a way I'd never anticipated. How exactly would one pretend everything was great in the face of the very person who broke your heart? The person whose heart *you* broke? The person who was now dating a guy who used to be your friend—a guy who was now my sworn enemy.

Chapter 2

ATTICUS - PAST

Who. Is. She?

I'd been hanging out in Cassius's basement for two years and had never seen that girl before.

A mysterious girl with long, black hair lay on the old tweed couch, watching us practice. She was officially the most beautiful girl I'd ever seen—with the biggest eyes and the rosiest, full lips.

Cassius had a lot of female friends who came down here to hang out and watch us jam. But *she'd* definitely never come around before. I would've remembered.

After all, this basement was pretty much the main place I hung out. Cassius sang while I was on drums, and Julian played the electric guitar. I guess you could say we'd formed a band, although we didn't have a name or anything.

People were always coming in and out of the basement, listening to us practice, but never had I been stopped in my tracks by any of them, never had I worried about messing up or whether I was performing well. It was rare that anyone or anything could pull my attention away in the middle of a jam session. But not today. This girl was distracting.

When Cassius's dad called him upstairs for something, Julian asked me if I wanted to go for a smoke. I followed him out of the house. He handed me a butt and held the lighter out.

I took a puff. "Who's that girl on the couch?"

"Cassius's cousin."

"What's her name?"

"Nicole, I think."

"How come I've never seen her before?"

"She's hot, right?" Julian blew out some smoke. "Cassius said they just moved back to Monksville. Her father had a job out of state, but now they're back."

I was afraid to ask. "How old is she?"

"You mean, is she eighteen?" He smirked.

At nineteen, I was the oldest of the group. Cassius was eighteen, and Julian sixteen. They were both still in high school while I'd graduated a year ago.

He shrugged. "I actually don't know how old she is. I haven't seen her at school, so maybe that's a good sign?"

That didn't mean anything. There were private high schools, including a prominent all-girls one the next town over that many of the girls from Monksville attended.

I threw the cigarette on the ground and stomped on it. "We should head back inside."

The girl was sitting in the same spot when we returned to the basement. My eyes met hers for the first time. I nodded and smiled. Her cheeks immediately turned pink.

Damn.

Vowing not to be distracted, I did my best to focus on our next set. At one point, she got up and left, and I was actually relieved because I no longer had to give a shit about how I was playing. Ironically, *she* was the distraction causing me to play like crap today.

Not long after she disappeared, though, Julian said he wanted to head home, and Cassius announced that he needed to study. So we ended for the day.

When I got to the top of the basement stairs, I wasn't expecting to see his beautiful cousin sitting at the kitchen counter.

"Hi," she said.

The sound of her gentle voice startled me. She hadn't said anything all day.

"Hi." I swallowed. "You're still here…"

"I am. This is my uncle and aunt's house. Not sure if you knew who I was."

"Julian said you're a cousin?"

"I'm Nicole." She nodded. "Cassius's dad and my mom are siblings."

"Ah." I cleared my throat. "I'm Atticus."

"I know." She smiled. "But it's nice to meet you."

"You, too." I nodded, unsure what to do. I wanted to talk to her, but the whole thing made me nervous. What if Cassius came in and thought I was up to no good?

"You're heading home?" she asked.

"Yup. Everyone bailed on me. Can't exactly jam on my own."

She stepped down off the stool. "I'll walk you out."

Um… "Okay."

When we got to the front of the house, she asked, "Are you walking?"

"Yeah. I don't live too far from here."

"Where do you live?"

"On Maple," I said.

"I live on Chaste. Not far from you."

She started walking, so I followed. *I guess we're walking home together now?*

"You're really good on the drums," she said after a moment.

"Thank you."

"I hope you realize I'm not just saying that. The other guys—they're playing around. But I feel like you could really do something with this. I hope you do."

"Well, thank you. Not a lot of people tell me that. Certainly not my family. Even if they think I'm good, they'd never encourage me to go for it. My parents and sister think it's completely stupid to pursue music seriously. They think it's even stupider that I chose not to go to college."

"Not everyone goes to college." She shrugged.

"I haven't decided what I want to study, other than music. So it kind of felt like a waste of money right out of high school if I didn't have a clear path. Couldn't afford Berklee College of Music, which was the only school I might've wanted to attend."

"Well, college will always be there..."

"That's the way I see it." I sighed. "Anyway, if the music thing doesn't pan out, I'm thinking I might become a plumber. So that would be more vocational school."

She nodded. "They make a really good living. My uncle on my dad's side is a plumber. You should see his house."

"I'm hoping for a future as a musician, though. It would be nice to do what I love for a living. But that's not always possible."

"You have to learn to tune out the naysayers. But also, don't tell others about your dreams. Keep them close to your heart where no one can shit on them."

"That's interesting…"

"My grandmother taught me that. She says there's a lot of power in belief. And when other people get in your head, it feeds the doubt. If you don't tell anyone, that can't happen. They can't ruin it for you."

"That makes a lot of sense. I'll try that. Although, I just told *you* about my dream. Does that jinx me?"

"You got lucky with me." She winked. "Just don't tell anyone else."

This girl gave me a strange feeling—in a good way. Like a ghost or an angel that only I could see, even if I knew she was real. From the moment she entered my line of sight, it felt like she'd been put there for me. That was probably delusional. I didn't understand it, except to say that no one else had ever given me this feeling.

We fell into easy conversation, talking the entire way to my house. All I wanted was to see her again, but I couldn't entertain anything if I didn't know her age.

"Well, this is me," I said as we stopped in front of my house. "Thanks for the walk."

"Yeah. It was nice talking to you." She fidgeted, blushing a little before she walked away.

Just ask, you moron. I called after her. "Hey, I never asked. How old are you?"

She turned. Her face grew redder as she walked backwards a few steps. "Sixteen."

Well, damn.

Talk about dreams getting crushed.

Game over.

Chapter 3

ATTICUS

Mimi's new place was a small, one-level home about ten minutes from the street I grew up on in Monksville, New Jersey. She had moved out of the larger house where she'd raised her family and downsized in the three years since I'd been divorced from Nicole.

While Nicole and her mother were close, Mimi was a second mother to her. She'd helped raise her when her parents had to work. Nicole was an only child, and with her parents now divorced and living out of state, looking out for Mimi was mostly her responsibility. Nicole's mom had moved down to Florida after she met a guy who ran a business that required him to be there half the year. As for Nicole's dad, he lived a couple of hours away in Pennsylvania now. And he and Nicole hadn't been as close since the divorce.

I stood in front of the door, hesitant to knock, trying to mark the last moment of peace before what I knew was going to be two of the toughest weeks of my life. A set of chimes blew in the wind as I continued to linger in front of the little white house with blue shutters.

I finally rapped on the door, my heart beating faster with each second.

When the door opened, Nicole looked even more beautiful than I remembered—probably because I'd tried to *forget* how damn beautiful she was. The sun caught her blue eyes, her black hair even longer now. A breeze blew her signature scent—Egyptian musk—in my direction. I felt instantly feral.

I am not going to survive this.

She forced a smile. "You made it."

"I did."

My eyes stayed locked on hers. In a matter of seconds, my heart was practically jumping out of my chest, my hands itching to pull her close.

She stepped aside, letting me in, and pushed her hair behind her ear. "Thank you again."

"Stop thanking me," I muttered. "Like I told you before, I'm not doing this for you."

My harsh tone surprised even me.

"Of course you're not doing it for me," she whispered. "How could I forget that we hate each other now?"

"I don't hate you," I said.

I needed to be nicer and make more of an effort. My attitude was completely unnecessary. But it was a defense mechanism I couldn't seem to help, a sad attempt to stave off my feelings. Being rude seemed like the only solution right now. Because the opposite would turn me into an emotional mess. Admitting how much I'd missed her would open a can of worms that needed to stay closed if I had any chance of surviving my time here.

"Where's Mimi?"

Nicole pointed to a room off the living room. "She's right in there, but she's sleeping."

I nodded and looked around.

The living room was tiny and held only a small, floral loveseat and a table. Not much room for anything else. The surrounding built-in shelves, though, were full of trinkets and figurines. The walls were covered with framed family photos, one of which featured a little Nicole smiling with her two front teeth missing. Two black pigtails. *My girl.* My heart clenched as I imagined the daughter we'd never have who might've looked just like her.

Then I found a framed photo of Nicole and me, taken on the trip to Las Vegas when we'd eloped. It had been snapped by someone who worked at the little chapel there. I was holding her up, big smiles on both our faces. She'd worn a little white mini-dress she'd purchased that morning, and I had on jeans and a black T-shirt.

Nicole had deserved a real wedding, but we were young and so in love and hadn't wanted to wait. It was months before we'd even told our families we'd gotten married. This was the only wedding picture we had, but I remember Mimi gladly accepting it when we broke the news to her that we'd eloped. In retrospect, I was glad we hadn't waited to get hitched, because I'd always cherish those early years when life was normal. If we *had* waited, my music career might've taken off first, and that would've thwarted everything. At least I'd had the chance to call her my wife before everything went to hell. After our private ceremony in Vegas, we'd gone out for sushi and taken in a Criss Angel show. It was a simple couple of days, but still two of the best ones in my life.

Forcing my eyes away from the photo, I sighed. "This is a small space."

"It's tiny, yeah." She nodded. "After Mimi sold her house, she didn't want to deal with cleaning a big place ever again. And now, of course, she can't clean at all. So it's just as well that there's not much surface area."

I walked over to one of the shelves, lifting a figurine of a cat dipping its paw into a goldfish bowl. "I should've bought Mimi a better place than this."

"She wouldn't have let you."

That was probably true; Mimi had a lot of pride and always took care of herself. She'd worked for many years as a legal secretary and put away nearly every red cent she'd made beyond what she needed to pay her bills.

After rolling my suitcase to a corner of the living room, I heard Mimi call, "Nicole, is he here? I hear talking."

I guess she's awake now. I couldn't help but smile, although I felt ashamed all over again for how long it had been.

Following Nicole, I willed myself to stop staring at her butt. Of course, she had to be wearing cutoff jean shorts that taunted me. *The things I used to do to that ass.* I shut my eyes and swore at myself for letting my mind go there, for even a second. *She's not yours anymore.*

Mimi's eyes lit up when I entered the room. Her voice was hoarse. "Atticus..."

"Mimi," I replied softly.

She reached out her hand. "I can't believe you're finally here."

That broke my heart. There was no fucking excuse. "I'm so sorry I haven't been back to visit you these past few...years."

"It doesn't matter. You're here now."

"I am. And I'm so happy to be."

Mimi had aged quite a bit since the last time I'd seen her. Her gray hair had thinned, and the creases in her face were deeper. All to be expected, but just another sign of how much time had passed.

"How's the music?" she asked.

"It's going well."

Our last album going platinum was a bit more than *well*, but nothing seemed less relevant in this moment than my music career, and I didn't like wasting even a shred of this time focused on it. It had taken up enough of my life. Ruined enough of my life. I felt an equal mix of appreciation and resentment when it came to my sudden stardom, and mostly they canceled each other out, leaving me feeling numb about it.

I rubbed her arm gently. "How is it that you're more beautiful than the last time I saw you?"

"When did you become a liar, dear Atticus?"

"Come on now..." I chuckled.

"I wish I wasn't stuck in this bed. I could make you your favorite chicken and dumplings."

Mmm. She did make some damn good chicken and dumplings back in the day. "Well, how about I make them for *you*, instead?"

She struggled to laugh. "Oh, gosh...now *that's* funny."

I shrugged. "I could at least try."

"Well, Nicole does have the recipe. I gave her all of my recipes, but I don't think she does anything with them." She grinned. "They're somewhere collecting dust under all her hair tools."

"I wish I could cook like you," Nicole said. "But nothing comes out the same, even when I follow your recipe cards, which I actually have taken out, believe it or not. I'm convinced you're holding back some secrets you didn't write down."

Mimi smiled. "You're not able to get it to taste right because you have to cook with *love*. And if you don't, people can tell. That's the secret. But not everyone has to love to cook. I don't think Atticus married you for your cooking." She winked.

"That's for damn sure," I murmured.

Nicole rolled her eyes.

But Mimi was right. I'd married Nicole for her kind soul and, yes, her beauty. I'd married her because I'd never loved anyone like I loved her. It didn't matter that she wasn't the best cook. Well, with the exception of one meal. She made a mean white chicken chili.

Mimi squeezed my hand. "I haven't wanted to eat much lately."

I rubbed my palm over her fingers. "Maybe you're just not eating the right stuff. The woman who works here, what is she feeding you?"

"Louise usually just heats up whatever Meals on Wheels brings. She doesn't cook, either."

"Well, that's not right." I frowned. "You should eat what you crave. What can I get you?"

She cleared her throat. "Well, now that you have me thinking about chicken and dumplings, I wouldn't mind that."

Damn. I'd promised something I might not be able to deliver. But I was determined to try. "Done." I stood, letting go of her hand. "I'm gonna figure out how to make that for you, if it's the last thing I do."

Mimi grinned.

In that moment, I realized that my being here was so much bigger than Nicole and me. Mimi deserved some happiness in her final days, tender loving care that only her family could provide. No matter what happened with Nicole, Mimi *was* family to me. And she *believed* I was still her family. As long as I was here, I needed to act like it.

I turned to Nicole. "I'm gonna head to the market and buy everything we need to make chicken and dumplings. I'll survey the fridge and see what else we need for the week."

Mimi smiled. "You're an absolute sweetheart, Atticus. Always have been. I'm so happy you're here."

"Me, too," I said. "Get some rest. I'll be back soon." As Nicole followed me into the kitchen, I whispered, "Not sure what I was expecting, but it's hard to see her so frail. She seems weaker than I imagined."

"I know. It's hard to watch that happen to someone who was once so vibrant."

I placed my hands on my hips. "Please tell me you know where those recipe cards are."

She nodded. "I keep them in a little box and brought them with me."

"Good thinking."

Nicole went to find the cards while I rummaged through the cupboards. I decided I'd handle being here by throwing myself completely into cooking and catering to Mimi. I didn't need to focus on Nicole at all.

Yet as soon as I had the thought, I felt the warmth of her nearness as she returned to the kitchen. The brush of her long, black hair against my arm sent an unwanted rush of desire through me. *Fuck*. Didn't think I'd be eating my words *this* fast.

Nicole opened the small box of cards and sifted through them until she found the one for chicken and dumplings. There was an asterisk next to the title, and written in cursive were the words *Atticus's favorite*. My chest constricted. I'd missed Mimi. And I'd fucking missed Nicole.

"Thank you for asking me to come here," I muttered, staring down at the recipe card.

She simply nodded, probably too afraid to thank me again, since I'd bitten her head off every other time she tried.

I took a photo of the card and went straight to the grocery store in my rental car, making sure to pull up my black hood to avoid being recognized. The escape from the tension in the house was welcome, but I also needed to avoid getting stuck out here signing a bunch of autographs. Delirious Jones had risen to fame pretty quickly after one of our songs went viral a few years ago. I didn't get recognized quite as much as Tristan did, but I still experienced a fair amount of public interruptions. Ironically, the rise of my career had coincided perfectly with the demise of my marriage. Or maybe that *wasn't* so ironic, since one thing was the direct result of the other.

After I paid for the groceries, my phone rang as I was leaving the market. "'Sup, Ronan?" I asked in greeting.

"You don't sound like you're ready to jump off a bridge, so that's good..."

I put the bags in the trunk. "I'm actually heading back from the supermarket."

"Jesus. When was the last time you went food shopping?"

"I can't remember." I chuckled. "Anyway, what's going on?"

"Nothing. I was just calling to check on you. How's it going?"

"Well, I'm learning pretty quickly that me being here is bigger than my hang-ups with Nicole. It's basically her grandmother's last wish to have this time with us, and I need to be present and not stuck in my fucking head, living in the past. So I'm determined to focus on Mimi."

"God knows you do enough of that living-in-the-past shit already."

"Thanks, asshole. I'm aware of that." I sighed.

"Well, I'm glad things are going okay."

"Thanks. What's new with you?"

"Just chilling out here in L.A. Waiting for you to get back, so I'm not bored as shit. Almost bought another car today because I had nothing better to do. Walked my ass out of there and donated the money instead."

"You don't do well with time off."

"You're right. I'd rather be working, which is messed up." He groaned. "I need a woman."

That was funny. Ronan probably had the most women falling at his feet lately. But he hadn't met anyone he'd deemed worthy of more than one night.

"You're too damn picky, so not sure if that's gonna happen."

24

"Might fly out to New York to meet Tristan and Emily when they land from their trip. They're spending some time out there before coming back to L.A."

Tristan and Emily were currently on a European vacation.

"I'm sure they'll appreciate you third-wheelin' it."

"Well, it's better than me showing up to surprise them in Tuscany, which I also considered."

"I'm glad you held back on that one."

He laughed. "I'll let you get back to playing house with your ex and her grandmother. Call if you need me."

"Will do, brother. Thank you for the check-in."

When I returned to the house with the groceries, Nicole had already cleared off the counter to make space for our attempt at cooking.

For the next hour, she and I worked tirelessly but quietly together in the kitchen, splitting up the different steps to prepare the chicken and dumplings. At one point, our fingers touched as we both reached for the same item. It was the first time I'd touched her in a very long time, and even that little zap of awareness felt like torture.

Then Nicole's phone rang, and she left the room to take the call. She clearly didn't want me listening to her conversation, and I suspected I knew *exactly* who was on the line. Anger ran through me, and I nearly chopped my fucking finger off slicing a piece of chicken.

In her absence, I took over what she'd been doing, cutting out the dumplings, since I'd finished preparing the chicken on my side. But I was probably messing everything up, as I couldn't really pay attention since she'd taken that phone call. My imagination ran wild as I mindlessly went through the motions.

When Nicole returned, she stormed over to me. "What are you doing? That's my job."

"Well, if you'd been paying attention instead of talking to your boyfriend, I wouldn't have had to step in," I said bitterly.

"You don't know who I was talking to," she murmured. She washed her hands before shoving herself in front of me to take over on the task.

I hadn't thought it possible for the mood in this kitchen to get more tense than before, but it had.

When we'd finished preparations and had the meal cooking in the pot, I went to check on Mimi. She was sleeping, so I opted to take an early-evening walk for some much-needed fresh air to clear my head. It had been damn hot in that kitchen.

As I reached the sidewalk, the sun was setting on what had felt like a really long day. It seemed like just yesterday that I'd roamed the streets of this town, filled with so much hope for the future. I'd achieved all the professional success in the world, but I now knew that meant shit if your personal life was in shambles. No amount of public success can ever make you happy.

After returning from my walk, I peeked into Mimi's room and found her awake. Dinner had to be ready by now, too.

I greeted Mimi and went into the kitchen to find Nicole, who was standing by the stove.

"I'm gonna lift her out of bed and bring her to the kitchen for dinner," I said.

She shook her head. "You can't do that."

"What do you mean?"

"When I told you she was bedbound, I meant it. Mimi says it hurts to even sit up in a chair."

My eyes narrowed. "She doesn't get out of bed at all?"

"The physical therapist has tried, but Mimi can't do it."

That made me sad. There was a lot I didn't understand about this situation. "Well, then we'll bring dinner to her."

I wracked my brain for a way to make this a nice dinner in Mimi's bedroom. I eventually found a couple of TV trays in the corner of the living room and set them up next to her bed. Nicole brought in the pot, plates, and utensils, putting everything on trivets on top of the bureau.

"Tell me when it feels comfortable," I told her as I moved her adjustable bed to an upright position.

"That's fine," she finally answered. "You have to feed me like a baby because it hurts to lean forward." Mimi snorted. "Isn't that nice? Funny how we end life the same way we started. Completely helpless."

"It's all good, Mimi." I placed a small towel over her lap. "I've got you."

Nicole prepared a plate and handed it to me. Steam from the hot chicken and sauce rose from the dish. I blew on the food for a while before slowly moving the fork toward Mimi's mouth. "I hope this is edible."

Mimi leaned in as best she could and took a bite. As she chewed, it felt like the longest minute of my life. I really hoped we hadn't fucked this up.

"How is it?" Nicole asked.

Mimi spoke with her mouth full. "You didn't happen to forget salt, did you?"

Nicole and I looked at each other.

I shut my eyes. "Shit!"

"Language, Atticus," Mimi scolded.

I'd been in charge of the spices in the sauce, but I hadn't been able to think straight after Nicole took that phone call. "Sorry, Mimi. I *did* forget the freaking salt."

She licked the corner of her mouth. "It's delicious, otherwise," she said, chewing very slowly.

I wiped sweat from my forehead. "Well, I'm glad you think so."

Nicole went to get a salt shaker, adding some salt to her grandmother's dish.

Mimi managed to finish the entire plate, which brought me great satisfaction.

"On a scale of one to ten, how did we do?" I asked her.

She hesitated. "Seven, not using the salt against you. Take that as a compliment."

I had no idea if she was telling the truth. "Next time I'll strive for ten."

We served ourselves afterward and ate our dinner at Mimi's bedside while she ate a pre-packaged ice cream cone for dessert.

After we'd finished, Nicole and I went to the kitchen and cleaned up in silence.

"Nice going on the salt," she teased. It was the first thing she'd said to me in a while.

"I didn't forget. I just figured you were *salty* enough for both of us today." I flashed her a wicked grin.

Rather than replying, she smiled. And it physically hurt to be on the receiving end of that. I would've preferred that she snap back with an insult. There was nothing more painful than her smile directed at me. And the harsh truth was, for every smile she might give me, I knew she'd shed far more tears as a result of my decisions.

For the rest of our silent clean-up time, I felt the weight of unsaid words on my back. They would likely stay there the entire two weeks. At least for my sake, I hoped so.

After there was nothing left to clean, no further distractions from each other, I turned to Nicole. "I should go put my stuff away."

She wiped her hands on a kitchen towel. "I'm not sure if you noticed, but this house is small. There's only one spare room. Not sure how we should handle that."

My eyes widened as the logistics dawned on me: There wasn't just one spare room—it only had one bed.

Chapter 4
NICOLE

I obviously hadn't thought this situation through when I invited Atticus here. There was literally nowhere for him to sleep. I'd somehow thought the living room would be an option. But I'd underestimated how tiny that loveseat was. His long legs wouldn't fit.

"You can sleep in the bed," I told him. "I'll take the loveseat in the living room."

He laughed. "You might be smaller than me, Nicole, but no adult can comfortably sleep on that thing, not even you."

"Well, what do you suggest, then?" I put my hands on my hips.

He scratched his chin. "I don't know yet. I don't have a solution. I'll sleep on the floor in the living room for tonight, though."

Wait. That won't work. Neither of us could sleep in the living room. "You can't," I countered.

"Why not?"

"The living room is right outside Mimi's bedroom. If she hears one of us out here, don't you think she'll wonder why we aren't sleeping together?"

He grimaced. "I hadn't thought of that. Shit."

"But *you* especially can't sleep in the living room. You'll keep her up with your snoring."

"My snoring is not that bad. I only do it once in a while, mostly when I drink a lot. And I haven't had more than three drinks in one sitting in...years."

Interesting. A three-drink maximum certainly hadn't existed when we were together. "Okay, but when you do snore, it's bad," I told him. "Do you not remember the time you woke up the Mackey's toddler who was sleeping in the apartment next door?"

"She was a light sleeper." He chuckled.

"She told her parents she thought there was a bear in her room."

"Dramatic."

"A grizzly bear..." I laughed.

Atticus laughed, too. I'd forgotten how much I missed the sound of his laughter.

He went to fetch his suitcase and rolled it into the bedroom. "Anyway, I need to take a shower," he said as he unzipped it. "It's been a long day. We'll figure it out."

We'll figure it out wasn't a solution.

Atticus yawned and stretched. His shirt rode up a little, showcasing the ink on his torso, making me all too aware of the gorgeous body I'd craved every day for the years we'd been apart—a body that no longer belonged to me, but to the world.

"Be back," he said.

I managed a nod. *Take all the time you need. So I can breathe.*

After Atticus disappeared down the hall into the bathroom, I sat on the bed and let out a long exhale. It was the first moment of peace I'd had since he'd gone for that walk before dinner. But only a few minutes went by before I yearned for his return. I knew this experience would be difficult, but I'd underestimated this painful longing.

Honestly, how did that man keep getting more handsome with age? When we'd divorced, Atticus was thirty-one. At thirty-four now, he was hotter than ever. He looked younger than his age despite the few gray hairs around his ears that probably only I noticed. Even those were damn sexy. Whenever I found myself thinking this way about him, I promptly reminded myself of all of the women he'd been with since our divorce. I'd heard stories from a friend who worked on a Delirious Jones tour, and there was plenty of other evidence as well. That snapped me back to reality *real* fast—at least for a moment. I had no right to be jealous—we weren't together when any of it happened—yet it still hurt like a motherfucker.

The second Atticus came out of the bathroom, though, I was once again reminded how futile it was to try to forget my attraction to him. White towel hung over his neck, his sculpted chest glistened as beads of water traveled slowly down his torso to his carved V and into the tempting abyss beneath his shorts. The sad fact was, my ex-husband, Atticus Marchetti, would always be my dream man physically. He would always be the one I compared all others to. No amount of time apart from him had changed that.

Atticus ran the towel through his wet hair. "Did you come up with a magical solution to our sleeping issue?"

I stared up at the ceiling to keep from looking at him. "Yes. I plan to disappear into thin air, so we don't have to deal with it at all."

"Wouldn't that be an interesting superpower? I could've used it that night I ran into you and Julian. Except I still would've punched him. Just would've disappeared right when the cops came." He winked.

I really wished he hadn't brought up Julian. But since he did... "It wasn't necessary for you to go after him like that."

He glared. "Trust me, it was."

"You don't see me going after..." I tilted my head. "What's her name...Kylie?" A rush of jealousy shot through me. Of all the women I knew Atticus had been with, she seemed to be a regular in his life—at least from what I could surmise from photos taken whenever he was home in L.A.

"*Riley*," he corrected. "And I wouldn't care if you did go after her. In fact, I'd pop some popcorn and watch that shit."

I rolled my eyes.

He tossed the towel onto a chair in the corner. "But you see..." He walked toward me, causing my skin to prickle. "There are some key differences between the two situations. Riley wasn't your friend at one time, like Julian was to me. She's also not even my girlfriend."

I wasn't going to touch the subject of Julian being one of Atticus's former friends, so I focused on the second part of his statement. "Why do you waste her time, then, if she's not your girlfriend?"

"We have an understanding. She and I hang out when I'm in town, but it's not monogamous."

"Oh, that's right, you're incapable of that now. If I had a nickel for every text someone sent me about your antics on the road." My cheeks burned.

His ears turned red. "Really, Nicole? You wanna go there? I don't know what anything I do as a single man has to do with *us*. Because I *never* cheated on you. And you know it."

I *did* know it. I also knew Atticus had been a good husband and that at one time, we'd been very much in love. That's why it was so hard to believe we'd landed in this place—up until today, we'd been virtual strangers for the past few years. Too much damage had been done, though, to ever go back. As much as I still wanted to jump into his arms at times, I couldn't let my heart go there. I'd been working so hard to try to get over him. But I needed to chill on the guilt pushing. Because the demise of our relationship was just as much my fault as his. We'd burned it down together.

"I'm sorry," I whispered with a knot in my throat. "Let's just go to sleep. It's been a long day."

His eyes seared into mine for a few seconds before he reached for one of the extra pillows on the bed and dropped it on the floor.

"What are you doing?" I asked.

"What does it look like I'm doing? I'm setting up on the floor."

The room consisted of one full-sized bed and a small chair in the corner. The bed took up almost the entire room.

"There's barely enough space for you on the floor."

Atticus ignored my concern. "I found a blanket in the hall closet. I'll be good."

34

A moment later, I realized that if I allowed him to sleep on the floor, it might give him the impression that I couldn't trust myself around him. Wouldn't it be better not to make such a big deal about it? After all, if I could sleep platonically with Atticus, I could do *anything*. Maybe sharing the bed was exactly what I needed to get over him once and for all. Sort of like exposure therapy.

"I think you should sleep in the bed," I blurted before I could think any more.

Atticus shook his head. "I told you. I'm not letting you sleep on the couch."

"That's not what I mean." I paused. "I think we should share the bed."

His eyes widened. "You smoke something while I was in the shower?"

"No." I laughed nervously. "I just think we're two grown adults, and there's no reason we can't lie on the same hump of foam."

"*You* said the word *hump*, not me."

I rolled my eyes. "Can you be serious?"

His smile faded. "Look, if you're cool with that, I am, too. I sure as hell wasn't gonna be the one to suggest it, though."

"I *am* fine with it." I blew a breath up into my hair, wondering if he could sense my nerves.

"Okay, then. Bed sounds good." Atticus took a deep breath and let it out. "Thank you."

"You're welcome."

After an awkward moment of silence, I grabbed my stuff and went to the bathroom to take my own shower. And boy, was it needed. I planned to take my sweet time, hoping I'd get lucky and he'd be asleep when I returned.

The hot water helped calm me at first. But then my nerves kicked in again as the reality of the situation began to register. Two weeks of sleeping in the same bed with Atticus every night but not being able to touch him would be absolute torture.

When I returned to the room, Atticus was already in bed and seemed to be out like a light. From the sound of his breathing, I assumed he was asleep. He'd had an early flight, along with the stress of the situation. I knew this was no easier for him than it was for me.

I slid under the covers next to him, immediately registering the warmth of his body. I lay flat on my back, careful not to veer too close to him. But after a couple of minutes of staring at the ceiling, I couldn't relax. I turned toward him, watching the rise and fall of his breaths as he slept soundly on his stomach. It seemed like just yesterday that this had been my norm, sleeping next to the man I loved. *This* man. But so much was different now. It was easy to pretend for a second, though, that I was back in that place of safety, the memories all too close for comfort, his familiar scent a taunting pull toward nostalgia.

As my body stirred, it was hard to remember why I'd ever thought I could handle sleeping next to him.

∼

Atticus's groggy voice startled me as he entered the kitchen the next morning. "You woke me up last night."

I turned to find his sexy abs staring me in the face. Of course he had to be shirtless, his beautiful hair tousled from sleep. I itched to run my hand through it, to taste his full lips just one more time.

36

I cleared my throat. "Excuse me?"

"You were talking in your sleep again."

My stomach dropped. "What was I saying?"

Atticus smirked. "I'd repeat it, but I don't want to embarrass you."

I did occasionally talk in my sleep, mostly when I was stressed. The problem was, I had no way of knowing whether he was telling the truth. This was a game Atticus used to play with me. There were times when I actually had talked in my sleep; he'd recorded me to prove it. But he'd also occasionally told me I was saying crazy things when I wasn't. And later, he'd admit he'd just been messing with me. I didn't know what to believe now.

"I'm gonna choose to believe you're lying and go on with my day."

"You do that, Nicole." He grinned mischievously. "You do that."

But while Atticus brewed some coffee, an unsettled feeling came over me. I'd had a lot of inappropriate thoughts swirling through my head while watching him sleep last night. It was conceivable that some of those might've come out in my dreams.

Atticus handed me a steaming cup of joe. "Here you go." He winked. "Be careful. It's smoking hot."

Smoking hot. Did I call him that in my sleep? *The mindfuck continues...* "Thank you." I took a sip and realized it was exactly the way I liked my coffee. Medium cream with one sugar. Despite everything, he'd remembered. I wished that fact didn't hurt.

He crossed his arms, his stare incendiary as he watched me drink it. "What's on the agenda today?" he finally asked.

I set my mug on the counter. "When Mimi wakes up, we need to try to get her out of bed and put her in a chair to sit, even for just a little bit."

"Why does she hate sitting so much?"

"It hurts her legs and back, but the PT says she has to get out of bed to prevent bedsores and to improve her circulation. So, we pretty much have to force her."

He nodded. "Whatever it takes, we'll get her sitting."

I was so lucky to have Atticus here with me. Lifting Mimi alone would've been next to impossible.

When he and I wheeled the chair into Mimi's room a little while later, a look of fear crossed her face. "You're not gonna make me sit, are you?"

Atticus leaned down and kissed her forehead. "Afraid so, beautiful. But I promise you don't have to sit for long. I hope you trust that I wouldn't do anything to hurt you."

Those words stung. I could've sworn Atticus had promised *me* the same thing once.

Mimi winced as Atticus lifted her off the bed, as if she were light as a feather. I could never have lifted her myself.

I steadied the wheelchair. "Mimi, hold on to Atticus. You'll be fine. I'm right here to receive you."

He set her down gently in the chair.

She wailed in pain. "Ow!"

"I know it hurts, but you're doing the damn thing, Mimi. I'm proud of you." Atticus grabbed a pillow and placed it behind her back. He turned to me. "Can you grab another pillow from the living room? Just any of the ones on the sofa."

"Sure." I ran to find one.

When I returned with it, he placed it between her legs.

After about a minute, she stopped complaining of pain.

He patted her thigh. "Better?"

Despite the lingering look of pain on my grandmother's face, she nodded.

"How did you know to do that with the pillows?" I asked him.

"I did some googling after you told me we were gonna have her sit. The pillow between her knees helps keep her spine aligned. That eases pressure on the joints. I ordered a foam leg wedge, which should work even better, but it won't be here until tomorrow."

I nodded, impressed that he was able to learn all that so fast this morning. But Atticus always stepped into action when you needed him. He was the person people called when they were in a bind. That take-charge quality was one of the many things I loved about him.

"We have to turn her every few hours in bed, too," he said. "You know that, right?"

"That I did know, yes. Louise explained that before she left."

He smiled. As tense as things were, I once again felt a wave of gratitude for not having to do this alone.

The feeling of appreciation was short-lived, however, when Mimi looked between us and asked, "So...when are you two gonna make me a great-grandma?"

Chapter 5

ATTICUS

It had been yet another damn long day. The woman who was supposed to stop by to bathe Mimi was apparently sick and had to cancel, so Nicole had to handle that task alone while I worked on something for dinner. I'd helped Nicole carry her grandmother to the bathtub before leaving the room so they could do their thing. I'd offered to assist, but Mimi wasn't comfortable with me seeing her naked. I couldn't blame her. But as a result, Nicole also got stuck with having to change her multiple times a day.

Nicole and I had managed to get through today without biting each other's heads off, though, and that felt like a reason to celebrate.

I'd picked up a bottle of red while I was out earlier buying groceries but had forgotten to open it during dinner. That was just as well, since drinking didn't seem to go well with spoon-feeding Mimi.

After we cleaned up supper, I popped open the bottle of wine. "Want a glass?"

"Yeah." Nicole nodded. "I could use it after today."

"Me, too."

I poured her one and walked it over to where she was sitting at the kitchen table.

"Thanks for handling dinner," she said as she took it. "And all your help with Mimi."

"That's what I'm here for." I poured my own glass. "Wanna take these outside?"

"Yeah."

She stood, and we headed out back, taking seats at the table in the yard. For late August, it was a pretty cool evening.

We sat in silence for a bit, sipping our wine and de-compressing. This reminded me of better times, when we'd drink wine together after dinner and talk about our future, our hopes and dreams. This tense moment of quiet was nothing like that, yet it still felt like a gift to be with her.

"How are the guys doing?" she finally asked.

"Tristan and Emily are engaged," was the first thing I thought to say.

"Wow." She smiled, but it seemed strained. "That's... great."

"And Ronan..." I grinned. "Well, Ronan is Ronan."

"Yeah." She chuckled. "Somehow I know what you mean."

I swallowed a larger gulp of wine. "Does *he* know about this? That you're here with me?" I couldn't even utter his name.

Nicole stopped mid-sip and set her glass down. "He does."

"I hope it bothers him," I bit out.

She looked down and shook her head. "It doesn't matter."

"You'd better fucking believe it *doesn't* matter what he thinks of this."

"Can we not talk about that right now?" Her breathing quickened. "We've been doing so well today. I don't want to end up in a fight."

It was too late. Even that quick mention of Julian put me over the edge. "Have we really?" I cocked my head. "Been doing so well? Or have we just been suppressing everything better than we normally do?"

Nicole's face reddened. "You'd rather me talk about what's bothering me? I'm not sure you want that, because then we have to discuss all the women you've slept with since we've been divorced."

Heat rushed through me. So much for the wine calming me down. I straightened. "I have nothing to hide. I've been doing what anyone in my position would, whatever it takes to fucking survive after getting my heart broken." I stared into her eyes. "But I'll tell you one thing, you don't know a single one of those women." My bottom lip trembled. "I wouldn't fuck around with one of your supposed friends."

"No..." Her voice shook. "You'd do worse than that."

My chair skidded against the concrete patio as I got up. "You know what? Fuck this. I'm going out front for a smoke."

I was halfway across the grass when she called after me. "Atticus, wait. Don't."

I turned. "Why?"

"You haven't smoked since you've been here. I can tell because I haven't smelled it on you. And I heard you tell Mimi you've been trying to quit. You've been doing so well. Don't ruin it."

My eyes widened. She'd been keeping track? "Well, I know Mimi doesn't like it. She'd smell it on me, too. So I've been trying not to."

Nicole's eyes glistened. "Please don't smoke any-more."

She looked like she might cry. *What the fuck?* I wouldn't allow myself to speculate as to why she cared so much. But it fucked me up a little to see that she did.

"Okay," I whispered. "I won't."

I returned to the table across from her as we both attempted to recover. The peace didn't last long though. "How come you never responded to even one of my emails?"

She blinked. "Emails?"

"Don't act like you don't know."

Her eyes narrowed. "I *don't* know what you're talking about, Atticus."

"I've sent you dozens of emails over the past few years."

"I never received them." She shook her head. "Where did you send them?"

"To your main personal account—the Nicole Gellar one."

She shook her head again. "I stopped using that account. It kept getting infiltrated by spam. I haven't checked it in years."

"Seriously?"

"Yeah..."

"Well, shit."

"What did they say?"

I had to laugh. What *didn't* they say? Those emails were a series of brain dumps, many written in the middle of the night while I lay on a bunk traveling along a dark highway. It would be impossible to summarize them.

It was probably better that she hadn't read those messages. It wouldn't have changed anything. But at the time, I'd needed to let out some of my feelings and emailing them had seemed like the right choice.

"It doesn't matter what they said." I took another sip of wine and slammed the glass on the table harder than I intended. It did make me feel a bit better to know she hadn't just ignored them, though. I'd always assumed she had.

"I'm sorry if you thought I'd chosen not to answer you," she said softly.

I looked up at the sky for a while. When I turned back to her, my eyes fell to her cleavage, my mouth watering with a desire to taste her soft skin. *My* skin. *My wife.* I would never look at her as anything other than mine, even if that was far from the truth. I remembered the times we'd finished a bottle of wine together and taken our buzz back to the bedroom to fuck each other's brains out—drunk, uninhibited sex at its finest. Something about being angry at her made me want to fuck her so hard right now. That was all my body craved. Sex with Nicole was unlike anything I'd experienced with anyone else. It didn't matter if I lost my inhibitions with her. I could let myself go without worry.

She snapped me out of my trance. "What are you thinking about right now?"

I shook my head. "You don't want to know." I downed the last of my wine.

~

Thank God I was the first to wake up the next morning because my dick was hard as a rock. I'd somehow managed to avoid this situation until now, but it was only a matter of time. Since the first sight of her, my body had felt like it was on fire.

This morning's erection was brought to you by Nicole's supple ass. She'd been sleeping with her back toward me, but the covers had slipped down. Her pajama pants were so thin that they'd formed a wedgie. On anyone else, that wouldn't have done it for me. But on her? Every little thing turned me on, now more than ever since I couldn't have her. I wanted to fuck her so badly it hurt.

She also wasn't wearing underwear. She never did to bed. With each second staring down at her, I grew harder. How I missed morning sex with Nicole—the way I'd kiss down her neck, eventually waking her up. She'd squirm and complain that she wanted to sleep more but would inevitably back her ass up against my cock, initiating sex. I'd be inside her in a matter of seconds. I missed the raw feel of fucking her without a condom. These days I wouldn't dare have sex with anyone bare. That was a recipe for disaster. That was also one of the main reasons I never had more than three drinks. I couldn't risk losing touch with reality—not in the world I currently lived in. But with Nicole? I'd always been able to let myself go. She was the only woman I'd had that experience with. I grew even more turned on just thinking about it, the raw, wet feel of her tight pussy. I looked down to find a damn wet spot on my shorts. *Fuck.* I needed to go take care of myself before she woke up.

I crawled out of bed quietly and tiptoed down the hall. Unfortunately, any time one of us used the bathroom, we ran the risk of waking up Mimi. The layout of this house absolutely sucked.

I'd just taken my dick out to relieve myself when I heard, "Help!"

Shit. I panicked. Without thinking, I turned the water on, grabbing the small plastic cup on the edge of the sink and stupidly dousing my cock in the hopes that by some miracle it would bring down my erection.

"What's wrong?" I panted, running into Mimi's room.

"I'm freezing," she told me. "Please turn off the fan. It kept me up all night. I didn't want to wake you, but then I heard you in the bathroom."

"You scared the shit out of me, Mimi."

"Language, Atticus."

I tried my best to hide my still-semi-hard crotch as I lingered facing the fan before turning it off. Thankfully, my boner went down pretty quickly, but there was nothing I could do about having poured water on myself.

She looked down. "Did you pee your pants?"

"Yeah..." I swallowed. "You scared me so much I pissed myself." *Really?*

"I'm sorry." She laughed.

Of course, then Nicole had to walk in.

Her eyes fell to my crotch. "What the hell?"

"Mimi was yelling for help. Pissed myself."

Her eyes widened. "You need to have better control, Atticus."

You have no idea. I ran a hand through my hair. "I agree."

After I fluffed Mimi's pillow and made sure there wasn't anything else she needed, I joined Nicole in the kitchen.

She clearly hadn't bothered to get dressed this morning, because her nipples were like steel through the material of her shirt. A visual of ripping that shirt off with my teeth threatened to make me hard again.

"How about you go put a bra on, and I'll make coffee?"

"I'll put on a bra if you change those nasty pee pants."

"It's not really piss. I made that up."

"Why would you do that?"

"Because the truth would've been worse."

She narrowed her eyes. "I don't understand."

"You don't need to understand. But what you *can* do is start wearing underwear to bed, please." I leaned in and gritted my teeth. "For fuck's sake, Nicole. Are you trying to kill me?"

Her mouth dropped before she turned and walked away.

While she was out of the room, I prepared her coffee just the way she liked it. I'd nearly forgotten just how much I loved taking care of her. I felt nostalgic for a moment as I poured in just the right amount of sugar. But *taking care of her* wasn't my job anymore. I couldn't help enjoying these little moments of delusion, though, while I still had them. In less than two weeks, we'd be apart again, and I'd go back to my life without her. This time here would seem like a dream.

Nicole emerged again wearing a cute, floral dress that was almost worse than her shirt with no bra. It had a low neckline and her beautiful breasts were practically busting out of it. I had to wonder if she'd selected that outfit to torture me. She'd also sprayed on a fresh burst of Egyptian musk. I licked my lips.

"I'm sorry. I didn't realize my not wearing underwear was that noticeable." She looked down at her chest. "I'll cover up from now on," she said. But the glimmer in her eye told me she had no real intention of accommodating my request.

Okay. She's definitely fucking with me. "You drive me crazy," I growled under my breath.

Suddenly, my attention was diverted to Mimi's room. I heard voices. I narrowed my eyes. "Who the hell is here?"

"I don't know." Nicole walked down to her grandmother's room as I followed.

There was a woman standing there talking to Mimi.

"Hi there." She smiled. "I'm Lori McFadden. I live next door."

"Oh..." Nicole tilted her head. "Hello."

"I hope you don't mind. Adele gave me a key a while back, and I check in on her from time to time. It's good to see you both. She's always talking about her granddaughter and grandson-in-law."

"Aren't they the most beautiful couple you've ever seen?" Mimi beamed.

Nicole looked over at me. I was still fired up by her little dress and wanted an excuse to touch her. I decided to play the part for a moment. "Thank you so much," I said. "It's our pleasure to be here with Mimi." I wrapped my arm around Nicole, bringing her close. She flinched at first but then relaxed her body into mine.

I rubbed my thumb along her waist.

Nicole squirmed and cleared her throat. "I'm sorry if I seemed surprised to see you here, Lori. I didn't realize she'd given anyone a key."

"Only recently. Just in case her worker can't be here or is running late. She has my number if she ever needs me."

Nicole nodded. "Well, I appreciate that so much."

I tightened my grip around her waist and pulled her closer. "*We* appreciate that."

Nicole looked up at me; her face was beet red, and I fucking loved it. I leaned in and kissed her softly on the forehead. Her eyes were still slightly closed when I pulled back to look at her. As much as I wanted to hang on, I let go and put her out of her misery.

Nicole couldn't get away fast enough as she rushed past me through the kitchen and into the bedroom. She leaned against the wall and crossed her arms. "Don't do that again."

My stomach sank. It hurt to hear her say that, even if I *had* crossed the line. "Don't...*what* specifically?"

"Touch me." She lowered her voice. "Don't touch me again like that."

That felt like a knife to the heart. "I thought we were pretending to be married," I whispered. "Married people touch each other."

49

Her chest heaved. "Yeah, well, I can't handle that."

"Your *nipples* can't handle it, at least. They're hard as fucking rocks right now. It's obvious why you don't want me to touch you, Nicole. It isn't that you can't handle it. It's that you like it. And you don't want to like it."

She looked down as her cheeks turned pinker by the second.

My voice was strained. "You tell me not to touch you. And yet you're intentionally trying to torture me. That fucking dress. You wore it on purpose because you knew it made your tits look so damn good. And you wanted me to suffer."

Her gaze lifted to meet mine. "Maybe…"

"You don't think I'm tortured enough? You put that damn dress on and tell me not to touch you?" I leaned in so she could feel what she was doing to me. "You get off on edging me?" As her breathing became heavier, I inched closer. "You don't want me to touch you because it makes you feel things you're trying not to feel? Is that what it is?"

She looked away. "I don't know…"

I placed my hand on her chin, moving her face to look at me again. "You used to beg me to touch you."

She licked her lips, and it made me yearn to do the same, to taste her again.

"For the record, Nicole, I will *never* not be yours to touch. Nor would I be able to pretend for a second that I don't want you to touch *me*. You never have to ask permission." My chest pressed into hers. "You were looking at me our first night here like you *wanted* to touch me. When I came out of the shower, I could see it in your eyes. Desire. You weren't happy about it, but it was there. Tell me I'm wrong."

My dick hardened even more as she licked her lips again. I spoke close to her mouth. "Was that my imagination? I don't think it was. You're forgetting how well I know you. I know you inside and out, every inch of your body. And while someone else may be borrowing you, I think deep down you know who you belong to." We breathed together for a moment. "Other women have borrowed my body since we've been apart, but I have never once, not for one second, not belonged to *you*. You won't admit it, but you feel the same. It's why we're so fucked up. We both want something we can't have anymore. But even if we're not physically together, I'm yours. That's never changed. I'll *always* be yours, Nicole. Whether you like it or not."

I moved back suddenly, forcing myself away before I took things even further. I'd done enough.

She stayed in place as I left the room. I moved some things around in the kitchen without purpose, pretending I was doing something other than ruminating on all the words I'd just recklessly unleashed, even if they were the truth.

Then I sensed her behind me, my body instantly, painfully aware of her presence. I turned to her. "I forgot to mention that I'm gonna need to disappear for an hour once a week."

"Oh yeah?" She arched a brow. "Going to take care of that little *pissing* problem of yours in private?"

"No."

"Sneaking cigarettes?"

I shook my head. "Nope."

"Where are you going for only an hour, then?"

"Actually, I'll be seeing my shrink during that time."

"Oh." Her expression softened. "How long have you been seeing someone?"

"Back when everything went down with us, Doug, the band manager, was worried I wasn't gonna be able to function with our grueling recording and touring schedule. He insisted I talk to someone. Tristan and Ronan see her, too. But I probably need it the most."

"You see her every week?"

"Not always. Only during down times when we have breaks. But I recently asked her to fit me in once a week for the time being." I'd be surprised if Nicole didn't realize *why* I needed more therapy at the present time.

"I see." She nodded. "Well, I'm proud of you for seeking help."

"Thanks," I muttered. *Maybe someday it will help me wrap my head around losing you, although I doubt that.*

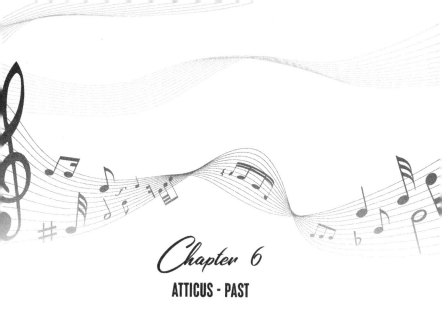

Chapter 6

ATTICUS - PAST

Julian came up behind me after our jam session in Cassius's basement.

"Do you think Nicole would go out with me if I asked her?"

The question felt like a punch to the gut. A rush of heat shot through my body.

Nicole and I had become very friendly over the past year, and I felt protective of her. But she was still only seventeen now, so it couldn't be more than that. I'd be damned if one of my friends moved in on her, though. Once she turned eighteen next year, I was considering telling her how I felt. But that wouldn't be possible if she was with someone else. Over my dead body would it be Julian. That would be worse than anything, having to see them together all the time.

"How would *I* know whether she wants to go out with you?" I finally answered. "Why are you asking me?"

"Because you're my friend, and I want your opinion..." His eyes narrowed. "Why are you so pissy?"

I deflected. "Don't you think Cassius would kill you if you made a move on his cousin?"

"Not sure I care about that. You know Cassius. You think *he* would hesitate to date *my* hot cousin, if I had one? I doubt it."

I crossed my arms. "Well, I don't think it's a good idea."

"Why, though?"

I had no damn answer. At least not one I was willing to admit. "I already told you," I huffed.

"I still might ask her out and see what happens. What do I have to lose? Cassius will get over it."

Angrier by the second, I snarled, "Why the hell did you ask my advice if you're not gonna take it?"

"Damn. What's gotten into you?" He cocked his head. "Wait...*you* like her?"

"No," I snapped. "She's too young for me."

"That's right. You could technically get arrested." He added, "But that doesn't mean you can't like her."

Asshole.

The age of consent here was sixteen, so while I couldn't get arrested, she was still too damn innocent.

"I like her as a friend. That's it."

He rubbed his chin, looking at me skeptically.

Is he testing me right now? Trying to bait me into admitting something? I needed to leave before he could see the truth written all over my face. "I gotta get out of here." I took off for my house.

I spent the rest of the day in a horrible mood. Julian was Nicole's age, and it made total sense that he would like her. He was a pretty decent dude, so I shouldn't have gotten so damn angry. But it pissed me off that he could make a move on her when I couldn't. Age aside, I also doubted I'd be good enough for her. She had plans to go away to college. Nicole had made it clear that she wanted to experience living away from home. She'd be leaving no matter what. And anyway, I didn't even know whether she liked me *that* way.

Later that afternoon, my doorbell rang. My mom had just left for her evening-shift job at a local factory, so I was the only one home. When I answered the door, there was Nicole. I'd been thinking of her a lot today, so it was odd that she'd shown up here. She'd never come to my house before—except for standing outside it the first time we'd taken that walk together. She and I had mostly gotten to know each other over at Cassius's house.

"Hey, you. What are you doing here?" I looked behind me. I hadn't had a chance to pick up the mess in the living room.

Nicole fidgeted. "Is this a bad time?"

"No. Come in." I stepped aside. "What's up?"

She bit her bottom lip. "I came by because I wanted to give you something."

"Okay..."

"I overheard you talking to my cousin the other day about not being able to go to that music workshop in the city because you couldn't afford the fee."

Damn. She heard that? My ears burned.

There was a workshop in Manhattan this summer, run by a retired member of a famous rock band. From what I'd read, they sometimes brought in big names to perform alongside the participants, and to mentor you.

It seemed like a dream come true. I'd applied for a spot with a video of one of my drum solos from the basement. But the cost was nothing I could afford. While I had a job working at a local tire shop, I'd given most of the money I'd made over the past few months to my older sister, Tina, to help with expenses after her husband's death. I wasn't even sure why I'd applied, since I couldn't afford it. Maybe I just wanted to see if I was good enough to get in.

"I know why you don't have money, Atticus, even though you work hard. You've been helping your sister out, and it's not fair that you should miss an opportunity because of your kindness." She handed me a white envelope. "I want you to take this."

Are you kidding me? I peeked inside. It was filled with cash.

"Two-thousand dollars," she said. "That's the admission fee, right?"

Whoa. I could barely breathe right now. "Nicole, this is the sweetest thing anyone has ever tried to do for me. But I absolutely cannot take this."

"Yes, you can," she insisted.

"Where did you even get this kind of money?"

"It's some of the cash I've made babysitting over the years. I've been saving it for nothing in particular. Just a rainy day, I guess. But I don't need anything."

"You're gonna need this cash for school." I put the envelope back in her hands.

She shook her head. "There's a good chance I'm gonna get a scholarship. I probably won't need it."

"You'll always need spending money, even if your tuition is paid."

"Atticus..." She pleaded. "I've told you this before. You're so talented. I don't mean to be cruel to the other guys, but they're just playing around when you all practice together. *You* have real skills on those drums. You can go somewhere with this. It made me so sad to hear you say you'd have to give up this opportunity because you don't have the sign-up fee. You never know. You could make an important connection there." Nicole shook her head. "Anyway, I won't take it back." She shoved the envelope of cash into my hands. "I'm not taking no for an answer."

Then she threw open the door and ran off before I could say anything else. Literally *ran* down the street.

What the heck?

I debated chasing after her, but I was still frozen, in a state of shock. My heart was bursting with an unidentifiable feeling. Gratitude couldn't even begin to describe it. I'd thought this girl was incredible before. But this? I was speechless.

Up in my room, I paced with the envelope in my hands for the next hour. There was no way I could accept this money. I'd done nothing to earn it. That wasn't up for debate. But I was still baffled as to what to say, how to thank her, whether to go to her house now to give it back.

Was it tempting to take it? Sure. But more than anything, it was the meaning behind this that mattered the most. She believed in me. When we'd first met, I wasn't sure if she was just pulling my chain being so complimentary. But we'd gotten to know each other since then. She'd seen me perform countless more times. Nicole's opinion mattered more to me than anyone's.

Finally done deliberating, I grabbed my jacket and hopped into my beat-up car, heading straight to her house.

It was the first time I'd ever visited her there, and I hoped her dad wouldn't want to kill me if he got the wrong idea about me stopping by. But as I was pulling up, I saw another car pulling out. Not just any car—Julian's.

My blood started pumping. There weren't any other cars in the driveway, so it didn't look like her parents were home. She'd been alone with Julian?

After he pulled out of the driveway, Julian took off in the other direction. So he didn't notice me parked outside the house.

For a few minutes, I sat in the car, unsure what I was gonna say to her, especially now that I'd seen him leave.

Forcing myself to get out, I walked up to her front door. This was no longer just about the money. Now I *had to know* what the hell was going on with Julian. As I knocked, I felt my heartbeat accelerate. I had to be careful. I didn't want to come off as jealous, even if that was the damn truth.

After a moment, she opened. "Hey," she said, surprise on her face.

"Can I come in?"

"Sure..."

I looked past her. "Are your parents here?"

"No. They went to church for a holiday bazaar planning meeting. My mom is on the board, and she dragged him along."

I kept nodding. "Did I just see Julian leave?"

"Yeah. He came by."

I tilted my head. "Just a visit or...?"

"Well, yeah."

I swallowed hard. "What did he want?"

Her face turned beet red. "He asked me out, actually."

Clearing my throat, I willed myself to remain calm. "Really..."

"Yeah."

My stomach was in knots. "What did you say?"

"I...told him I'd think about it."

"What's your hesitation?"

She looked down at her feet. "I don't know if I'm into him that way."

That gave me intense satisfaction, though it didn't sound like she'd totally made up her mind. "Well, if you're not sure, you shouldn't sell yourself short."

She lifted her gaze to mine. Her eyes were piercing. For a second, I was tempted to admit that it wasn't just Julian who had feelings for her. *I* liked her, too. But then I remembered the repercussions. I was twenty. She was seventeen and I was pretty sure still a virgin. So I kept my mouth shut.

"What made you stop by?" she asked. "I hope it's not to give back the money."

I pulled the envelope from the inside pocket of my jacket. "I can't take it, Nicole. As much as I would love to attend that workshop, I just can't do it."

She frowned. "I really wish you would."

I stepped closer to her. "You have no idea what you offering it to me has meant. My sister and my parents think I'm crazy for believing I could make a career out of music. You're the first person who has *ever* told me they believed in me."

Nicole placed her hand on my face. Her skin felt so damn soft. I closed my eyes momentarily, yearning to kiss her. But just like I couldn't take that money, I couldn't take *her*. Not *yet*, at least.

"While I won't be accepting your generous gift, you've given me an even *bigger* gift that will stay with me. Thank you for believing I was worth your savings. I'll never forget it." I exhaled. "And mark my words, if I ever do make it big, I'll make sure to repay your act of kindness."

She opened and closed her mouth multiple times like she wanted to say something but thought better of it.

I chose not to say anything else, either. Maybe someday the time would be right to tell her how I felt. Maybe I'd get to a place in my life where I felt like I deserved her. But today was not that day.

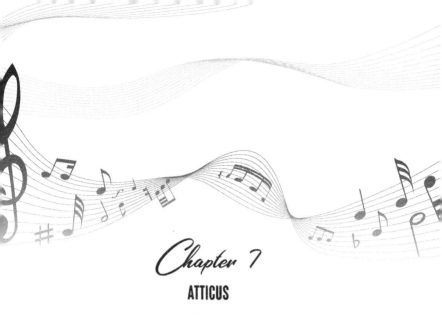

Chapter 7
ATTICUS

As always seemed to happen, Dr. Jensen popped up on the screen before I could get the damn sound to work on my end.

"Can you hear me?" I asked for the third time.

She shook her head no, and her mouth moved as she said something I couldn't make out.

"Shit..." Then my sound suddenly started working. "Can you hear me now?"

"I can now, yes." She nodded. "Hi, Atticus. Long time no see."

"I know. I finally have a chance to think straight with the band on break."

I'd decided to do this session from my car, which was parked outside Mimi's. There was no sense in going somewhere else around town where I might be recognized. I also hadn't told my family I was here in Monksville yet, since I knew I wouldn't have time to see them right away. I planned to visit them after the two weeks with Mimi were over. Then I'd actually have time to hang out with my sister and her kids. Like Nicole's mom, my parents had moved down to Florida, so I wouldn't be seeing them this trip. But there was a chance my sister would find out I was in town if the press got wind of it. The tabloids didn't target me nearly as much as they did Tristan, but occasionally I'd catch someone on my tail when I went for a coffee run back in L.A. It was unlikely anyone was camped out here, though, but you couldn't be too careful.

"I'm glad you scheduled an appointment," Dr. Jensen said. "Why don't you fill me in on what's been happening since we last spoke."

My mind had been in a tailspin lately, and I needed that to end. There was only one way to make that happen. I let out the breath I'd been holding. "I think I'm ready to talk about her." I shut my eyes, feeling immediate regret about committing to something I wasn't sure I could handle.

"You're ready to talk about what happened with you and Nicole, you mean?"

"Well, *ready* is not the best term. It's more like I *need* to talk about it or it's going to kill me. I'll probably never be ready."

"What brought you to this decision?"

"Funny you should ask..." I chuckled. "We're temporarily living together, actually."

Dr. Jensen's eyes went wide. I explained the situation with Mimi and the favor Nicole had asked of me. All Dr. Jensen had known prior to this was that I was divorced, that Nicole was dating a former friend of mine, and that I wasn't willing to talk about any of the things that had led to the demise of our relationship. Needless to say, we could only get so far in therapy without my full participation.

"Well, this news is certainly a surprise."

"Yeah. For me, too," I said.

She scribbled something down. "I think for me to understand the impact Nicole has had on your life, we need to go back to the beginning. Are you willing to do that? It would require reliving some of the happier times, which might be difficult. But I think it would be good for you to feel all of that in order to release any trapped emotions."

This is going to be fucking hard. I rubbed my eyes. "Okay, well, you're gonna have to guide me because I have no clue where to begin."

"Of course. Like I said, we'll start from the beginning. Why don't you tell me how you and Nicole met?"

An image of Nicole lying lazily on the tweed couch in Cassius's basement flashed through my mind—her long, black hair splayed across the sofa, her sweet smile as she watched us practice. Younger and forbidden. I detailed for Dr. Jensen how I'd met Nicole and how we became friends while I waited in the wings for her to turn eighteen, the age at which I'd mentally decided she was no longer too innocent for me.

"She'd usually linger after we were done practicing, and we'd walk home together," I explained. "Sometimes we'd stop halfway and just sit and talk. Nicole and I could talk about anything. I could tell her about my insecurities and not worry about being judged. It really was platonic in the beginning..."

Dr. Jensen smiled. "Sounds like she was the whole package."

"Yeah. On top of everything else, she was the most beautiful girl I'd ever laid eyes on. I also loved that she didn't take shit from anyone and could hang with us guys and handle all our crazy, lewd talk without batting an eyelash. It was like she was one of us, aside from the obvious fact that she was very much female and a knockout."

"And I'm sure you weren't the only one of the guys who had eyes for her…"

"You'd be correct. That was stressful."

She grinned. "So, once you and she started dating, what was that like?"

"It was amazing. I couldn't get enough of her, physically and otherwise. On top of that, my family became like her family, too. Nicole is an only child, so she and my sister became close. I knew early on that Nicole was the one, that I'd ask her to marry me someday. We both wanted the same things out of life—a family, to laugh, to love, and to just…be happy. I really would've been okay with a simple life. I didn't need the fame or the money I have now. I just needed her. Drums weren't my passion. She was." I paused. "But at some point…she started to believe she wasn't enough for me."

Dr. Jensen nodded and wrote something down. "I feel like we're getting a bit ahead of ourselves. Back up and tell me more about Nicole's home life before you and she got together."

"Her parents' marriage didn't end well. Her father cheated on her mom. But Nicole didn't find out about it until she was in her twenties. And I think that had a lot to do with her lack of trust down the line."

"Her grandmother that you're taking care of, is that her mother's mother?"

"Yeah. Needless to say, Mimi's not a big fan of Nicole's dad, even though he was a pretty good father. Just a terrible husband, as we all found out after the fact."

"Were *you* a good husband?"

"I thought I was." I stared out at the trees lining the street. "I loved being a husband."

"Do you think you'll ever get married again?"

"No," I said immediately.

I couldn't fathom a world where I was married to anyone else. Nicole was my wife. She'd always be my wife. It wouldn't be fair to let anyone else believe they had a place that belonged to someone else in perpetuity, even if only in my heart. Even if a bit delusional.

"Tell me more about the early days of your relationship with Nicole, before you were married."

"Well, soon after we started dating, she went away to college while I stayed behind and pursued my music. But we managed to stay together all four years while she was studying at BU. We'd visit each other on weekends when we could. After she graduated with a business degree, she did a one-eighty and decided she actually wanted to be a hairstylist. That was more her passion. She'd attended cosmetology classes during the summers while she was in school and had always dabbled in it on the side, doing hair for friends and family. Despite pressure from her parents to use her business degree differently, I was proud of her for being true to herself. She's really good at it. She rents a chair now at one of the top salons in New York City."

"That's amazing. How old were you guys when you got married?"

"We eloped when I was twenty-five and she was twenty-two. So, we'd been together for four years. Flew to Vegas on a whim."

"Wow. None of your family attended?"

"No, it was just us. But that's what made it perfect."

"What were things like after you got married?"

"Those early years of our marriage were amazing. We settled into a routine and were genuinely happy. Shortly before that, I'd met Tristan and Ronan in an online music forum. It wasn't until about five years after the band got together that Delirious Jones hit it big. That was when things started to go downhill with Nicole."

"She wasn't supportive?"

"She was. She always told me I was destined for success in music. But turns out being a rockstar wife wasn't the life she wanted. After I met Tristan and Ronan, my life changed. We were signed to a label, and things moved very fast. Even in the years before Delirious Jones really rose to fame, I was traveling a lot." I hesitated. "But it was manageable before we went viral. I don't think either of us expected my music career to take off the way it did."

"You became famous overnight..."

"It felt like overnight in some ways, yeah. No one was prepared for it."

"So, would you say your career was what ultimately cost you your marriage?"

"At first, that was the cause. But it wasn't *ultimately* the case." I paused. "It's not why we're not together now."

Dr. Jensen tilted her head. "What's the reason you're not together?"

My chest constricted. "Definitely not ready to go there today."

"Okay. Baby steps. Let's return to the present for a moment." She smiled reassuringly. "What has it been like living with Nicole under the recent circumstances?"

I sighed. "Things are tense, but more than anything? I just feel grateful to have time with her again. I can thank Mimi for that."

"Why do you think she believes her grandmother can't handle the truth about your divorce?"

"I know Mimi would be heartbroken. Her generation didn't believe in divorce. She took Nicole's parents' split really hard, even knowing what Nicole's dad had done. And Mimi really believed in Nicole and me, that what we had was true love and unbreakable. We were her hope for the future. She's an old romantic."

Dr. Jensen smiled. "Mimi is the *only* old romantic in this situation? Sounds to me like you're holding a lot of romantic feelings yourself."

I nodded. "I do have a romantic side. And I'd give anything to be able to love on my wife again." I picked at my callused fingers. "Unfortunately, that's not possible."

"Your *wife*. It's interesting that you still refer to her that way." Dr. Jensen wrote in her notebook again. "Anyway, why have you given up hope?"

I swallowed. "Because some damage is irreparable."

Chapter 8

NICOLE

Somehow I woke with my ass up against Atticus the following morning. I had no idea how long I'd been sleeping like that. But I'd felt his hardness against my backside the moment I opened my eyes. And I'd chosen to stay in this position for a while, allowing his heat to slowly light me on fire. It felt too good to move.

Atticus's breathing was still steady. He remained fast asleep, unaware of his own vulnerability. Only when I forced myself away did he rustle awake. I hopped out of bed, feeling guilty for having stayed up against him for so long.

"What's going on?" he asked groggily.

"You need to stay on your side of the bed," I snapped.

He looked down at himself. "Sorry. I can't be responsible for anything that happens when I'm sleeping."

Of course I knew that. But per usual, I didn't know how to handle my own weakness for the man. "I'm sorry. I know that. I'm just..." *Horny.* And desperate. *Desperately still in love with you.*

He tugged at his hair. "It hasn't been easy for me."

"What specifically?"

"Sleeping next to you." He grimaced. "When you suggested it, you didn't seem to think it was a big deal. But it's been hard for me. I can't just pretend I don't want you every second you're near me. Maybe I *do* need to figure out some other sleeping arrangement."

I gulped, afraid to admit that I'd felt the same.

"I'm sorry if I wake up hard," he said, eyes boring into me. "Or if my body naturally veers to your side of the bed because it remembers how damn good that felt. I'm sorry if I still can't help the way I look at you. I'm sorry if I still think you're the most beautiful woman in the world. I'm sorry if I'm not perfect at this. I'm sorry that being here is harder than I ever fucking imagined, Nicole. Way harder than my fucking dick could ever be." He threw a shirt over his head and pulled on pants before storming out of the room.

My legs felt weak. I was a fraud. It had been hard for me, too. I just wasn't willing to admit it.

When I finally garnered the courage to meet him out in the kitchen, Atticus set his empty coffee mug down in the sink.

"I made you one." He pointed to a mug on the counter. "You might need to heat it up in the microwave."

"Thank you."

He reached for his keys. "I'll be back in a bit."

"Where are you going?"

"Mimi needs a few things from the store. You need anything while I'm out?"

Actually, I did. I'd gotten my period this morning. That might've explained my heightened reaction to his boner earlier. My hormones were going crazy.

2

"Tampons?" I said.

He nodded. "Okay."

"Do you need to know which kind?"

"I remember."

That surprised me. "You do?"

"Yeah. I remember everything." He took a deep breath. "I wish I didn't."

Yeah. Boy, do I get that.

⁓

While Atticus was out at the store, I logged into my old email account. Ever since he'd mentioned emailing me over the years, I'd been debating whether to go in and see if the messages were there.

After a couple of security steps to regain access, I searched his name in my inbox and sure enough, up popped several unread emails from him. After sorting the messages by date, I decided to start with the oldest one, the first he'd sent after our breakup.

Nicole,

I know I'm probably the last person you want to hear from today. But it's your birthday, and I can't let it go by without saying something.

It's the first time you've had a birthday since we stopped talking, and I'm having a hard time with this. I can't tell you how many times today I've felt like I should be doing something—buying flowers, ordering a cake, shopping for jewelry. I now realize those little things were such a privilege. Loving you freely was a privilege and the greatest experience of my life.

What happened doesn't change the fact that I love you. It doesn't change the fact that your birthday will always be one of the most important days of my life because it was the day you came into this world. Not being your husband anymore doesn't change the fact that I love you, but it does change how I'm able to express that love. Sometimes loving someone means letting them go. That's especially the case when you know your presence in their life will only cause them pain.

It hurts.

It hurts so fucking much to not be able to celebrate with you today. But when you told me it would be better for you if we didn't see each other anymore, I took that seriously. You asked me not to call or come by. And I've tried to respect your wishes, which is why I'm writing this email. It's my compromise.

It pains me to think that your smile is dimmer this year because of me. Hurting you so profoundly made me wish I'd never existed. Some days I fantasize about not being here. It would be so much easier. Please don't take that to mean that I would ever hurt myself. I couldn't do that to my family or you. Because I know, after everything, that you still love me, and that if anything ever happened to me, you'd be devastated. So I have to be strong. I still have a lot to live for.

My greatest wish is to see your beautiful smile directed toward me again someday. I'll take it even if we're old and gray, and that's the last thing I see before I leave this Earth.

Sorry this message has taken an ominous turn. I just wanted to wish you a happy birthday. I hope whatever you're doing today, you take time to celebrate yourself and appreciate the wonderful woman you've become, one I'm so proud of.

I'll light a candle in your honor tonight and make a wish that someday you can forgive me for letting you down.

Always lost without you,

Atticus

～

I was out back doing yard work when Atticus returned from the store. I'd heard his car pull into the driveway.

A few minutes later, when I walked through the side door into the kitchen, he was nowhere to be found. But he'd left the bag of tampons on the counter. Except when I opened the bag, it wasn't just tampons inside. He'd also bought my favorite candy: Rocher chocolates and Sour Patch Kids. He knew I craved sugar when I was on my period. The gesture nearly made me cry because it was the nonverbal version of *I love you*. And it didn't take much to make me emotional lately.

I went over to the kitchen sink and splashed water on my face. Reading that email had taken a toll on me and made me immeasurably sad. I wanted to assure him he was most definitely wanted and appreciated in this world. But then I'd have to admit to reading it, which I wasn't prepared to do.

After I turned the faucet off, I could hear Atticus talking to Mimi. When I walked into her room, my jaw dropped: Atticus was painting Mimi's nails.

"What the heck is going on in here?" I couldn't help but grin.

"She told me this morning she was feeling frumpy. So I asked what I could do. She gave me the name of the nail color she wanted and asked me to do her nails."

A smile bloomed on my face. "I could've done that, Mimi."

She turned to me. "I think Atticus does a pretty good job, don't you?"

He chuckled. "I paint my nails all the time."

"That's true. I forgot." He often wore them black when performing. It went with the whole dark-drummer vibe.

He blew on Mimi's fingers. "And the women at the store got a kick out of helping me look for the *Lollipop Kisses* color."

I wanted to hug him. Not only because of what I'd read in that email, but because of how damn sweet he was being to my grandmother right now. Seeing Mimi so happy made my heart melt.

Since everything seemed under control, I went to the kitchen to make myself something to eat. Except once again all I could think about was Atticus, and I lost my ability to think straight. Forgetting about a meal, I ended up eating half the candy he'd bought me instead.

When I went to check on them a second time, the sight before me was even crazier than the last. Atticus had set up what looked like a mini, inflatable pool behind Mimi's head at the back of her bed.

I covered my mouth. "Where did you get that?"

"Medical supply store. It's a portable washing basin for her hair. She wanted a blue rinse put in. It's got this storage bag for the water to rinse her."

"I didn't know we were doing her hair today. I would've helped."

"It's spa day. Get with the program, Nicole," he teased. "I've got it under control."

Mimi had her eyes closed, like she was in ecstasy. Atticus began to massage her head and rub something into her hair. He looked up at me for a moment and winked before returning his attention to the task at hand.

If I'd thought my heart was full before, it was ready to burst now. My eyes welled up, and I escaped to the bathroom to let my tears fall. It had been a long time since I'd cried over Atticus. It was kind of odd that what finally did it was the sight of him coloring my grandmother's hair. But emotions were funny and unpredictable. I really needed my hormones to calm down.

The doorbell rang, and I quickly wiped my eyes.

"Can you get that?" Atticus hollered from Mimi's room.

"On it!" I yelled as I dabbed my face with toilet paper.

When I opened the door, I was surprised to see Atticus's bandmates: Tristan Daltrey and his fiancée, Emily, along with Ronan Barber.

"Hey." I swiped a hand down the length of my hair, praying my eyes weren't swollen or red.

"Hey, Nicole." Tristan smiled. "Long time no see."

"I know." I smiled over at Emily, whom I'd never met before. "What brings you guys to town?"

"Sorry for the surprise," Tristan said. "But Atticus wasn't answering his phone. Emily and I just got back from Europe. Landed in New York overnight. Figured we'd stay a week in the city before heading back to L.A. Since you're only a couple of hours away, we thought we'd also spend a night here in Monksville—come say hi to Atticus and check out this side of New Jersey."

I turned to Ronan. "You were with them in Europe, too?"

He shook his head. "Nah. I was bored back in L.A., so I flew in to meet up with them in the city."

"I thought I heard Ronan's big trap." Atticus's voice came from behind me. "What the hell are you guys doing here?"

Tristan's eyes widened. "What the hell is all over your hands?"

"It's blue rinse. Probably should've worn gloves. I was doing Mimi's hair."

"Damn. Can you try that on me next?" Ronan laughed. "I could use my streaks touched up. Was thinking of going blue at some point anyway."

Tristan looked over at me and muttered, "Sadly, he's serious."

Our surprise guests stepped into the house and followed us to Mimi's room.

"Mimi, we have visitors," I announced.

"Do you remember Ronan and Tristan from the band?" Atticus asked.

"How could I forget...such handsome boys." My grandmother turned to Emily. "And who is this lovely lady?"

"I'm Emily Applewood, Tristan's fiancée. It's so nice to meet you."

"You as well, dear." Mimi then turned to Ronan. "Will you do me a favor?"

"Of course." He grinned.

She pointed over at Atticus and me. "Will you tell these two to get the heck out of here and have some fun for one night? They've been fawning over me for days, and I can't get rid of them."

"I don't want to leave you alone," I told her.

"I'll be fine for a couple of hours. Louise is never here twenty-four-seven, you know. She pops in and out all day. So I'm used to being alone at times. I have a phone in case of an emergency, and you met my neighbor. She's around, too. Not like I can get up and fall or anything. I can't move, so I ain't going anywhere."

Atticus bumped my shoulder with his. "It'll be good for you to get out. I think Mimi will be fine for a little bit. We won't go far."

"I've got a better idea." Ronan lifted his index finger. "Why don't *I* stay with Mimi so you both can relax for a couple of hours and not have to worry at all?"

He flashed me a serious look to let me know he wasn't kidding. I had such cabin fever. I needed to take him up on his offer.

"Well..." Mimi said. "I've never been one to turn down the companionship of a handsome young man."

"Nor I the companionship of a lovely MILF such as yourself."

Mimi squinted. "Milk?"

Everyone broke out into laughter.

Before Ronan could explain, I intercepted. "That would be really nice if you could stay with her."

Ronan placed his hand on her shoulder. "It's a done deal, then."

"Take them to Laurentano's," Mimi told Atticus.

"What's that?" Emily asked.

"A really good Italian restaurant here in town," I explained.

"Tell them Adele sent you and see how you're treated," Mimi added.

"They love my grandmother over there." I turned to Ronan. "You sure you're good with staying here?"

"Of course! I don't have a grandma. Lost both of mine. So this will be fun."

I sucked in a breath. "Okay, then." *I hope I don't regret this.*

Chapter 9

NICOLE

It felt so good to be out of the house and enjoying a cocktail. My emotions had calmed down considerably from earlier in the day.

One cool thing was that we could check in on Mimi remotely via a camera set up in her room. Louise had used it to gauge when she needed to return to assist Mimi, and I was able to access it via an app on my phone. Ronan had no idea he was being watched as he played guitar for my grandmother. Mimi had a huge smile on her face while he entertained her.

We'd stopped at a bar before heading to Laurentano's, since we weren't able to get a table for dinner until eight. Skip's was a hole in the wall but a popular speakeasy in our little town.

"I'm surprised Atticus and Tristan haven't been recognized yet," I said to Emily as we waited for them to come back from fetching us a second round of drinks.

"True." She nodded. "Normally at least one person would've asked for a photo by now. But you know, there's something about a small town. People don't seem to care as much about celebrities as they do in the bigger cities. They're nowhere near each other, but Monksville sort of reminds me of Shady Hills in Missouri, where I'm from. Same kind of vibe."

She was about six years younger than me, but Emily seemed very mature.

She looked over her shoulder at the guys before turning back to me. "So how are you doing *really*? This living situation can't be easy on you."

I swirled the last of the drink around in my glass. "I'm hanging in there. It's been a bit stressful, as you might imagine. But there are some beautiful moments to make up for the tense ones."

I thought about Atticus doing my grandmother's nails today and coloring her hair. Definitely something I would never forget.

Emily once again looked over at the bar. "I don't have a lot of time before the guys come back, so I hope you don't mind me being frank with you."

I licked my lips. "Okay..."

"For so long, you were like this mythical creature to me, Nicole. Every time anyone mentioned your name, the room would go quiet. I've been so curious about you. And it took a while for anyone to even explain to me what happened between you and Atticus."

My heart began to race. "You know...everything?"

She nodded. "I do. And I just want to say..." Emily exhaled. "Despite all that's happened, Atticus is still hopelessly in love with you. I know you don't know me well, and I have no right to interfere, but it's one thing I know for sure about him."

She didn't need to convince me of that. I felt it. Lack of love had never been the reason Atticus and I were apart.

"I'm not sure what to say to that..."

"You don't need to say anything. I just needed to get that off my chest." She sighed. "It's really great to meet someone I've heard so much about. And no matter what happens, I hope you end up happy. You deserve it."

I liked this girl. She seemed genuine. Good that Tristan had found someone like her to spend his life with. "Thank you for being so open and for trying to get to know me, though I tend to put up a pretty big wall. Thank you, too, for being honest about what you know rather than tip-toeing around me—I hate that."

"You're just as stunning as I imagined." She smiled. "I often wondered how beautiful a woman had to be to keep a man like Atticus so transfixed."

"If you're trying to be my friend...it's working." I laughed.

"Good." She giggled.

The guys returned, bringing our conversation to an end. Atticus placed a cocktail next to me, along with an extra cup filled with cherries.

"I got you maraschinos." His eyes lingered on mine.

"Thank you."

I always loved to snack on those when I drank. Atticus might not be perfect, but he was thoughtful.

Tristan looked between us. "Can I say something?"

"Depends." Atticus sipped his beer.

"It warms my heart to see you two getting along. Like, more than anything has warmed my cold heart in a really long fucking time."

"You should be a fly on the wall back at the house if you think we're getting along," Atticus quipped. He winked at me.

"There's been no shortage of arguments." I laughed. "Except we have to whisper-fight, so poor Mimi doesn't figure anything out."

"Yeah, no shit," Atticus agreed. "I've never whispered so much in my life."

"Well, from my perspective, to have him go from not being able to say your name, to hanging out with you and having a couple of drinks?" Tristan placed his hand on Atticus' shoulder. "I'm proud of you both. That's all I'm saying."

I popped a cherry into my mouth. "It's the magic of Mimi, I guess."

Emily grinned. "Your grandmother is so sweet."

"Speaking of which, let's check in on Ronan." Atticus took out his phone and pulled up the camera app. He faced the screen toward us.

Mimi was flapping her arms like a chicken from her bed. Ronan was doing the same, except standing and spinning around from time to time.

I covered my mouth. "What the hell?"

Atticus shook his head. "I'm not even gonna ask what the fuck is going on there."

"Ronan is involved." Tristan laughed. "That should tell you everything you need to know."

Atticus and I shared a smile. Going out tonight had been a good idea. It felt good to laugh. It felt even better to laugh *with him*. I felt myself falling all over again. *What are you doing, Nicole?*

I cleared my throat and turned to Emily. "How do you like living in L.A.?"

"I wasn't sure I would like it, but I really do. You should come out and visit us sometime. We have a huge pool and two beautiful fur babies: a dog and a rabbit."

"The rabbit is bigger than the dog," Atticus added.

"Leave my Bertha alone." Emily smacked him on the arm. "Seriously, Nicole, open invitation. Anytime."

I loved visiting new places and had only been to L.A. once before. "There's a hair convention out there once a year," I said. "If I go again, I can let you know when I'm in town."

"That would be awesome." She smiled. "And if it's during recording season, I would especially love the company when my honey abandons me."

I remembered the days of Atticus disappearing for hours to record. He'd always make things up to me in his own special way. I shook my head. *There I go again.*

Not long after that, we left the bar and moved our party to Laurentano's restaurant. Emily and I continued chatting over dinner. Not only was she the perfect distraction from Atticus, but she was quickly becoming a friend. She and I talked throughout the evening, and she told me the long and complicated story of what she and Tristan had to overcome to be together. I'd had no idea about their backstory and holy hell, I could hardly believe it. Someone should write a book about that.

When we returned to the house, the smell of marijuana immediately registered.

The four of us entered the bedroom together. Mimi had her eyes closed but was smiling. She looked damn relaxed. She looked...*high.*

I sniffed the air. "Ronan, were you smoking pot with my grandmother?"

"She said she was in pain. So I gave her a few hits of my joint."

"Well, that explains the chicken dance." Tristan chuckled.

Mimi opened her eyes. "I was able to sit up in the wheelchair for a whole ten minutes!"

My jaw dropped. "What?"

"Seriously, it helped her pain," Ronan explained. "She said she wanted to try to sit because she hadn't been able to. So I lifted her into the chair."

I crossed my arms. "Mimi has never smoked a day in her life, and she's going to start now?"

"Why the hell not?" Mimi slurred. "Now is the *best* time, if you ask me."

I guess she has a point.

"Ronan says he can hook me up with the good stuff," she added.

"Anything that takes away your pain is fine by us, Mimi." Atticus put his arm around me, sending a chill down my spine. It didn't seem like he was touching me for show this time or to tease me. It just felt natural, like he'd forgotten for a second that we weren't married anymore. That was sort of how tonight had felt in many ways.

After the crew left, I helped get Mimi settled for bed. The smell of marijuana still lingered in the air as Atticus and I headed to the spare room.

I felt even more nervous than usual to sleep next to Atticus tonight. He'd stuck to his three-drink rule, but I couldn't say the same for myself. Always a lightweight, I had a pretty significant buzz after four drinks. All I wanted was for him to touch me again. And that scared me.

As I turned my back to him and faced the wall, I took my shirt off to change into my sleep top. Somehow I felt his eyes on me as I unclasped my bra. The hairs on my arms prickled, and my body became tingly all over. As I heard the sound of his shirt coming off behind me, my nipples stiffened. I slowly slipped my pajama top over my head, hesitant to turn around and face this crippling need head on. Finally, I removed my pants and underwear, then reached for my pajama shorts.

When I did turn around, Atticus's cheeks were flushed, his eyes dark with desire. It proved what I'd already sensed and only intensified the growing need between my legs. My nipples were hard as ever and prominent against the material of my shirt.

Atticus was shirtless, of course, as he typically was at bedtime, wearing only the gray track pants he often wore to sleep. The thin line of hair leading down from his waistline taunted me. His Adam's apple bobbed as his eyes fell to my chest. *What was going to happen next? Would he try to kiss me? Would I let him?* Things were a little hazy from the alcohol—a little hazy and *a lot horny.*

"Goodnight," he finally said, his voice throaty.

"Goodnight."

My knees felt weak as we got into bed. I realized I was stupid to think Atticus would try anything while he believed my judgment was impaired. I was more sober than he was likely giving me credit for, though. The only thing I was guilty of right now was an intense hunger for sex. And I respected him for not taking advantage of what

I knew he could sense. I wanted him to ravage me tonight. And that was unsettling.

It took several minutes for my body to calm down, but it eventually did. Yet I still couldn't sleep. And it seemed neither could Atticus. When I turned to look at him, his eyes were wide open as he stared up at the ceiling.

"Mimi seemed to have had a good time with Ronan," he said after a moment.

I chuckled. "She was high. Of course she had a good time."

"Right." The low rumble of his laughter vibrated through me. He shifted, moving a little closer, awakening the nerve endings in my body. "You seemed like you had a good time tonight, too. Was I reading that correctly?"

Turning more fully toward him, I rested my hand under my chin. "I love Emily."

He sighed.

"What?" I asked.

He opened his mouth then shook his head. "Never mind."

"What?" I repeated.

"It's just that..." He paused. "I can't tell you how many times I've hung out with Tristan and Emily, thinking how you and she would get along. And what a shame it is that we..." He stopped. "Anyway."

Yeah. What a shame it all is.

Silence replaced our conversation for several minutes. But there was one more thing I needed to say. "Thank you for today."

"What are you referring to specifically?"

"Everything. The candy. For being so sweet to Mimi, doing her nails and hair, and just...being here. And especially for encouraging me to go out. It was fun, and I needed it."

"You don't ever need to thank me. Being here is a privilege, Nicole. Not just because I get to give back to Mimi. But because it's time with you I never thought I'd have." He paused. "And I'll take whatever you'll give me. The good. The bad. Anything you're willing to share, I'll take."

My eyes welled up. "I read one of your lost emails earlier. I'm not ready to read them all, but I read the first one."

"What did I say?"

"It was my birthday." I paused, getting choked up. "You said there were times when you wished you weren't here, that you fantasized about that. It made me so sad." I placed my hand on his cheek and turned his face toward me. "Don't think for a second that this world would be a better place if you weren't here. So many people are blessed to have you in their lives. Including me. Despite everything, I'd never survive in a world without you in it."

"I'm sorry if I scared you. That was a dark time for me."

My voice was barely audible. "I know."

"I'm not perfect, but I'm so much better now. I don't want you to worry, okay?"

Wiping a tear from my eye, I nodded. Thoughts and questions swirled around my head. "There are things I want to ask you that I'm afraid to—things I want to know but I'm not ready to face."

He reached for my hand and locked his fingers with mine. "It's okay."

"I really want to get there. I feel like I owe it to you. I'm sorry I'm not strong enough yet."

"You owe me no apologies, baby." He reached out and wiped my eyes with his thumb. "Do you understand that? You owe me nothing. And every second you give me, it's a gift."

Atticus leaned over and kissed my forehead firmly. I closed my eyes, relishing the warmth of his lips on my skin. And even if I yearned for a real kiss, the tenderness he'd given me was what I actually needed right now.

I doubted any man would ever love me the way Atticus did. Least of all, not Julian. But I wasn't ready to admit to Atticus where things stood with his former friend. Julian—or at least the idea of him—was a safeguard right now, one I needed to keep up more than ever, because I was starting to feel my protection slipping away.

That night, I didn't turn away from him in bed as I normally did. Instead, I curled my body into his, falling asleep to the sound and feel of his gentle breaths.

Chapter 10

NICOLE - PAST

I looked forward to Friday nights more than anything—not just because the long school week would be coming to an end, but because I'd be seeing Atticus.

I was what you'd call a good girl, for the most part—*too* good, some would say, a virgin who attended an all-girls' Catholic school. I studied hard and tried my best to do the right thing. But Friday nights down in my cousin's basement were my reward for all that. Friday nights and the weekend were my guilty pleasure.

It wasn't just that I got to listen to my favorite drummer practice; I got to hang out with him after. I loved our chats and the way he looked at me, even if I was starting to think all hope was gone when it came to us ever being more than friends.

I'd turned eighteen three weeks ago.

I'd been holding out hope that my age was the only thing keeping Atticus from asking me out, and that maybe when I became a legal adult, he'd make a move. But we'd hung out twice since my birthday, and nothing had changed between us.

Had I been a fool, holding out for him all this time?

I tried to tell myself it was for the best since I'd be going away to college, but that didn't help. I still only had eyes for him. My crush on Atticus Marchetti was the most insidious thing I'd ever experienced.

Finally, I decided I couldn't take it anymore. At the end of this particular Friday night, I was going to ask Atticus out. If he rejected me, at least it would save me months of anguish waiting for him to make a move. At least I'd know where he stood.

But when I arrived at my cousin's basement that night, I got a rude awakening: Atticus had brought a girl. I didn't realize she was *with* him at first. The girl was sitting on the couch, but I'd never seen her before. A sinking feeling developed in my stomach because she was really pretty.

"Hi," she said. "I'm Kayla."

"I'm Nicole."

"How do you know the guys?" she asked.

"I'm Cassius's cousin. Who are you?"

"I'm Atticus's date."

Excuse me? My cheeks burned. "I didn't...know he was dating anyone."

"We've gone out a few times now, yeah."

The room swayed as a rush of heat shot through my body. Not only did jealousy consume me, I also felt deflated given what my plans for tonight had been. How much time had I wasted over the past couple of years, fantasizing about the day he'd finally come around?

Was this my fault? Should I have told him how I felt about him sooner? Or maybe he just never felt the same about me?

Kayla and I made small talk as the guys practiced. I did a pretty good job of pretending like my world wasn't ending. I kept my eyes fixed on Atticus's amazing hand movements as I normally did, getting lost in the beats and crashes of the cymbals. He commanded attention even when I was pissed.

But then during a break in the music, Kayla moved to the other side of the room and sat on Atticus's lap. She began running her fingers through his hair. It felt like my worst nightmare.

Then Julian came up to me. "Hey, how's it going?"

"Good," I lied, my eyes still fixed on the sight across from me.

"I called you earlier this week, but it went to your voicemail. I wanted to see if we could check out that new 3-D movie theater that opened in Brunswick."

"Oh. I'm sorry." I turned to him. "I didn't know."

Julian had been trying to date me for the past couple of years, but I never gave him the time of day. There was nothing wrong with him. He was good-looking and sweet. His only flaw was that he wasn't Atticus Marchetti.

My cousin seized everyone's attention when he brought down a case of beer.

Things went from bad to worse because I knew as soon as everyone started drinking, anything could happen. My imagination ran wild. Atticus could lose his inhibitions and sleep with this girl. He probably already had. Was I naïve enough to think he hadn't been with other girls? This was just the only time it had happened in front of my face.

I felt sick. My stomach churned. I knew I needed to leave, but felt too weak to get up.

All of a sudden, Atticus was next to me. "Are you okay?" he asked.

Refusing to look him in the eyes, I blew out a breath. "Yeah, I'm fine. Why do you ask?"

"I don't know. You just look like something is wrong."

I hesitated. "I think it was this...seafood I ate earlier." *Really? What the hell?* I guessed that was better than telling the truth.

"Seafood?" he asked. "You're sick to your stomach?"

"Yeah," I murmured. "You'd better stay away so you don't get sick, too."

His brows drew in like he didn't know whether to believe me, but he went back to the other side of the room.

Kayla, who'd gone to the bathroom, I assumed, returned and sat on his lap again.

That was it. I needed to conjure the strength to get the hell out of here. I forced myself up off the couch and left. An evening that had held so much promise was instead one of the worst nights of my life.

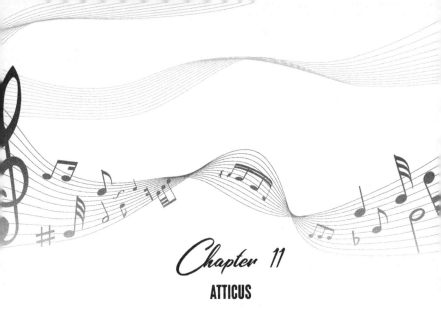

Chapter 11

ATTICUS

I was cleaning up in Mimi's room the morning after we'd gone out with our friends when her words stopped me in my tracks.

"I had a dream about your baby last night."

I froze for a second and then gulped. "Oh yeah?" *What is she talking about?*

"Yes. I couldn't tell if it was a boy or a girl, but it was the most beautiful, dark-haired baby that looked just like Nicole."

"Lucky kid," I murmured, a hollow feeling in my chest. That baby was not likely to ever exist. Then a flash of panic hit. What if Mimi's dream was a premonition about another baby? What if Nicole was pregnant? It certainly wouldn't be mine.

After a moment, relief washed over me as I remembered she had her period. *Thank fuck.*

"The last time I asked you guys about children, you both went quiet," Mimi said. "I'm sorry if I overstepped. But is there something you're not telling me?"

My heart pounded. *Something we're not telling you, Mimi? Why ever would you think that?* I cleared my throat. "Like what, Mimi?"

"Are you two having trouble in that area?"

I stalled. "What kind of trouble?"

"Trouble conceiving."

I hated lying to her. Yes, this entire façade was a lie, but when she asked me direct questions, it somehow felt worse than just being here and taking care of her under the guise of still being married.

"No, there's no trouble there," I assured her. "It just hasn't happened for us."

"Did I upset her when I asked about it the other day?"

"Not that I know of."

"Does she say she's not ready to be a mother?"

My chest felt tight. "I just...don't think it's the right time yet. Nicole will make a great mother someday, though. There's no doubt about that."

It hurt to think I wouldn't be the one to experience that with her. It hurt even more to think I'd wasted some of her best years and could be to blame if it *didn't* happen for her. That thought wrecked me like no other.

"Okay." Mimi sighed. "I guess I'm a little old fashioned. In my day, when you were over thirty, you had to worry about being too old. But in this day and age, with all the medical advances, I guess that's not something people are concerned with anymore."

"Nicole is thirty-one. She still has plenty of time."

Plenty of time to have a family with *someone else*. Guilt morphed into sadness.

Mimi stared into my eyes for a few seconds. "Are you okay, Atticus?"

Feeling like the biggest fraud in the world, I felt my cheeks heat. "Sure, why?"

"You look upset."

I would've given anything to get Mimi's take on our situation, to tell her everything and get her honest advice about whether she thought I had a chance in hell of ever getting her granddaughter back. But I couldn't.

"No, Mimi. I'm fine," I lied. *You just reminded me of something I try hard not to think about. Something that eats away at my soul every time I allow in the thoughts of what never will be.*

"What are you guys talking about?" Nicole asked as she entered the room.

"Nothing. Just life," I answered, praying that Mimi dropped the subject. "You need help in the kitchen?"

"No. I have it covered."

"She told me to stay out of the kitchen, Mimi. I think she's up to something. What are you making in there anyway?"

She winked. "You'll find out."

I wished she wouldn't wink at me like that, because it made me want to kiss her senseless. It wasn't my imagination that Nicole had been softening to me lately. We'd had a moment in bed last night after she'd mentioned reading my email. I hadn't been able to resist kissing her on the forehead. And she hadn't pushed me away. Not only that, she'd slept close to me. For one night I'd had my wife back, even if it was just in my head. And now the wink. I had to warn myself not to read into it.

"Well..." I sighed. "By the time I get back, maybe you'll be ready to tell me."

Nicole's smile faded as she followed me out into the hallway. "Where are you going?"

I hated the pleasure I felt when she seemed disappointed that I was leaving. It was the opposite of the permanent ache I carried in my chest every second of every day that we'd been apart.

"I'm going to get weed for your grandmother."

Her eyes went wide. "Are you serious?"

"Dead serious. This is a thing now. She said it helped her, and a friend of mine works at the dispensary. He's gonna hook me up."

Nicole looked apprehensive. "Why not get gummies this time?" she suggested.

"I read that smoking is actually more effective for pain."

"Can you pick up some wine while you're out?"

"Any particular kind?"

She wriggled her brows. "Surprise me."

I smiled. *Surprise me.* That was something she'd always said when we were together. I'd loved surprising her with a hell of a lot more than just wine. And there she was being playful with me again. Definitely not my imagination.

Later, after I returned with the weed and wine, I realized why Nicole had wanted me out of the kitchen. The aroma had given it away. Her white chicken chili—and the only thing she ever cooked—was fantastic.

I leaned over to see inside the pot. "This is for me?"

She dug her elbow into my side. "Who else?"

"Wow. Thank you."

"Well, you've given up your life for two weeks to be here. It's the least I can do."

I wanted to tell her I had no life without her, that there was no place I'd rather be than this little house with her, that I'd give everything up in a second to do life with her again.

But instead, I said, "This wasn't necessary. But I appreciate it."

We brought the pot of chili and some bowls into Mimi's room and enjoyed a quiet dinner.

Afterward, I helped adjust Mimi forward so she could smoke her joint. Unfortunately, when we tried to have her sit up in a chair a little while later, her pain hadn't subsided. Ronan's success seemed to be a fluke.

After Nicole and I helped Mimi back into bed and left her to sleep, I lifted a spare joint from my pocket.

"What's that?" she asked as we walked back to the kitchen.

"It's for us. Let's go out back and smoke it."

She shook her head. "I don't know."

"Come on, Nicole. Everyone's doing it," I teased. "Even your ninety-three-year-old grandmother."

"Not a good idea. I need my inhibitions around you. And I have to be careful."

That comment pleased me. I loved the thought of her losing her inhibitions. Even better? Maybe she'd magically lose her memory of the bad stuff.

"You had four drinks when we went out and managed to survive. This is safer than alcohol. It will just relax you. You won't lose your mind."

"Okay…" She exhaled. "I suppose sharing one joint won't kill me."

We went outside to the yard and sat across from each other in the two Adirondack chairs. It was a cool night, and when I noticed her shivering, I took off my hoodie and placed it over her shoulders.

"Thank you." She wrapped it around herself.

I lit the joint, and we began passing it back and forth. It was quiet aside from the sound of crickets. After a few hits, Nicole seemed to relax into her chair. I was happy that she was letting her guard down.

"The other night..." she said. "I was telling Emily about how we met. I hadn't allowed my mind to go back to those days in a very long time."

I blew out some smoke before passing the joint to her. "It's funny you say that because I did the same recently... with my therapist."

"Really?" She took a puff and handed it back to me.

"Yeah. The first thing I thought of was sixteen-year-old you on the nasty couch in Cassius's basement, watching us jam. That's the first memory I have of you. I'll never forget the first time I saw you. I thought you were the most beautiful girl in the world." I glanced over at her. "Still do."

She took one last hit, then passed it to me. "Well, you never would've pursued me in the first place if I hadn't freaked out when you brought a girl to the basement. I was so damn jealous. Do you remember what I did?"

"How could I forget? That was the best night of my life up to that point. It was so damn sexy that you made the first move."

She shrugged. "I couldn't help it."

"I can't believe I never saw it coming, never knew you had the same kind of feelings for me that I'd had for you."

"Well, you were blind, then, apparently."

"Maybe," I said. "But I'm glad you took your shot with me."

Her smile faded. "Are you? We could've avoided a lot of unnecessary pain if I'd never said a damn thing."

I felt an ache in my chest at the thought of never having gotten to love her. "That's where you're wrong. I don't regret any of it. Not for a second. I'm just sorry for how it ended."

"Yeah, me too," she whispered. She looked up at the sky before abruptly changing the subject. "What's the next adventure for Delirious Jones?"

"We start recording again soon. Then we have a tour early next year."

"I'm surprised you haven't practiced the entire time you've been here. You almost never go this long without your drums. They're a part of you."

"It's funny you mention that. I actually have someone delivering a set tomorrow. Just a rental."

"Where are you gonna put them?"

"Have you been in the garage? It's pretty empty."

"I haven't. I just assumed she was using it for storage."

"Me, too. But there's next to nothing in there. It's perfect and far enough away from the main house that hopefully I won't be too loud. I figured I could go out there in the evenings before Mimi goes to sleep and get some beats in."

Nicole stared at me intently, and I loved it. "What's up?" I asked.

"Your hair's getting long."

I ran my hand through my mane. "Yeah. I guess it is."

"I brought my shears with me."

"For a reason other than stabbing me in my sleep?"

"Believe it or not, yes. I brought them to trim Mimi's hair."

"Ah."

"Want me to do you really quick before bed?"

God, do I ever want you to do me really quick before bed, woman. "Yeah. That would be awesome. You're not gonna hack all my hair off while stoned, are you?"

"No. I'm not that high off half a joint."

"Okay, then."

She stood. "Let's go."

Her ass looked so damn good as I followed her inside. Not sure if it was that little bit of weed or what, but I was damn horny right now. Even more so than usual.

I pulled out one of the kitchen chairs and waited as Nicole went to get the black pouch she kept her hair supplies in. This felt like old times. I couldn't count the number of times she'd cut my hair over the years.

Nicole sprayed my hair down and began trimming the ends in the meticulous way she always did, grasping piece by piece between her delicate fingers with a snip-snip here and a snip-snip there; somehow it always came out like magic. Not only had I lost a wife a few years back but also the best damn hairdresser I'd ever had. What I'd missed most about this, though, was now also my current torture. I closed my eyes so as not to have her tits in my face while she trimmed my bangs. They were at eye-level. The way her warm body grazed mine as she moved around the chair made my temperature rise. And that damn Egyptian musk she wore drove me crazy. Fuck, what I wouldn't give for just one more night with this woman. How many times had she done this very thing for me—cut my hair, teasing me with her body—before I ended up carrying her away and making love to her, loose hairs and all still fucking stuck to the back of my neck. Sometimes I wouldn't even make it out of the chair. I'd just pull her on top and let her ride me.

A small mirror suddenly appeared in front of my face, snapping me out of my salacious thoughts.

"You like it?" she asked.

I ran my fingers across the top of my head. "Amazing as ever. No one cuts my hair like you."

There's no one like you.

Never was, never will be.

"You should be good for a couple of months."

I didn't want to consider where I'd be two months from now. Because she wouldn't be there.

There was a knock at the door, and both of us turned our heads. It was just after eight-thirty PM.

My brows drew in. "Are you expecting someone?"

She shook her head. "No."

Unfortunately, there was no peephole. And after I opened the door, I wished I hadn't. Because standing in front of me was the closest thing I'd had to a girlfriend since Nicole and I broke up. "Riley, what are you doing here?"

Chapter 12

ATTICUS

Riley shot me a look. "I should be asking you the same question."

Nicole stood behind me quietly, and all I could think about was protecting her feelings. That meant getting Riley the fuck out of here.

"Let's step outside, please," I told Riley, leading her down the block where there was no way Mimi or Nicole would overhear.

When I felt comfortable that we were well beyond earshot, I stopped and faced her. "Why didn't you call before showing up here?"

"You told me you were dealing with a family situation, Atticus. You conveniently left out the part where your *ex-wife* was involved."

I exhaled. "You shouldn't have come."

"Why? Because you didn't want me to know what you're up to?"

"Riley, even if I *were* having an affair with my ex-wife, which I'm not, you and I are not exclusive."

"Yes, but I thought we had an understanding that when you weren't touring...you and I would spend time together. Why did you lie and tell me you were coming to New Jersey to visit your family?"

An understanding created by you that I'd never agree to? "I didn't lie. I said I had a family *situation*, and that's what this is. Nicole and I aren't married anymore, but she'll always be my family."

I owed Riley the decency not to continue this conversation on the street, so I texted Nicole that I would be back soon.

We got in Riley's car and drove to a bar in town.

Once there, I explained the full situation. While she wasn't happy, Riley calmed down a bit once she realized the situation with Nicole wasn't as cut and dried as she'd assumed.

"Will you tell me now how you found out where I was?" I asked.

She stirred the ice in her drink. "I called your manager and told him I needed to reach you. Doug said you'd had him order a set of drums to be delivered here and gave me the address. Said he knew nothing more than that. But what prompted me to reach out in the first place was a photo posted online—you and Tristan out with two women. One I recognized as his girlfriend, and I knew the second woman was your ex."

I narrowed my eyes. "I've never shown you photos of Nicole."

"No, but come on, Atticus. Of course I've peeked at your old social media posts over the years."

THE Drummer's HEART

"That's creepy."

She raised an eyebrow. "You mean to tell me you've never stalked someone's social media before?"

Only Nicole's, although she never posted much. I guess I couldn't blame Riley for stalking me. I couldn't blame her for being pissed, either. She knew I dated other people, but she'd been around long enough that I owed her the truth. I had nothing to hide, but somehow I *had* been trying to hide the fact that Nicole was the family I'd been referring to. I still had feelings for my ex-wife. And I couldn't admit that to Riley without getting her more upset than she already was.

"I'm sorry I wasn't clearer about why I was here. Would you have taken it well if I'd told you the truth, though?"

"Probably not. But I would've accepted it. What choice do I have when it comes to you? I've accepted a lot, like the fact that our relationship, if you want to call it that, won't ever go beyond friends with benefits."

"Are you not happy with our dynamic anymore?" I asked.

Riley crossed her arms. "I've never been happy with it."

I could not handle Riley developing feelings. She'd been a good friend and lover, but it was nothing more than casual for me. Never had been. If she wanted more, she deserved better than to be strung along by a man who would never love her. Maybe now was the time to set her free, even if she wasn't technically mine to let go of.

"Riley, listen, I don't want you to hate me. You've been a very good friend, and your companionship has helped me through a hard stretch in my life. I've appreciated having your company when I'm home in L.A. but also the fact that you never question what I do with my time when we aren't together. It's been the perfect situation for me, but not a really fair situation for you, if what you want is someone who prioritizes you. I'll never be a true boyfriend." I forced the words out. "Maybe it's better if we end this now."

She moved back in her seat. "You're breaking up with me? Is that what you're trying to say? Here, in this podunk bar?"

"I'm suggesting that you not waste your time with me anymore because I can't give you what you need."

Being around Nicole again had confirmed that I had no room in my heart for anyone else. And if even a piece of my heart was what Riley wanted, this had to end. Because none of it was hers to have.

Her bottom lip quivered. "What if I just want to keep things the way they have been?"

"You really came all the way out here to tell me you want things to stay the way they are? You wouldn't have come if you didn't care about me. And you deserve to have that reciprocated."

She looked away. "God, you're right."

I reached for her hand. "Riley, you deserve better than *me*. Okay? That's what I'm trying to say. I could've said, 'Yeah, let's keep doing what we're doing when I'm back in L.A. because it's convenient for me.' But I don't want to do that to you. I don't want to hurt any more people in my life than I already have."

Riley closed her eyes for several seconds then opened them. "Sadly, I needed this reality check. The moment I saw the photo of you and your ex, I went ballistic. That says something. I guess I've been lying to myself."

It hurt to see her upset. But I didn't have the bandwidth to give her more of my time. I squeezed her hand. "The last thing I ever wanted was to lead you on. The most honest thing I can tell you is that...if I were you, I wouldn't waste any more time with me."

Riley wiped tears from her eyes, further proof that I'd taken this too far.

To my surprise, she eventually flashed a smile. "I wish you weren't so damn hot." She chuckled. "I'm gonna miss having sex with you."

"That's one area we've definitely been compatible. And I don't regret a second spent with you, Riley."

She tugged at the hairs on my arm. "You should... come back to my hotel for one last time before we say goodbye."

While that sounded like a fun way to end things and could have been a solution to my perpetual boner, no part of me actually wanted that. There was only one woman my body, mind, and soul craved right now. Even if it made no sense, given the reality of our relationship—or lack thereof—going to Riley's hotel would feel like cheating. As long as I was here in Monksville with my ex, I was hers, even if she wasn't mine. That was the sad reality.

"Are you back together with her?" Riley asked.

"No." *I wish.*

"Then why not one last time with me?"

I sighed. "I just...can't."

"Okay." She moved her hand away. "Well, how does one end this conversation? Have a nice life?"

I stood and smiled. "We end it with a hug. Then you leave, and I walk my ass home."

Opening my arms, I hugged her before placing a chaste kiss on her cheek.

Then she was gone.

I lingered at the table for a bit.

It felt strange to think I might never see her again. At the same time, it was a huge relief. I no longer had to worry about hurting her.

Just as I was heading out of the bar, I heard a voice call out, "Hey, asshole!"

Who the fuck did I piss off now?

But a second later, I realized it was my sister. My mouth curved into a smile. "Hey!"

"What the hell? You're in town and you don't tell me?"

Shit. "I swear I was gonna tell you I was here."

"Really?" She poked my chest with her index finger. "When?"

Beads of sweat formed on my forehead. There were very few people I had to answer to in life. Very few people who scared me. But of those who did, my big sis, Tina, was at the top of the list.

"Very soon. What are you doing here?"

"I was just picking up some fries to go. You know I love the fries here."

Tina was a widow and had three kids, two sons and a daughter. Kieran and Kenzie were twins, both twenty-four. Kieran had worked on one of Delirious Jones's tours, and my niece, Kenzie, was a photographer. The youngest, Kyle, was a junior in high school. Their dad, Brian, had passed away after a cardiac event related to a disorder he never knew he had. The kids had been small when it happened, and I'd been just a few years out of high school. My sister was my hero for the way she'd handled raising those kids alone, even if she'd had no choice. I tried my best to be there for them whenever I could. I'd take the boys camping or invite them to New York or L.A. for the weekend. But Kenzie was my princess. That girl could just look at me, and I'd give her whatever she wanted.

"Did you tell any of the kids you're here?" she asked.

"No one knows I'm here."

"When did you get in?"

"Five days ago."

"What the hell?"

"I'm not hiding from you. I just knew I wouldn't have time until these two weeks are over."

"Why two weeks? By the way, you had time to come to the bar tonight."

I sighed and then spent the next twenty minutes explaining everything to my sister, who thankfully calmed down once she understood I wasn't simply ignoring her.

"Wow, I'm so sorry to hear Mimi isn't doing well. She's such a sweet lady."

"Now that you know I'm here, you should come visit her."

"I would love that. You think Nicole would mind?"

"If she doesn't mind *me* being around, she certainly won't mind you. She always loved you."

My sister flashed a sad smile. "I love her, too."

I love her three. I needed to get back to Nicole, especially with the way I'd left tonight, but there was no chance in hell my sister was gonna let me go that fast.

"Are you doing okay with all this?" she asked.

"I've upped my therapy sessions to once a week, if that answers your question."

"It does, but I'm happy to hear you're still seeing someone."

"Yeah, well, I'm still seeing Dr. Jensen, but I haven't been willing to talk about the tough stuff, which sort of defeats the purpose." I tugged at my hair. "What? You look like you want to say something."

"I do. But it's nothing I haven't said before."

"Okay..."

"Come sit for a bit." My sister took what was supposed to be takeout fries to a table and opened the greasy bag. She bit into one of them. "Losing Brian all those years ago taught me that nothing else matters in life if you don't have the person you love. I never got to say goodbye, and there's nothing I wouldn't do for more time with him. There's nothing I wouldn't give for just one more moment, no matter how brief. I will always believe that if the person you love is on this Earth, there's nothing you shouldn't be willing to do to get them back."

"She doesn't want that, Tina. She can't get over what happened, and there's the not-so-small complication of her dating someone I hate now." I felt my blood pressure rising.

"Doesn't matter."

"Really..." I gritted my teeth.

"Really. I'm telling you none of that matters. But how you get her back is up to you, little brother. I don't have all the answers. I just tell you what to do, not how to do it." She winked.

I shook my head and looked at the time. "I have to go. I have to get home to Nicole."

Tina looked at me a moment. "You realize what you just said, right? *Home* to Nicole."

"It was just a figure of speech."

She winked again. "Sure it was."

Chapter 13

NICOLE

Every second Atticus was out with that woman was more excruciating than the last. I'd spent the entire time pacing. Also, most of my fingernails were gone after I'd bitten them off.

Tonight was the first time I'd been face to face with a woman Atticus had been with since me. She was pretty, of course, and blonde, my total opposite, which added insult to injury. I'd thought *I* was his type. Guess not.

Needing a distraction, I'd once again logged in to my computer and checked my old email account, reading another of Atticus's messages to me.

Nicole,
I don't understand anything anymore.
I don't recognize my life.
Someone told me something today that I'm hoping isn't true.

They said they saw you with Julian.

But only you can tell me the truth.

Is it true?

Are you with him now?

This is the first time I've really needed to get drunk since I quit drinking more than three drinks at a time. It's really fucking hard not to get fucked up tonight.

I get why you'd want to hurt me.

I'm not even debating the fact that I deserve it.

I just don't know what to say.

I'm broken.

I'm sorry.

I still love you.

But this one fucking hurts.

Although nothing hurts more than losing you.

Always lost without you,

Atticus

My eyes watered as I shut my laptop. It took me several minutes to decompress.

This was the email I'd selected today? It served quite effectively to remind me how out of line my jealousy toward Atticus's "girlfriend" was. I *deserved* to feel this way.

Mimi must not have been able to sleep, as I could hear her moving around in her bed. I hated the thought of going in there because having to lie to her about why Atticus was gone was going to suck. But if she was still up, I needed to check on her.

After stopping in the bathroom to splash water on my face, I went into her room.

Of course, the first thing she said was, "Where's Atticus? I don't hear him."

He's out with some bimbo. "Oh, he went to get some stuff we need for the house."

"This late?"

"Yeah..." I cleared my throat. "You know there's that twenty-four-hour Walmart."

"Can you tell him to get some of those mint candies I like? The green and white starlight ones?"

"Oh, um..."

No way did I want to text him. He'd think I was making up an excuse to interrupt.

"He's already left the store and is on his way back. Sorry."

"That's okay, honey."

Not sure how I was going to explain if she stayed awake and noticed he never came home tonight, which was certainly a possibility.

I covered her with a blanket. "I'm sorry you're having trouble sleeping. Try to get some rest."

"Is everything okay with you and Atticus?"

I gulped. "What do you mean?"

"I don't know. I've just sensed something lately. I can't put my finger on what it is."

I would've loved some advice from her, but I was too deep into this farce to back out now. At this point, she might be more disappointed that I'd lied to her than the fact that Atticus and I were divorced. Still, I decided to give her some semblance of the truth.

"You picked up on that, huh?"

"Am I right?"

"You're right that things have been better between us, yes."

"Is it about kids? Are you having trouble getting pregnant? I asked Atticus about it the other day, and he didn't seem comfortable talking about it."

My stomach sank. "It's not about kids, Mimi. I just struggle with the life Atticus leads sometimes. It's not easy to be married to a famous musician." *It wasn't, at least.*

"But that's the life you signed up for when you agreed to marry him, wasn't it?"

Guilt hit me as her words sank in. She was absolutely right. I'd agreed to marry him knowing his career could take off, and when it did, I couldn't handle it. I'd had a hand in the demise of our relationship. Her words were a reminder of my own weaknesses and insecurities—a reminder that if Atticus had given in to his past thoughts about not existing, my actions could've caused far worse than just the end of our marriage.

When I didn't say anything, she added, "Is it because of your dad that you can't fully trust Atticus?"

There was no doubt that my father cheating on my mother had a huge impact on me. A man I'd trusted implicitly had ultimately betrayed us both. The man I trusted most in this world had lied to me, and everything I'd thought to be true simply wasn't.

I nodded. "That definitely affected me, Mimi. It's a trauma I still haven't properly worked through. As much as I want to be a confident person, I do feel like what Dad did has impacted my ability to trust people."

She struggled to speak as she looked me straight in the eyes. "Atticus is *not* like your father. I can see how much he loves you. I know *you* have to believe that, though, for it to matter. I've observed many people in my lifetime, and I've never seen anyone look at someone the way Atticus looks at you."

I shut my eyes. What she'd said was true. I felt it in every inch of my soul.

The front door opened, and I heard footsteps. *He came back.* Atticus couldn't have orchestrated his return better considering what I'd told my grandmother about him being at the store. The timing was perfect.

Atticus stood at the doorway. "Hey, Mimi. What are you still doing up, beauty? You were asleep when I left."

"Well, Nicole and I were just talking."

"You were, were you?" He bent to kiss her forehead.

I wondered where those lips had been tonight. I searched his face for signs of lipstick, examined his hair to see if it looked out of place. It didn't, really. My eyes landed on his big, beautiful hands as I wondered where they'd been tonight, too.

"What did you get from Walmart?" she asked him. "You don't have any bags."

Atticus looked over at me and lied, "Uh...just a few things for the house. I left the bag in the car because I'm feeling too lazy to put anything away tonight."

"Next time you're out, can you please get me some starlight mints? The green and white ones?"

"Of course."

She nodded and closed her eyes. "You two can leave me be. Shut off the light on your way out."

"Yes, ma'am," he said.

Atticus and I walked silently down the hallway. The tension in the air was thick as my heart thundered in my chest, jealousy pumping through my veins.

I headed straight to the bedroom and planned to give him the silent treatment while he hopefully stayed in the kitchen. But when he followed me into the room, I couldn't help but whisper, "How was your girlfriend?"

He shut the door behind him. "She's not my girlfriend."

"She sure acted like it, showing up here and looking at me with daggers in her eyes. Doesn't she realize we're not together anymore? What's her problem?" My tone was filled with spite. I knew I must've seemed jealous. But I was. And I hated this feeling.

"Well, I never told her what I was doing in Monksville. And Doug stupidly gave her this address because I had him order the drums to be sent here. And you and I were apparently photographed while we were out the other night. Somehow she saw those photos."

"Great." I huffed. "So she, what, thought you were having an affair with me?"

"She was jealous, yeah. Came to confront me about it."

"Did you set her straight?" I crossed my arms. "You told her there's absolutely nothing going on between us?"

"I ended things with her, actually." He looked down at his shoes. "Not that there was much to end, because I thought we'd had an understanding about not being in a relationship, but apparently that wasn't clear enough to her."

A wave of relief hit me. "So that's why you were gone so long? You were breaking up with her this whole time?"

"You can't break up with someone you're not with. But yes, I was ending our limited relationship."

"How did she take it?"

"She wasn't happy, but she accepted it. I think she realizes she's better off. I'm relieved because she deserves to find someone who can give her the time and attention she needs. It was never anything more than..." He hesitated, seeming to catch himself.

"Yeah..." I rolled my eyes, feeling sick. "Say no more."

He exhaled. "But then after she left, as luck would have it, my sister walked into the bar and reamed me a new asshole for not telling her I was in town. You know Tina. She wouldn't let me go. So that's why I'm late."

I couldn't help but smile at the thought of Tina. I'd always loved her and her kids. For a long time, I'd looked at Tina like a sister, and her daughter, Kenzie, as my own niece.

"How is she?"

"She's okay."

"You should've told her you were in town from the beginning. Not sure how you thought you were gonna be able to get away with that. Someone was bound to find you."

He shrugged. "I wanted to be able to focus on Mimi. If my family knew I was here, they wouldn't leave me alone. There's plenty of time to see them after Mimi's aide comes back."

"So...you're gonna stay in town for a while after this is over?"

"For a little while. I'm not totally sure. Eventually I have to get back to L.A. so we can start recording. I won't have an opportunity to come home for a while after that, either, because we'll go on tour."

"I see." I bit my bottom lip.

"What's that look for?"

"Nothing..."

"As soon as I mentioned the tour, your face changed."

He was right. Just the word *tour* triggered me. It brought visions of Atticus doing God knows what with God knows who. Atticus had been with a lot of women since me, and there wasn't one time I'd thought about that and not felt sick. But even before that lifestyle became a reality for him, my fear of it contributed to our end.

"You ended things with Riley so you don't have to feel guilty for screwing around on tour anymore?" I blurted.

His expression went from concern to anger. "Yeah, Nicole. That's exactly it," he snapped.

"I'm sorry," I muttered, attempting to backtrack.

"No, by all means. It's the truth, right? I'm nothing but an out-of-control manwhore without a soul. That's how you see me." He walked toward me, causing my blood to pump faster. "Well, I've got news for you." He paused. "I became the very man you feared I would. But I was *never* that person when we were together. Not even close. But after you ended things for good, I had to turn to other people to try to get over you. It wasn't going to be alcohol or drugs, so it was women. When you started dating Julian, I needed to forget reality." He paused for a moment, gritting his teeth. "And no...ending things with Riley had nothing to do with needing more freedom to fuck around. Sadly, she was always aware of my activities on tour and didn't seem to care so long as I hung out with her when I came back to L.A. She didn't seem to care about anything—until she saw me photographed with you."

I wouldn't look at him. "Well, she had nothing to worry about there, did she?"

He inched closer, and now I could feel his breath on my face. "If you're implying that I no longer have feelings for you, you're mistaken. And you're forgetting that *I'm* not the one of us in a committed relationship." He tilted his head. "How is Julian, by the way? We haven't talked about him much. But since you seem to think I'm the insensitive prick here, we might as well talk about how *he* took advantage of our pain and made it his prize."

My stomach dropped at the mention of Julian. I'd known exactly what I was doing when I let Atticus's former friend into my life, let him help me heal from the pain of my divorce. I'd known Atticus would be devastated when he found out. Yet I'd allowed it anyway, hoping that would cancel my own devastation over what had finally ended us for good. It was something I'd always regret. It had been a mistake.

"You don't like it when I bring him up, do you?" His voice trembled. "I don't like it, either. I wish it were a nightmare I could wake up from."

I hadn't been ready to admit what happened with Julian and me—I was still using him as a shield. It felt like without the idea of him, I was too vulnerable. Without Julian, my heart was still in the place it had been when my marriage ended. But right now, I couldn't stand the hurt in my ex-husband's eyes. I needed to ease the pain I knew he was feeling right now at the mere mention of Julian's name.

I needed to tell Atticus the truth.

"I'm not with him anymore," I admitted.

My revelation, though, only seemed to make him angrier.

Atticus gritted his teeth. "What did he fucking do? I'll kill him if he hurt you. I—"

"No." I placed my hand on his chest. "He didn't do anything. I ended it."

His erratic breaths softened. "Why?"

"Because he and I were...a mistake."

His chest heaved. "Why were you a mistake?"

"You know why, Atticus."

Atticus's eyes were glassy. I couldn't tell if it was because he'd had more than three drinks tonight or if he was about to cry.

He moved in closer. "I need to hear you say it."

I swallowed. "He and I were a mistake...because I only attached myself to him to forget you and to spite you, and I'm a horrible person for it. At the time I let him in, I needed a distraction from how badly I was hurt, and I didn't care that I hurt you in the process."

Atticus nodded for a while. "Well, mission accomplished." He exhaled. "But you know the hardest part for me?"

"What?"

"I can't even blame you for it. Because I wanted to hurt me, too."

A shooting pain sliced through my chest.

He closed his eyes as the room filled with silence.

"Can we not talk about this anymore, Atticus? It's been a long night."

He nodded.

We said nothing further as we changed for bed, once again back to back so the other couldn't see things we'd already seen a million times before.

Then we got into bed and lay together in more silence. I'd thought maybe he'd fallen asleep until he spoke into the darkness.

"I hate the person I am without you," he whispered.

My chest tightened. His words mirrored exactly how I felt about myself. I hated the person I was without him, the person I'd become in the years since our separation. I didn't want to be that heartless woman anymore.

I wanted to comfort him right now, to roll over and hold him. But I was so afraid to let my guard down. The need to touch him in some way became too intense, though. I reached my hand over to his chest and placed it on his heart. It was beating so fast. I didn't have to wonder why. I *knew*.

He placed his hand over mine, locking it in. I fell asleep to the rhythm of his heart beating for me.

~

When I walked into the kitchen the following morning, Atticus threw me for a loop.

"Did you mean everything you said last night?" he asked.

"What are you talking about?"

"Everything you said in your sleep."

A rush of adrenaline hit. *Oh no.* "What did I say?"

"You don't remember?"

"Of course I don't remember what I said while I was *sleeping*." Dread filled me. "What did I say?"

He flashed a mischievous grin. "It's too obscene to repeat. I don't want to embarrass you."

Great. "Your little game is such a mind fuck. You know that?"

He flashed his teeth. "It is, isn't it?"

The smirk on his face was so damn sexy. I hated that this man could make me feel like my body was on fire just by looking at me. I wanted to run my hands through his hair so badly that my fingertips tingled. I wanted to kiss him and forget about the past for one damn day.

These feelings were troubling, to say the least.

"Heard you get up," he said, "so I prepared your coffee. Mimi's also had her breakfast. She should be good for a while but probably needs to be changed soon. She still won't let me do it." He turned to leave the kitchen.

"Where are you going?"

"My drums are about to arrive. Got a text from the delivery guy that he's only a few minutes away." Atticus disappeared down the hall.

After I tended to my grandmother, I returned to the kitchen and heated up the coffee Atticus had prepared for me earlier.

Still consumed by our conversation last night, I took advantage of him being out of the house and went back to the room to open my laptop. Though I knew it would upset me, I clicked into another of Atticus's lost emails.

Nicole,

You could at least let me know you're receiving these messages.

I wrote a song for you.

Ready?

There once was a girl named Nicole.

She ate me up and swallowed me whole.

But I got what I deserved.

My beautiful wife.

I ruined her life.

Anyway, I'm too messed up to finish it, but you get the point.

That's why I don't write songs. I leave that to Tristan.

SO fucked up right now.

Not alcohol, but I took something. I don't even know what the fuck it was. Someone gave it to me. Stupid, I know.

Kind of defeats my three-drink rule if I'm moving on to other things, I guess. But I really need to forget today.

I need to forget that you're not mine anymore.

That you're with him now.

So, I got fucked up.

Did I mention that?

It won't happen again.

He posted a photo of you and him.

And I can't unsee it.

I hate you. (I love you.)

Always lost without you,
Atticus

Staring at the screen, I felt empty, certainly not strong enough to read another one. Each of those missed emails hurt me more than the last. The only solace was knowing they'd been written far in the past and that instead of being in the state he was when he'd written that, Atticus was currently okay and setting up his drums in the garage.

Shutting the laptop, I busied myself cleaning the kitchen, all the while ruminating about that email and what I may or may not have admitted to him in my sleep last night.

A half-hour later, the sound of drumming rang out in the distance. I shut my eyes for a moment, appreciating the nostalgia of hearing Atticus practice. It had been so long since I'd heard that sound.

It was no surprise that Mimi heard it, too, though, since it was louder than he probably realized.

"What's that racket?" she asked when I entered her room.

"Atticus just had a drum set delivered. He's taking full advantage of you being awake this morning."

"Well, that's one way for him to get out his frustrations."

"Is it bothering you? I can tell him to stop."

"No, no. It's nice to have something to focus on besides the thoughts racing in my head. I sort of like the noise."

"What have you been thinking about?" I sat by her bedside. "Are you okay?"

"Well, you know, when you get to be my age and close to the end, you have all sorts of crazy thoughts. We don't know whether we'll wake up from one sleep to the next. Every sunrise is a miracle. And every night, all we can hope is that we've finished the day with some peace in our hearts. Just in case it's the last time."

"Do you feel a sense of peace right now?"

Mimi nodded. "I think I do, yes. My daughter and granddaughter are settled. Your uncles and cousins, too. It's really you and your mom I would worry about. As for me, I've lived. I've loved. I don't want to leave this Earth, but I've had the privilege of living far beyond the age of most. At some point, I have to say goodbye and move onto whatever's next. Can't be here forever, as much as I'd want to be for you, honey."

"Well, I hope we have you for many more sleeps to come. I don't ever want to lose you. I'll never be ready for that day."

She turned her head slowly toward me. "Can I give you some advice?"

"Of course."

"Don't fight with your husband."

Uh-oh.

Last night.

Were we too loud?

I was pretty sure Atticus and I had been whispering behind that closed bedroom door last night, but you never know.

"Did you hear us fighting?"

"Yes."

My stomach dropped. "Did you hear what we were fighting about?"

"No. Couldn't make it out, but like I've told you, I sense that things are not right with you two, even if I don't know exactly what's going on. Life is too short to spend your time bickering, you know. You should be making love, laughing, doing all the wonderful things youth allows. If I could have just one day back with your grandfather, the last thing I'd be doing is arguing with him."

I felt like such a fraud for making Mimi believe I was settled in life, but it was more important that she die in peace than anything else. It was more important than my own sanity, apparently.

I nodded. "Thank you for the reminder of what's important. I'll take it to heart."

After I left Mimi's room, I wanted to peek in on Atticus practicing. Before opening the door to the garage, I leaned my back against it, closed my eyes, and let the beats vibrate through me, Atticus's passion consuming me more and more with every strike. Echoing through my bones. Through my soul. How I'd missed listening to him play. Suddenly, I was sixteen again, enthralled by my cousin's older friend.

I lost track of how long I stayed there in that spot against the door. When the drumming abruptly stopped, I nearly fell back as the door opened behind me.

"What the heck?" I shouted.

Atticus's eyes flashed with anger. "He's here."

"Who's here?"

"Fucking Julian is out front. I set up a Ring camera on the house, and it alerts me whenever someone's at the door."

Chapter 14

ATTICUS

He had some fucking nerve showing up here. I'd never wanted to break someone's neck more in my life.

But I couldn't risk Mimi hearing anything.

"Why are you here?" I spat as I rounded the porch, my ears throbbing.

Nicole took Julian by the arm and led him down the street. "We need to talk down here away from the house," she explained.

No way I was leaving her alone with him, so I followed. "You didn't answer my question," I said to him. "Why are you here?"

"I don't need to explain that to you."

"She dumped you. Why would you come if it wasn't to make trouble?"

"She dumped *me*? You're thinking of *your* situation."

My blood boiled. "You need to leave. You know why she and I are here. Now is not the time for your bullshit."

"I don't really think that's for you to decide. You have no right to tell me what to do."

"I have *every* right to protect my wife."

"Your wife?" He huffed. "I believe that ship sailed long ago."

Nicole stopped walking and held out her palms. "Stop! Both of you." She turned to me. "Leave us for a bit, please."

Me? My chest heaved as I looked between them. She wanted *me* to go? It pained me to turn around and leave her alone with him, but I did as she asked—mainly because I didn't want Mimi to suspect anything was off if we'd both disappeared. If I came in bruised up, that wouldn't have been a good look, either.

"Call if you need me," I said as I walked away.

Much to my chagrin, I got back to the house feeling like I'd left my heart out on that sidewalk with Nicole. I felt hollow inside, and most of all, ashamed—ashamed that my actions had caused all of this. Ashamed that I'd ever allowed her to land in the arms of another man, especially him.

I checked in on Mimi, hoping she hadn't sensed any commotion outside.

She looked up at me. "You stopped drumming."

Running my hand through my hair, I sighed. "I did."

"Did I hear someone at the door?"

"Yeah...uh, it was just someone selling something."

"Where's Nicole?"

"She stepped out for a bit." I walked over to the window and looked out, tapping my foot.

"What's so interesting out there?"

"Nothing. It's...a nice day. That's all."

I arched my neck to see better, though I knew she was too far down the street for me to see from here.

"Why don't you go back to your drumming?" Mimi asked. "It was relaxing me."

Turning around, I arched a brow. "Relaxing? I worried I was disturbing you."

"No, my love. It's the quiet that causes my mind to race. The drumming gave me something to focus on."

"Well, that's how I feel too. Great minds think alike." Even though I felt dead inside, I smiled. "Alright, then. I'll get back to it."

I forced myself to return to the garage, repositioned myself at my seat, and began beating the shit out of the drums. Each strike only fueled my anger. Sweat beaded on my forehead as I pounded out my fury. Better the drums than Julian's face.

When the door to the garage opened about an hour later, I stopped.

Putting my sticks down, I rushed over to Nicole. "Are you okay?"

"Yeah. We just drove to the center of town and had coffee."

Even that made me insane. "Is he gone?"

"No, actually. He's staying in Monksville tonight."

"Why?"

She shrugged.

"What the fuck does he want from you?" I yelled.

"Not sure you want to know."

I gritted my teeth. "He wants you to take him back..."

"He wants another chance, yeah, after I return to the city."

A flash of panic hit. How could I compete when he'd be in New York with her, and I'd be all over half the fucking world?

My palms began to sweat. "What did you tell him?"

"I told him I wasn't interested in resuming things."

"Why couldn't he have waited for you to be back in New York to say what he needed to say?"

She shook her head and looked down at her feet. "I don't know."

"Yes, you do. He came here to fucking rattle me. He wants to get his ass beat." I tightened my fists. "Where's he staying?"

"Why? You're not going after him."

"I just want to talk to him." *While I bash his face into the pavement.*

"Nothing good can come from that, Atticus, and you know it."

What *did* I hope to achieve by confronting Julian again? The rage inside me right now made me realize I was still holding out hope for Nicole and me, and I saw Julian as an impediment. That was likely delusional. I needed to protect myself from getting hurt. But first I wanted to hurt *him*.

"If you won't tell me where he is, I'll find him anyway. There aren't that many hotels in town nor places to hang out. And I know where his mother lives. He's staying with her, I assume, if she still lives here?"

Nicole refused to confirm.

She followed me as I exited the garage and headed to my car.

"Atticus, don't be stupid."

I ignored her, turning on the engine and taking off. As much as I hated to upset her, I couldn't help it. I needed him to know that if I wasn't going to have her, he certainly wasn't either.

Since I knew Julian's car, I figured I'd drive around town to see if I spotted it.

It took me a few hours of scouring Monksville, but I finally located his Range Rover parked outside a local bar around happy hour.

I parked and stormed inside.

He was seated in the corner, watching a game on the TV mounted to the wall.

He jumped in his seat as I pulled out the chair across from him and made myself comfortable.

"Surprised to see me?" I cracked. "You shouldn't be. You knew coming here would risk getting your ass beat, yet you chose to come anyway."

"Come on." He rolled his eyes. "Really? You're following me around now?"

"Actually, I just want to talk."

"You mentioned beating my ass a second ago. Now you want to talk?"

"I don't want to upset her any more than I already have, so no, I won't be attacking you. You can thank Nicole for that. But please, by all means, come for me first and give me an excuse. Then I'll have a perfectly legitimate reason to knock your teeth out in the name of self-defense."

Maybe I'd knock his teeth out either way. But first, I needed a drink. I'd definitely be taking advantage of my three-drink maximum today.

I headed to the bar and ordered a beer. Before I could return to the table, a woman recognized me and asked for a photo. Forcing a smile, I appeased her before settling back in the seat across from Julian. I had to give him credit for not leaving.

I took a long sip and set my glass down. "What can I do to get you to stay away from Nicole?"

"Why should I? She's your ex-wife, *ex* being the operative word. You have this unfounded belief that she somehow still belongs to you. She doesn't. After you and she broke up, she chose to be with me. You can't seem to understand that."

"She only chose you after you manipulated the situation. You knew what had happened, and you were conveniently right there to pick up the pieces—pieces you had no right to."

"Whether you think the timing of my relationship with her was convenient or not isn't the point. She and I developed something real. It didn't happen overnight. You weren't there, and you have no idea what she and I built. You're only seeing what you want to see. You're also forgetting that Nicole is a grown-ass woman and can do whatever the hell she wants with her life. She doesn't need you to dictate who she falls in love with."

"In love with *you*? She broke up with you!"

"Yeah, well, I think that was a mistake."

"You're telling her how she's supposed to feel?" I slammed my glass on the table. "A mistake on what basis?"

"I don't think what happened in our relationship is any of your business. No relationship is perfect. It takes real work. Unlike, you know, being a musician who's not even around to put effort into things."

I sucked in a breath. He'd hit a nerve. He seemed to know exactly what to say to get to me. The likelihood of this talk ending well was diminishing by the second.

I rolled up my sleeves. "You know what? This *was* a bad idea. I thought I could talk to you and not want to smash your face in, but I was wrong."

"I'd love to see you do that because it would solidify for Nicole what a nutcase you are."

"You're a piece of shit, Julian. I can't believe we were ever friends. You can think whatever you want about yourself, but the truth is, it takes a real shitty human being to move in on his friend's wife."

"Again, she's not your wife. And she wasn't when I started dating her."

I leaned in. "She'll always be my wife. And if you know her as well as you seem to think you do, you'd see in her eyes who she belongs to. Just mention my name around her and you'll see what I mean."

"Don't be so sure she would ever go back to you. Do I need to remind you *why* she ran to me in the first place?" He glanced down at my beer and raised his chin. "Why don't you have another drink? Make some great decisions..."

My body trembled with rage. That was it. *Why don't you have another drink?* That's what caused me to snap. My chair skidded against the wood floor as I stood, my glass shattering to the ground. I grabbed him by the neck, dragged him over to the wall, and slammed him against it.

I squeezed his neck and spat, "Go ahead. Say it again. Tell me to have another drink."

Two men rushed over and pulled me off of him. When one of them threatened to call the cops if I didn't immediately leave the bar, I decided I couldn't risk staying. Mimi had relatives who were cops in this town. She'd find out what happened. Then what?

So I left without so much as looking at Julian again, secretly thankful that they'd stopped me. Because I really would have hurt him.

I debated how to explain to Nicole what I'd done—or almost did—on the ride home. What I'd *wished* I'd done to him. My behavior certainly wasn't going to score me any points.

Ashamed, I wasn't ready to face her. So I detoured to my sister's first. I needed to decompress.

"You look like shit," Tina said when she opened the door.

"Yeah. I feel like it." I followed her to the kitchen. "Are any of the kids here?"

"No."

"Good."

I didn't want my niece or nephews to know about today. I always tried to set a good example for them, even if Kieran had gotten a taste of my bad behavior when he toured with us.

"What happened, Atticus? Is it Mimi?"

I shook my head.

My sister wasn't surprised one bit after I explained what had gone down at the bar. Thankfully, she and I were on the same page.

"That guy had some damn nerve coming here to stir up trouble. I wish you *had* knocked his teeth out."

And *that's* why I loved my sister.

I nodded. "Me, too."

"But no skin off your back. You got out of there, and no one was killed. Why are you still so down?"

I rubbed my temples. "I don't have a lot of time left here with Nicole and Mimi. I guess I hoped that somehow

Nicole and I would've reconnected more by now. But I take two steps back every time we make some progress, making things worse each day. Not to mention, Julian coming back reminded me that he's not out of the picture. He'll have the home court advantage." I tugged on my hair. "I don't know what to do."

Tina poured me a glass of water, sat down, and slid it across the table. "If the love wasn't still there, it would be easy, you know? The reason things have been so tense for you is because it's very much still alive. And I wish more than anything that I could convince Nicole to see things differently, to give you another chance, but it has to come from her. She has to be ready for that."

"I know." I sighed deeply. "That's the thing. I'm not sure she'll ever accept what happened. And I can't blame her."

"Don't give up hope, not as long as you're both still alive."

I reached for her hand. I'd give anything to bring her husband, Brian, back for her. I sighed. "The reality is…I think I need to focus exclusively on Mimi for the rest of this trip and stop thinking there's any other reason Nicole invited me here. Because I'm setting myself up for major disappointment."

"Well, you'd better be spending some time with *us* before you leave town. The kids will never forgive you if you don't."

"I'm looking forward to seeing them. Freaks me out that they're all adults now, though." I chuckled.

It was dark by the time I left my sister's.

Once I got back to the house, the first thing I did was peek in on Mimi. Thankfully she was sleeping soundly.

Then I walked into the kitchen to find Nicole sitting with a cup of tea.

Her expression was sullen, and she wouldn't look up at me. "Where were you all this time?"

"It took me a while to find Julian, and then I went to my sister's after I left the bar."

She nodded.

Placing my keys on the counter, I hung my head. "I assume he told you what happened."

"He did. I was worried because it was a while ago that he said you left."

"Of course..." I gritted my teeth. "He called you as soon as he could. I'm sure he spun it that I attacked him unprovoked."

She lifted her gaze to meet mine. "Did you?"

"He brought up the very thing he knew would trigger me. He was asking for it."

I couldn't even repeat it.

A look of sadness crossed her face. I couldn't tell if she was upset at the whole thing or just disappointed in my actions.

"I tried," I told her. "I really did. I thought I could have an adult conversation with the guy, but apparently, it's just not possible for me to be in the same room without wanting to kill him. I'm sorry."

"No, you're not," she said with a hint of a smile.

I waited, expecting her to scold me for my loss of control.

Instead, she stood, walked over to me, and put her hands around my face. "Are you okay?" she asked softly.

Taken aback, I nodded.

She shocked me even more when she brought my face to hers and kissed me on the forehead.

I closed my eyes, appreciating every second. "You're not mad?"

Instead of answering, she patted my face. "Did you eat dinner at your sister's?"

I shook my head. "No."

"I made a fresh batch of chili, if you want some. It's in the crockpot."

Is she really giving me a pass?

"I would love some," I said with a sigh.

Nicole left me alone in the kitchen. I didn't understand why she hadn't given me a harder time about my behavior, but I was damn grateful for it.

My stomach grumbled as I went over to the counter and got myself a bowl of chili.

I ate it in silence, unable to stop thinking about what had transpired—mainly that kiss on the forehead, which had given me more hope than anything in a very long time. It spoke a thousand words. Among them, that she understood me, she was sorry, and maybe she still loved me. Even if it was false hope, I'd hang onto it. It was better than feeling like I'd lose her again once the time here ended.

After I finished and took a shower, Nicole already seemed to be asleep when I got to the bedroom. Her long black hair was splayed across my pillow as her body rose and fell with her gentle breathing. In all the days we'd been here, I'd never longed to hold her more.

Instead, I ran my fingers gently through her hair before moving her tresses off of my pillow. What I really wanted, though, was to bury my face in that hair and inhale it all night.

I lay down facing her back, continuing to wish I could wrap my arms around her. But getting to lie next to her was better than nothing. It was certainly better than a lonely bunk on a tour bus, where I'd spent endless nights wishing for this. Actually, lying next to Nicole right now was better than *anything*. And you know what? Even though I hadn't had a chance to win any fights with Julian today, I *had* won. At least for now, in this moment. Because I was the one here with her.

A few minutes later, I heard her voice. It was barely audible.

"Atticus..."

Surprised that she was awake, I straightened a little and answered softly. "Yeah, baby?"

"Atticus..."

I'd thought she was trying to get my attention, but she was talking in her sleep. For real this time. I'd been messing with her this morning when I'd told her she was saying obscene things while unconscious. This was the first time I'd heard her do this since we'd been here.

"Atticus..." she repeated.

I closed my eyes, loving the way she called my name and wishing so badly that I could see inside her mind right now.

Why was she calling for me?

What were we doing in her imagination?

Did she forgive me in her dreams?

Did she *love* me in her dreams?

Chapter 15

NICOLE

The following week, Atticus told me he had to go to the city for the day. Made sense since he was this close, rather than in L.A. He'd left in the wee hours of the morning and had likely only gotten a few hours of sleep.

We'd been here now for twelve days, and this felt more normal with each day that passed. It was hard to believe we'd be parting ways soon. I'd grown attached to having him around, and I wasn't ready for it to end.

With Atticus gone today, the afternoon dragged. Mimi slept for most of it, so I did everything I could to keep myself busy and sane. I cleaned the kitchen from top to bottom and took a quick drive out to the coffee shop, checking in periodically on her via the app on my phone. That fifteen minutes out and about was like heaven after being stuck in the house most days.

More than anything, I found myself missing Atticus, which was disconcerting to say the least, considering he'd only been gone a few hours. It felt like all the work I'd done to try to get over him these past few years was slowly coming undone. I missed his coffee in the morning. I missed anticipating his return from the store. I missed his smell. His laugh. And the sweet way he spoke to Mimi. He'd be back tonight, and I knew I'd wait up if it turned out he came back late.

As if the universe knew I was going stir crazy, later that afternoon, there was a knock on Mimi's door.

When I opened, I found Atticus's beautiful niece, Kenzie, standing there, the sunlight casting a glow on her strawberry blond hair.

"Hi, Nicole." She smiled. "I hope it's okay that I stopped by."

"Oh my gosh, Kenzie. It's so good to see you." I opened my arms and gave her a hug.

She squeezed me. "It's been so long."

"I know." I waved. "Come in. Please."

Kenzie had grown into such a beautiful woman. She looked just like her dad, Brian, with the same color hair and complexion. Both Tina and Atticus had dark hair, but the only one of Tina's kids who looked like the Marchetti side was the youngest, Kyle. Kieran, Kenzie's twin, also resembled their dad.

Kenzie looked around the small living area. "Am I disturbing you?"

"No. Not at all. Actually, I'm happy for the company. I was going a little bonkers all alone today. Well, Mimi is here, of course, but she's catching up on sleep. She must've not slept well last night."

"How *is* Mimi?"

"She's good most days, all things considered."

"Where's my uncle?"

"He went to the city for the day. He should be back tonight."

She looked over at the photos on the wall. "I see."

"I'm glad you came by, though," I said. "I haven't talked to you in a long time." I led the way. "Let's go in here so we can chat."

We walked past Mimi's room into the kitchen.

"Can I get you something to drink?"

She took a seat. "Do you have any wine?"

Her question gave me pause, because the last time we were together, I was pretty sure she wasn't quite legally able to drink. But she was most definitely old enough now. "Absolutely I do." I smiled. "Is red okay?"

"That's perfect."

"That's your uncle's favorite. So that's what we have." I took out a bottle and poured us each a glass.

I handed her one and sat down across from her. "It feels weird to be drinking wine with you."

"Yeah, well, a lot of time has passed, hasn't it?"

"Are you still living at your mom's?" I asked.

"Kieran and I have an apartment in town now. Kyle is the only one still living at home."

I took a sip. "What are you, twenty-three now?"

"Twenty-four." She sighed. "Yup. Getting old."

"Hush..." I laughed, gliding my finger along the stem of my glass. "Listen, I just want to get something out of the way."

"Okay..."

"I feel really guilty for not communicating with you all this time. What happened between Atticus and me wasn't your fault, and you shouldn't have had to pay for it. I'm sorry I didn't keep in touch after he and I split."

Kenzie shook her head. "Everyone in the family understands why you had to leave. And what happened was very difficult for all of us to accept at first."

"I know. I just...I've missed you. Your mom, too. And your brothers. All of you. You were my family. And I'm sorry."

"I did always see you as a big sister. I'm not gonna lie. It was difficult. But I never blamed you, you know?"

"Do they all hate me deep down? Your mom and the boys?"

"For what?"

"Any number of things. Not sticking by Atticus. And... well, I'm sure you heard about Julian and me, right?" I hated bringing it up, but I owed her the truth at this point.

"That was definitely surprising. Out of all the men in the world, I don't understand why you had to choose him, but..."

I could see disappointment in her eyes.

"Your reaction is fair. I know it seems hard to believe." I paused. "Julian found me in a very bad state one night. He wasn't trying to pursue me. We literally ran into each other in the city. Nothing turned romantic between us for a long time." I took a long sip of wine. "Then I heard some rumors about your uncle. It shouldn't have bothered me so much, because we were divorced, but it did. It still felt like a betrayal, even if I knew my leaving was what had caused him to spiral. During that time, I became closer to Julian. He cared about me, and in some ways, I grew to care about him. But if I'm being honest, I knew I was only with him to try to forget about Atticus."

She nodded. "Are you still with Julian?"

"No." I shook my head. "I ended things."

"How did he take it?"

"Not well. He says he fell in love with me and wants me to consider getting back together. He came to Monksville to try to talk me into giving things a second chance. Atticus and he got into it last week."

"Oh my gosh. What a mess."

"Atticus tracked him down at the bar, and things got a bit ugly. Thankfully, no one got hurt."

"Well, Julian may care for you, but he should know that you and Atticus are soulmates. The fact that you're not together doesn't change that."

My eyes widened. She seemed completely confident in what she'd said. Maybe that's why I could never seem to feel at peace—because life had ripped me away from my soulmate, and every day since had been about trying to find my way back to him. "The truth is, Kenzie, I live with a lot of regret about how I handled the situation. I'm not proud of it. There are many things I would do differently, if I could go back in time."

"Like what?"

"For one, I wouldn't have allowed my fear of Atticus's fame to control my actions."

"I never understood why you didn't trust him."

"I think I have some trauma that I haven't dealt with when it comes to my father."

"What do you mean?"

I sighed. "My dad cheated on my mother. It had been going on for years, and we had no idea. I'd always believed I came from the happiest family, that it was safe and sacred. That my parents were so in love that nothing could ever break that bond. When we found out, it was quite a gut punch. It felt like my entire life had been a lie. My hero turned out to be a fraud. I found that out around the time Atticus and I got married, so I'd lived most of my life believing my dad was a stand-up guy."

"Atticus would never cheat on you."

I nodded. "Strangely, in the years we've been apart, as I see how badly our separation has affected him, I do believe that now." I shook my head as I felt a teardrop fall.

"Well..." She sighed. "No matter what happens, I'm always here for you, Nicole. And I hope now that we've broken the ice, you and I can stay in touch."

"I would love that, Kenzie. Truly." I wiped my eyes. "Enough about me. What's going on with *you*?"

She shrugged. "I'm just trying to figure out life. Photojournalism wasn't exactly the wisest major for getting a job."

Kenzie was so smart. She'd run track in high school and earned a full scholarship to Boston University, my alma mater.

"What have you been doing in the meantime?"

"Wedding photography." She rolled her eyes.

"What's wrong with that?"

"There's nothing *wrong* with it. It just feels like a waste of my skills. It's always the same thing. But I have to say, it really pays the bills and then some. I've been continuously booked."

"Well, that's awesome. At least you're getting paid."

"But if I could do it on the side and have a main gig at a newspaper or something, that would be ideal. The best of both worlds. I wouldn't mind getting to travel."

"Well, don't give up on that, if it's your dream." I shook my head at the grown woman in front of me. "Can I just say how proud of you I am? As someone who's known you since you were a little girl?"

Kenzie smiled, but my phone rang, interrupting our conversation. When I saw it was Mimi's caretaker, I picked up right away. "Hey, Louise."

"Hi, this is Lynn, actually, Louise's daughter."

Something about her sullen tone brought dread to my gut. "Oh, hello. Is everything okay? I've been waiting for your mother to confirm that she'll be back in a couple of days as planned? I'd tried to call her, but—"

"I'm really sorry, but I'm afraid I'm calling with some bad news."

My heart sank. "What happened?"

"My mother had a heart attack on the ship two days ago. And I'm sorry to say..." Lynn hesitated. "She passed away."

Chapter 16

NICOLE

Atticus' smile melted to a frown the moment he walked in. I'd been pacing near the door, anxious for his return.

"What's wrong, Nicole? Your eyes are red. Have you been crying?"

I just kept shaking my head. He pulled me into his arms without hesitation.

He spoke low into my ear. "Tell me what happened."

"Come into the bedroom. Mimi can't hear us."

I explained everything to Atticus about Louise passing away on the cruise. She'd apparently had a heart attack after attending some dancing event on the ship. She was only in her early sixties. How could someone so young and energetic just drop dead without warning? Life was so unfair.

Rubbing my arms, I continued to pace. "I don't know what to do. I don't want to tell Mimi. She won't be able to handle it."

Atticus sat on the edge of the bed, scratching his chin. "I think we need to tell her. There's no way around it. We could get away with some crazy story about why she's not back yet for a little while, but forever?"

"Okay, you're right." I exhaled. "I think I need a few days, though. You and I were supposed to be gone in a couple of days. But I can't leave now. I'm gonna have to let my clients know I'll be gone longer than anticipated."

He stood and squeezed my shoulder. "We'll figure it out together. I've got you. I won't leave Monksville until there's a solution."

His gentle touch calmed me for a moment. But then reality set in. "You have to get back to your life."

"There's nothing more important than you. Fuck the rest."

I shook my head. "I don't know how you can say that, Atticus. After everything…"

"I'm not just saying it. I mean it. I'll drop everything for as long as you need me to stay."

His eyes glistened as he looked deeply into mine. I could see my reflection in them. Those beautiful eyes had once held my entire future, the promise of children, and a life of laughter and love—eyes that were constantly begging me to reconsider that dream, even if he didn't come out and ask me.

"How was your trip?" I asked, willing myself to focus.

My question seemed to break his trance. "It was good. Very good. Thank you for asking."

I nodded, shooing away the pangs in my chest.

"Do you want me to tell you more?" He swallowed.

My heart raced as I shook my head. *You're a coward, Nicole.*

"Okay," he whispered.

It was too much to go there tonight. I needed to keep my focus on the problem at hand. What the hell was I going to do with Mimi now that she had no one to take care of her?

"Don't hold the entire world on your shoulders, okay?" he said. "We're not gonna come to a solution tonight or even tomorrow. But we'll find a good person to watch over her. Might take a couple of weeks. But I'll make sure she gets the absolute best care, even if we have to pay more."

"I don't want to take your money."

"It wouldn't be you taking it. It would be for Mimi, and I think we can both agree that we just need to do what's best for her at this point."

I'd been adamant since the divorce about not taking a single cent from Atticus. If I couldn't handle his fame, I didn't want his money. But he was right. If he was willing to help pay for someone we otherwise couldn't afford, that would be in Mimi's best interest, and I'd need to get over it. Atticus was a multimillionaire. If he wanted to give money to Mimi, who was I to interfere?

"It's going to be very hard to replace Louise because it was a unique arrangement," I explained. "Rather than being here eight hours a day, she'd come in and out since she lived nearby, keeping tabs on Mimi with the camera and the app. She took much less money than anyone else probably will."

Since I'd been using Mimi's savings to pay for her care, I really appreciated not having to pay double or triple what Louise charged. Mimi needed around-the-clock assistance, but the going rate for that was through the roof.

Atticus shook his head. "Please don't worry about the money, okay? We'll figure it out one step at a time."

Letting out a long breath, I nodded. "I'll try."

He looked into my eyes again. "I'm not exactly upset about the prospect of staying here longer until we can find someone. I still have time before I'm needed in L.A."

That brought me some comfort. "Kenzie came by today," I told him.

His expression brightened. "Really?"

"Yeah, I think she was looking to say hello to you, but since you weren't here, she and I had a nice talk."

"That makes me so freaking happy. I know how much she's missed you. I'm glad I wasn't here, if it gave you a chance to talk to her."

"Yeah, it surprised me how easy it was to open up to her. I can't believe she's twenty-four. We're only seven years apart, but I still see her as the eleven-year-old she was when you and I started dating."

"Sadly, I do, too, which makes it a problem if I ever meet any of her boyfriends."

"I definitely fear for any man who hurts her."

"She's gonna be Tristan and Emily's wedding photographer, you know," he said proudly.

"Oh, no way." I smiled. "She was telling me she's been doing a lot of weddings but wants to get into more journalistic stuff."

"Yeah, she's really talented. Have you seen her photos?"

"I follow her social media, yeah. She's definitely found her calling." I paused. "Just like her uncle, who followed his dream and made it happen. Even after everything, I'm so damn proud of you, Atticus. I don't say that enough."

"Well, you were the person who made me believe in myself enough to stick with it." He smiled sadly. "It's hard for me to appreciate my career sometimes with how complicated it's made my life."

"*I* made it complicated when it didn't have to be. My own fears. You're an amazing musician. Don't ever regret following your dream."

His stare was incendiary. "Don't you realize *you* were my dream?"

I froze. His words cut straight to my heart.

"You couldn't help your fears. I just wish..." He trailed off. "Well, I wish a lot of things."

There was torment in his eyes. Maybe he'd already figured this out about me, but it felt like a long-overdue explanation. I took a deep breath. "One of the things Kenzie and I talked about today was my dad. How I thought his cheating on my mother had given me trust issues."

Atticus blinked. "I'm surprised you went there with her."

"Me, too. I guess when you're around the right person, it brings out certain emotions. It was strange to talk about it with someone I hadn't seen for years. But maybe that made it easier."

"Well, I can see why you feel she's easy to talk to. She's like Tina in that way."

"You and I have never really discussed my father in great detail, the way he's impacted my life. There's a lot I've figured out over the past few years, but I think I need to follow your lead and see a therapist. That seems like it might help."

"I think that's a great idea. I've always figured your dad had something to do with your fears about our marriage. How can you not have trust issues when the man you trusted the most failed you?" He nodded. "I get it, Nicole. I never pushed you to talk about it because I knew how much it upset you. But even before you brought it up just now...I knew the connection."

I shook my head. "I felt bad for even mentioning my father to Kenzie. It hit me afterward that I'd been complaining about my dad when she didn't have hers. But I didn't have time to apologize for that because the call about Louise came in. I—"

"I'm sure she didn't see it that way, but I get what you mean." He sighed. "I think about Tina and Brian a lot, whenever I find myself lamenting what happened with us. As painful as it's been being apart from you, at least I can still *see* you. You know? I can still be here like this and look into your eyes. See you smile back at me—sometimes, when I'm lucky. And even laugh with you. I'll take anything I can get over nothing at all, no matter how painful it sometimes feels. That's why I don't want this time here to end."

"But it will," I whispered.

Atticus took my hand. "Ever since we broke up, I've looked forward to going on tour more than anything because there's nothing worse than being home without you. Home was always where you were. And it doesn't matter if I'm at my house in L.A. that you've never been to, or our old apartment in New York, being in one place just reminds me of the emptiness I've felt since losing you." He looked away. "But on tour, everything is erratic and moving, and it doesn't give me a chance to think. On tour I'm someone else. Which is just as well because there is no me without you. Being here? This is the first time in a long while I've wanted to stay in one place. But it's only because you're here."

My fingers tingled as I yearned to touch him. Eventually I gave in and ran my hand through his hair. "Atticus..." I whispered.

"Fuck." He bent his head back. "You touching me feels so good." He exhaled and shut his eyes. "The other night, you were calling my name..."

My hand froze. "What do you mean?"

"In your sleep...you kept calling my name over and over."

I had no recollection of that, but given the lack of mischievous look on his face, I had a feeling that this time, he was telling the truth about my sleep talking. I swallowed. "I was?"

"Yeah..."

"Was that it?"

"That was it. You were calling for me, yet I was right there. It's sort of the way I feel every moment you look at me when you're awake, Nicole. You try so hard not to feel anything, but I see it in your eyes. It's all still here, isn't it?" He wrapped his hand around my neck, the cold metal of his rings a contrast to the heat of his palm. "You'll always be fucking mine. You can move on. But you will always belong to me." He rubbed his thumb along the center of my neck. "Look at the effect I still have on you. It doesn't matter whether I look at you or touch you like this. I see how you change instantly. You still want me."

My breaths quickened.

He moved closer. "You can tell me it's over. But is it really? Not as long as we're both alive."

His amazing scent overpowered me as his touch continued to set my body ablaze.

"Everything I want in this world is right fucking here in front of me." Atticus lowered his hand to my back, placing his lips gently against my neck. I could feel his breath against my skin.

I wanted more, so badly. That scared me. If I went there, I wouldn't be able to handle being apart from him again. I'd worked so hard to get to the place I was before our time here. I couldn't say I was *over* him, but I was learning to live without him. And if I couldn't accept all aspects of his life, we couldn't go backward. Time hadn't just stood still these last three years.

My brain battled with my heart and body. All my heart wanted was to immerse itself in the love I could feel emanating from him. And my body wanted him inside of me.

His chest pressed against mine. I could feel his erection straining through his jeans. My legs grew weak, and I felt myself losing control. But the lust consuming me right now was no match for the fear.

I pushed away suddenly as my brain won out. "I think you should sleep on the floor tonight."

Chapter 17

ATTICUS

The next morning, Nicole got up before I did, so I didn't have a chance to make her coffee. I'd overslept because I hadn't fallen asleep until around four AM after tossing and turning on the floor.

She stood at the counter buttering toast, and I came up behind her. She flinched as she became aware of me.

I spoke low into her ear. "I'm sorry I lost control last night. It won't happen again." But even as I said it, I found myself turned on as my chest grazed her back. I knew my promise was a lie.

She turned around to meet my gaze. "I'm sorry I made you sleep on the floor."

"What did I tell you before about apologizing to me? You owe me nothing. Certainly no apologies for reacting to my bad behavior." I shrugged. "Anyway, my sleeping on the floor was probably a good idea."

I reached for a mug and poured myself some coffee. "I'll be gone for an hour."

She stopped mid-bite. "Where are you off to?"

"I have my therapy session at noon. I wasn't expecting to oversleep."

"Oh, that's right." She licked the corner of her mouth. "I guess you can always count on me for new material, right?"

"Yeah." I chuckled. She was definitely the star of my therapy sessions. I took a sip of my coffee and lowered my voice. "Later we should talk about when we're gonna tell Mimi about Louise."

She cringed. "We do have to tell her."

I usually hated therapy, but I'd take a session with Dr. Jensen any day over having to tell Mimi that her caretaker had passed away. That wasn't gonna be fun, and I dreaded it.

I downed my coffee and found my laptop before walking out to my car. After logging in to the chat portal, I waited for Dr. Jensen to appear on the screen.

She finally popped up and smiled. "Atticus. How have things been going in New Jersey?"

The first thing that came to mind was last night. "I fucked up."

Dr. Jensen tilted her head. "What do you mean by that?"

"I crossed the line with Nicole."

She drew in her brows. "What did you do?"

"I came on to her physically."

"How did she react?"

I smiled slightly. "She seemed turned on, to be honest, but also uncomfortable with her reaction. Ultimately, she pushed back and told me to sleep on the floor. So that's what I did, tossing and turning all night. Served me right."

"What do you think caused you to act in such a way?"

"I'd gone to New York for the day, and I really missed her. Then we found out Mimi's caretaker passed away. It was an emotional day. I guess it fucked me up a little, made me feel like I needed that physical contact."

Her eyes widened. "Her grandmother's caretaker died?"

"Sorry. Yeah." I sighed. "What a shock. She had a heart attack while on vacation, and we need to find a way to tell Mimi. It's gonna suck so bad." I exhaled. "It looks like I'm going to be here longer than I originally thought."

"Well, that's horrible. I'm so sorry to hear that."

"The messed-up thing is... I'm sort of happy about it." I raised my palms. "I mean, not that Louise died, of course—didn't mean to imply that. Just happy that I have a little bit of extra time here with Nicole. I feel like, at the very least, we're working our way back to a friendship, even if she'll never consider more than that with me again."

She jotted something down. "You keep talking about your relationship as if it's completely unsalvageable. From what you tell me, it seems like the two of you still have a lot of unresolved feelings for each other. So I'm surprised you don't seem to have any hope."

I rubbed my eyes. "It's complicated."

"I know we haven't delved into what happened between the two of you. I haven't wanted to push you into reliving what was clearly a trauma until you're ready. But I *do* think we need to go back a little today and continue your backstory with her."

I swallowed. "Okay."

"Let's talk about the time when Delirious Jones started hitting it big. You said that was when your relationship with Nicole began to deteriorate..."

"Yeah." I sucked in a breath and repositioned myself in the seat. "A couple of our songs went viral, and suddenly everyone was listening to our other stuff, too. We just blew up overnight. Or at least, it felt that way. Our manager set up our first multi-city tour soon thereafter, and everything started happening really fast."

"What stage of your marriage were you in at the time?"

"Nicole and I had been married for about five years. We were living in Brooklyn at the time. Tristan and Ronan lived in New York back then, too, so we were all there. Nicole had built a big clientele in the city with her hairstyling. She'd been making all the money while I was a struggling musician."

She nodded. "So that part changed almost overnight, too."

"Right. I was suddenly making more money than we'd ever dreamed of. But Nicole loved her job and was taking steps to open her own salon. I didn't want her to give up her dream just because mine was coming to fruition. When I had to go on tour for the first time, she stayed behind to continue working. I thought that was the right decision because she would've lost everything if she'd dropped it all to come on the road with me. Back then, the tour amenities weren't what they are now, either. We mainly stayed on the bus—no hotels the break things up. It wouldn't have been comfortable for her. I didn't want her to give up her life to sleep in a bunk for months."

"So she stayed back, and you went on your first adventure..."

I nodded. "Yeah, and it was harder than I ever imagined. The distance really tested us."

"Were you loyal?"

I narrowed my eyes. "Yes. I've never cheated on Nicole."

"Okay..." She paused. "So tell me more about why it was hard."

"We argued a lot. Just about the future. What was best for us..."

"She didn't want you to continue your music career?"

I shook my head. "No, that wasn't the issue. It was more like...she started expressing concern about whether us being married was the right thing, in light of my new life. She never discouraged my career, just the opposite. She's always been my biggest cheerleader. But her doubts about *us* wrecked me. I'd get off the phone with her and my performance would be shitty. Or at least what *I* considered shitty. Our fans don't tend to notice the difference. I was ready to quit, though. But Nicole wouldn't let me. She kept saying how hard I'd worked to get where I was."

"How long was the tour?"

"Only a few months, but she knew it wouldn't end there. She knew my life would never be the same, that our lives as we knew them had changed. She pushed me away slowly—until one day she admitted that she didn't think she could do it. She didn't think she could be a rockstar's wife." I shut my eyes.

"So *she* asked for the divorce?"

I nodded. "I would've left the band if it came down to a choice between Nicole or my career. But again, she refused to let me give it up. Refused to give me a choice. She sent the message loud and clear by filing the papers."

"That must have been quite a shock. Where were you when you got them?"

"It was right after the tour. She waited until I got home. I think she truly believed it was best for me not to have the pressure of a marriage. Maybe she felt like we'd made a rash decision when we eloped and I might've chosen differently if I'd known what was gonna happen with the band."

"Is that true?"

"Fuck no. But maybe *she* would've chosen differently." I leaned my head back on the seat. "I didn't understand how she could give up on us. Her filing put me in a really bad place. But even then, I knew it was about more than just me. Nicole has trust issues."

"In what way?"

"Her father. He cheated on her mother, had a long-term girlfriend no one knew about. That really messed with Nicole's head. She found out when she was twenty-two, shortly after we got married. So the emotional wounds were still fresh. Deep down, I know her decision had to do with her father, even if she never wanted to talk about it."

Dr. Jensen nodded. "So it was maybe partly trauma from her past and partly that she felt like she was holding your career back by staying married to you?"

I nodded. "But no matter the reasoning, she was wrong to ever think I was better off without her. I've proven that in the years since. I'm all kinds of fucked up now, and I'm unhappy every day that we're apart." My head was starting to hurt.

"What happened after the divorce papers were filed?"

"Everything went down so damn fast at that point. I kept trying to convince her to give us another chance, but she insisted it was best for us to not be married anymore. She refused any money from me, and we didn't own much together at that point, so there wasn't much holding up the process. Everything moved faster than I wanted."

"You signed the papers?"

"What choice did I have? I didn't want to force her to be married to me if my life wasn't what she'd signed up for." I closed my eyes for a moment as I resisted the pain of one of my worst memories. "The night the divorce was finalized was the first time I ever went off the deep end. I drank so much I blacked out." I blew out a long breath as shame washed over me. "About a week later, though, I got this clarity that the divorce was just a bunch of papers that had been born of her panicking. I didn't give a shit whether we were legally married or not. *She* was all that mattered to me. And I thought maybe the divorce was enough to take some of the pressure off. I wondered if I could still make things work with her without the pressure of having to maintain the perfect marriage."

Dr. Jensen tapped her pen against her chin. "Interesting that you went from rock bottom to hopeful again, even though nothing had changed."

"Well, there's nowhere but up to go from rock bottom. So, yeah, I decided to not give up on us. She meant too much to me to just throw away everything we'd built. But I did it quietly. Nicole used to tell me not to share my dreams, that no one could dissuade me if I kept them to myself. So that's what I did. I didn't tell her I was hanging on to hope. I didn't tell anyone. I just chose to believe that everything would work out, that somehow the universe would bring her back to me."

"Based on the current situation, I assume that never happened?"

"Not exactly. It *almost* happened. I moved out to L.A. after the divorce, but we talked a lot on the phone, many times late at night East Coast time. We were still in each other's lives, slowly finding our way back to one another. It was like we were falling in love all over again—this time without the pressure of a marriage or a label." My eyes followed a cat walking across the street. "Our conversations ran pretty deep during those calls. She admitted that she was freaked out by my sudden fame. But more than anything, she admitted that she still loved me. And I think my resilience when it came to us after the divorce helped her see how much I loved her. She told me she'd consider moving out to L.A. and building a clientele there. She had a friend who was gonna hook her up at their salon. Life was all of a sudden good again. But it didn't last long." I looked back at the screen. "Then my world turned upside down."

"What happened?"

I looked over at my phone. There wasn't much time left. No way I was gonna go there today. "You usually stop us by now. Session is about to end."

"We can go a little longer today."

Of course this would be the one time she would say that. But *I* wasn't ready. "No." I shook my head. "I need a breather."

Dr. Jensen nodded and closed her notebook. "Next time, then."

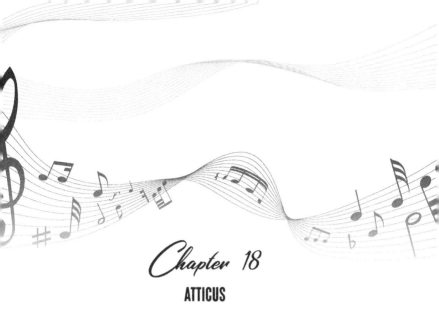

Chapter 18

ATTICUS

Today had been a day.

My mind wandered as I drove to my sister's house that evening, mentally reviewing everything that had happened since I woke up late.

After my therapy session, Nicole and I had decided to bite the bullet and tell Mimi about Louise's death. As expected, she took it really hard, cried for a while, and kept saying how unfair it was, that God should've taken her instead.

It was heartbreaking. But in the end, I was glad we'd been honest. It might've been tougher lying about why Louise was suddenly gone or trying to justify why someone Mimi loved and trusted had seemingly chosen not to come back.

I pulled up in front of Tina's. She'd invited me to dinner because all three kids would be home. When she called, I'd initially told her I didn't want to leave Nicole and Mimi. But Nicole had overheard my conversation and encouraged me to go, pointing out that there were few nights where my niece and nephews were all in one place. Mimi had fallen asleep by early evening, so in the end, I decided to go to Tina's after all.

My nephew Kyle began busting my balls the second I walked in.

"So, someone has to literally die for you to stay in Monksville long enough to see us, Uncle Atty?"

Tina slapped her son on the arm. "Kyle…"

I shook my head. "You know if you really needed me, I'd drop everything and come back to New Jersey, right?"

"Well, that's sort of what you're doing for Nicole," my sister added.

My niece, Kenzie, gave me a hug. "Did Nicole tell you I stopped by?"

"Yeah. She said you guys had a nice talk."

"We did." She smiled.

"Good."

"How's Emily?" Kieran asked. He knew Tristan's fiancée from the tour.

"Wouldn't you love to know…" I taunted.

Kieran asking about her was a running joke. "*How's Emily?*" was always the first thing he said to me. I liked to tease him about his little crush on Tristan's fiancée. They'd even gone out to dinner once, but nothing ever came of it, because unbeknownst to him, Emily had already been obsessed with Tristan.

As we sat down to dinner, I grilled Kieran about his new job. "What's the latest with that TV gig? What are you doing there again?"

"I'm working in the control room at a cable station here in New Jersey," he told me. "I'm liking it. Most especially I like the cute morning news anchor I've gone out with twice now." He winked.

"Nice."

"Yeah. Only problem is, she's looking for other jobs in bigger markets, so I don't know how long she'll be here."

"Well, not like you have too much going on. You could always move and find a similar job somewhere else, couldn't you?"

Tina glared at me. "Don't encourage that, please. I don't need my son following some girl around the country."

"Sorry. But he needs to do what he needs to do. Spread his wings." I reached for a roll. "Although, I have to admit, there's no place like home. It's just that sometimes you have to leave home to figure that out."

Kyle put his hand on his mother's shoulder. "Don't worry, Mom. You'll still have me when the other two are gone."

Kyle had one aspiration in life, and that was to become a firefighter like his dad. He wanted nothing more than to do that right here in Monksville and had pretty much been guaranteed a position. The current fire chief had been a good friend of Brian's. He was just waiting for Kyle to finish the appropriate training.

I grinned. "Dude, I can't wait to see you in that uniform. Your dad would be so damn proud."

"Thanks, Unc."

I turned to my niece. "What about you, princess? Tell me what's new."

"Just weddings up the wazoo."

"I know you're not too happy about that."

"I'm not. I feel like my creativity is stifled. But the weddings pay the bills."

I smiled at Kenzie, though I knew Tina wasn't thrilled about this. "Do you think you'd want to go on tour with us...as the band photographer?"

"Get out of town." Kenzie dropped her fork. "What are you saying?"

"Well, Layla, who's worked for us up until now, just got married and is pregnant. She can't travel anymore. So, we're looking for a new photog. I asked Doug if he'd be okay if I offered you the position."

"Oh my God." She looked over at her mother. "Did you know about this?"

Tina nodded. "He mentioned it to me, and while I'm apprehensive, I think it would be cool for you. So I'm not gonna discourage it, even if you going on tour freaks me out a little."

Kenzie turned to me. "This is a dream come true. When is the tour?"

"Early next year. I can send you all the dates once I confirm them with Doug. Can you swing it, though, if you're already committed to weddings?"

"I'll figure that out. I work under a larger company with a group of photographers, so I'm sure with enough notice they can help me get coverage." Her eyes sparkled. "Are you serious about this, Uncle Atticus?"

"I am. The only thing is, I might have to kill someone if they mess with you. The crew can be pretty rowdy. That whole scene is nothing to play with. So you have to promise me you won't get into trouble."

"I survived just fine," Kieran told her. "I'm sure you will, too."

I took a bite of chicken. "I'll tell Doug we talked, and I'll have him get in touch with you."

She nodded. "You have no idea how much this means to me."

Her look of joy made my heart happy. I loved being able to afford my niece this kind of opportunity, though I hoped I didn't regret it.

~

I stayed at Tina's pretty late, chatting with the kids. When I returned to Mimi's house, it was quiet. I peeked in on Mimi, and given the time, I assumed Nicole might also be sleeping.

When I opened the door to the bedroom, I found her in bed as expected. But she wasn't asleep.

She turned to face me. "Hi," she said groggily.

"Did I wake you?"

"No. I was having trouble sleeping. How was your visit?"

"It was great. I love those kids, even if they're not really kids anymore."

"Yeah, it's funny to think there's only ten years between you and the twins," she said. "It doesn't seem like as big of a difference as it used to, now that they're in their twenties."

"How was Mimi after I left?"

"She cried a little more. I wish I knew what to do to make it easier."

"You're doing everything you can by being here," I assured her.

"That's true."

"Is your mom coming at all?" I asked.

She shook her head. "I haven't told my mother about Louise yet. I want to see if we can find someone so she doesn't feel obligated to come back. After everything she went through with my dad, I just want her to be happy. And her fiancé, Joe, makes her happy."

"Earlier, I spoke with this staffing agency Tina told me about," I said. "Filled them in on Mimi's needs. They're working on finding us a permanent home-health aide."

"That's amazing. Thank you."

I knew I'd be able to find help for Mimi, and soon, because I'd be willing to pay more than they were used to getting. Money talks. But that left me anxious about leaving Nicole. Julian would be waiting with open arms back in New York while I was forced to return to L.A.

"Is that why you were having trouble sleeping?" I asked. "You were worried about the Mimi situation?"

"Partly. But also, my stomach is upset for some reason."

"What, did you eat some bad seafood or something?" I winked.

Her mouth curved into a smile. She knew exactly what I was referencing. Bad seafood was a running joke from our past.

"Not this time," she said.

"Well, that's good."

Nicole turned around and within minutes seemed to be asleep.

As I climbed into bed, I tried not to analyze the fact that she'd so easily relaxed into sleep after I was back. Had she been waiting up for me?

I, on the other hand, was wired. I couldn't stop thinking about her. Her little stomach-upset problem reminded me of the first time Nicole ever told me she had feelings for me.

As I nodded off, my mind drifted back to that day. At the time, it had been the best freaking day of my life.

Chapter 19

ATTICUS - PAST

It was anything but a typical Friday night down in Cassius's basement. My nerves were fried because this was the first time I'd brought Kayla around. I'd only just started dating her. We'd hung out a few times alone, but never with my friends. More than anything, I was nervous about introducing her to Nicole.

I'd decided not to tell Nicole I had feelings for her before she left for college. I had a mad crush on her and always would, but it was better if we stayed friends, given the long-distance thing. She was such a good friend, and I wanted to make sure she stayed that way. That's what I'd told myself at least—that I didn't want to hold her back when she was about to leave home. Nicole was headed to the big city. And me? I was stuck in Monksville, still dreaming of some big break that would get me out of here and on my way to an actual music career. That was probably a pipe dream.

Anyway, I was pretty sure Nicole only saw me as a friend. She'd never given me any vibes that indicated otherwise. And I hadn't had the balls to test it out. I'd never been afraid of rejection, but getting shot down by Nicole was something I didn't think I could handle. That would make things awkward between us forever. So I kept my feelings inside.

We'd just finished playing a set in the basement—Cassius on the mic, Julian on guitar, and me on the drums. Kayla had been sitting next to Nicole on the couch the whole time, watching us practice. It seemed like they were getting along, which brought me some relief. But I still felt weird about it because the girl I was dating was talking to the girl I'd been obsessed with for so long. If Kayla knew my true feelings for Nicole, she wouldn't have been so friendly. It wouldn't be an issue for much longer with Nicole leaving for school in a month, though. I just needed to stay focused. It made sense for me to move on with someone else, rather than being stuck thinking about Nicole while she started her future in Boston.

After we stopped practicing, Kayla came over to sit on my lap. As she ran her fingers through my hair, I noticed Nicole looking over at us. Was she happy for me? Was she jealous? Was she just observing?

Cassius brought out some beer, and we all dove in. Well, everyone except Nicole. She looked pretty upset now, and that concerned me.

When Kayla left to use the bathroom, I went over to Nicole. "Are you okay?"

She wouldn't look me in the eye as she blushed. "Yeah, I'm fine. Why do you ask?"

"I don't know. You just look like something is wrong."

She hesitated. "I think it was this...seafood I ate earlier."

"Seafood? You're sick to your stomach?"

Nicole continued to look away from me. "Yeah," she muttered before getting up from the couch. "You'd better stay away so you don't get sick, too."

Something seemed off, but I had no reason to question her. A few minutes later, when Kayla was back on my lap, Nicole left the basement. After that, I found it hard to focus on anything else. I couldn't ignore the prospect of Nicole being jealous.

Unable to help myself, I lifted Kayla off my lap and stood. "Excuse me for a minute, okay?"

"Where are you going?"

"Bathroom," I lied.

Nicole was nowhere to be found upstairs, so I assumed she had left, which bummed me out. I was about to return downstairs when I spotted her car in the driveway. I rushed outside just as she was backing out. I held up my hands, prompting her to stop.

She rolled down the window.

"Are you okay?" I asked.

She shook her head. "Not really."

"You're feeling sicker?"

Despite the darkness, I could see her face turning red.

"You don't know what's going on here, Atticus?" Her eyes glistened as she looked up at me. "You really don't know?"

"Why don't you tell me…" I walked around to the passenger side and got in.

She backed out and drove a ways down the road before parking on one of the side streets. Nicole shut off the engine. "I can't stand seeing you with her."

My heart beat faster. *I was right? She's jealous?* My chest filled with hope. I swallowed. "In what way? Like, you don't like her... Or you don't like her *with me*?"

"I don't like *anyone* with you. I thought I'd be able to handle this when the day came. Especially since I'm going away. But I've never felt so much jealousy in my life."

Before I could respond, Nicole got out of the car and hurled all over the street. I ran to hold her hair back.

After she finally stopped, she turned to me. "This is so mortifying."

"That must have been some fish..." I teased.

She held her stomach. "You're the fish, Atticus! It's you. Seeing that girl all over you made me sick to my stomach." She shook her head. "You must think I'm nuts."

"Are you kidding? This is the happiest night of my life. I didn't know you felt that way about me. I really didn't. If I'd thought for a second that you had feelings for me, I wouldn't have been with her at all, let alone brought her around." I brushed my hand along her cheek, not giving a shit if I got vomit on me. "Nicole, I've been so into you all this time. But I was scared you didn't feel the same way. I've dreamed about you telling me you had feelings for me. Can't say I imagined it happening like this, though." I laughed.

"You didn't imagine the barf?"

"Not quite. But it's all good."

"What do we do now?" she asked.

"What do you *think* we do? I'll drive us back to the house, take Kayla home, and tell her we can't see each other anymore. You wait for me to come back."

"Wait for you where?"

"Wherever you want. I'll go wherever you are. Just tell me where to meet you. But make sure no one else is around, because I want to kiss you like you've never been kissed before." I winked. "Just brush your teeth first."

Still looking embarrassed, she laughed nervously. "I've never been kissed before, Atticus."

I arched a brow. "Say what?"

"I know that's crazy. I'm eighteen, and I've never been kissed, but the opportunity just hasn't presented itself. I've spent the past two years wishing I was with you." She looked down at her feet and shook her head. "I haven't been interested in anyone else."

After she dropped me off at Cassius's house, I ran down to the basement and told Kayla we needed to leave.

Feeling a bit giddy, I drove her to her house and let her down as easily as I possibly could. Still, she got pissed, slammed the car door, and ran inside. Maybe that was a shitty thing to do to someone, but the girl of my dreams liked me so much that she'd thrown up.

That was pretty damn awesome.

Chapter 20

NICOLE

Atticus's large arm was wrapped around me when I woke up. This guest room bed certainly wasn't big, but until now we'd managed to avoid being *this* close. I should've moved away, but I didn't.

You'll wake him if you move, I told myself. But I knew better. The truth was this felt too good. Being in the warmth of his arms was the best place in the world. It was the only time I'd ever felt safe. He was sleeping and oblivious to it, so I didn't have to justify my actions.

But as the minutes passed, the feeling of safety transformed into something else: intense arousal. I hadn't been *this* horny since we'd arrived here.

My temperature rose as his breath warmed the back of my neck. My nipples stiffened. *Oh God.* The need to touch myself became too much. Without thinking it through, I slipped my hand into my pajama bottoms and began massaging my clit—ever so slowly so as not to wake him. I imagined Atticus waking up and taking me from behind without so much as a word. I pressed my fingertips to my clit and thought about his hard, thick cock entering me, filling me like he always did. No one had ever pleasured me the way he could. And no other man knew his way around my body like Atticus. When you were made for someone, any experience with anyone else felt broken. I shunned the pervasive thoughts of how many women had experienced Atticus over the past few years, determined not to let that ruin my current pleasure.

I shifted, and my ass grazed the hardness of his cock. I was pretty sure Atticus had woken with a stiff one every morning since we'd arrived. He was a sexual person, so morning wood was par for the course. I forced my hips forward, away from the warmth. Now I was more aroused than ever, circling my fingers faster over my clit, praying to reach orgasm before he woke up and also wanting to prolong this feeling.

I froze when I felt his hand grip my wrist. His voice was strained. "Need some help?"

Adrenaline rushed through me. Had he been awake this whole time? I gulped. "What are you talking about?"

He spoke against my back. "You're masturbating..."

My chest rose and fell as I said nothing. Denying it would've been stupid. Admitting it would've been even more stupid.

"Did you forget I used to catch you doing that all the time? I know what it looks like. Did you think I wasn't going to figure it out, with you moving your beautiful ass around in front of my cock for the past fifteen minutes? What warm-blooded man could sleep through that?"

I swallowed. "I really thought you were asleep."

"Were you thinking about me?"

I said nothing.

"I'll take no denial as a yes?"

I shut my eyes tightly, even more turned on now by the sound of his voice.

He moved in closer and spoke against my back, sending a shiver down my spine. "What did I tell you about not wearing underwear to bed? You haven't listened to me once. I can see the shape of your ass right through those thin little pants every single night. It fucking drives me crazy."

My breathing became heavier as I felt goose bumps form.

"You know how many times I've had to go to the bathroom to jerk off so I could fall asleep? Almost every damn night." He spoke behind my ear. "But you *like* driving me crazy. Am I right?"

I pleaded the fifth.

"Once again, I'll take your silence as a yes."

Atticus wrapped his hand gently around my neck. I closed my eyes, and rather than moving away like I should have, I surrendered to the need building within me, pressing my backside into him.

"That's it. Give me that beautiful ass." He pressed his erection against my crack. "Fuck, Nicole. Now I know you're trying to kill me." He ground his massively hard cock against me. "You know how torturous it's been to look down at your apple bottom every night, knowing I could be inside of it in three seconds? Knowing how damn good it always felt to fuck that beautiful ass?" He groaned. "You used to beg me to do it," he rasped. "You've been torturing me every night. You better believe now I'm gonna torture *you*."

"Atticus…" I begged, not even sure what the hell I was asking for. Did I want him to stop or keep going? I wasn't sure.

"Go back to what you were doing," he hissed. "Touch yourself. I want to help."

Willing away all the voices of reason in my head, I resumed massaging my clit.

"I bet you're nice and wet, aren't you? You're always so damn wet for me."

As he pressed his cock harder against my backside, I felt it move. "Is this okay?"

Letting out an unintelligible sound, I nodded.

"You feel how fucking hard I am? I'm imagining sinking inside that wet pussy right now."

My clit throbbed. "Mmm-hmm."

"You know what I would give to be inside you right now?" He slid his dick up and down my ass crack. "My left nut. All my freaking money. Anything."

The *need* to have him inside of me was almost too much to bear. I felt my orgasm threatening to rise to the surface.

He thrust his hips against me. "Feel me. Feel me right here. Feel what you do to me."

I moved my fingers faster. My clit was so wet, I could no longer get a good grip with my fingertips.

I felt his hand on my inner thigh. "Can I?"

I nodded, not even understanding what he was asking, but it didn't matter. Whatever it was, the answer was a resounding yes.

Atticus slipped his hand down my pants. His low groan vibrated against my back. "Holy shit, Nicole. I knew you were wet, but this is..." He sank his fingers inside of me, moving them in and out as I backed my hips against his rigid cock. My orgasm was ready to explode.

As he continued to move his fingers in and out, he pressed his thumb against my clit and moved it in slow circles. "I missed this beautiful pussy so much. I want to come inside it so bad right now..."

I opened my mouth to beg him to do it, but the words wouldn't come out. That would be a terrible idea. And I knew he was holding back, that he wouldn't really. Because Atticus would've been inside of me by now if he'd planned on going that far. *This* Atticus was towing the line but very likely wasn't going to go there.

"I want to taste you, but I can't," he murmured. "Because once I start, I won't be able to stop."

I needed to come to put us both out of our misery. But also, I *never* wanted to come. I wanted this to last forever, just Atticus and me in our own little world as he continued to push me over the edge. I rubbed my ass harder against him.

"You're gonna make me come right up against that pretty little ass of yours? Is that what you want? I haven't come in my pants since the first time you rubbed your pussy against me. Remember that fucking day?"

I moaned in response.

"Don't worry, baby. Let go. I know you want to. It doesn't have to mean anything. Enjoy it. Let yourself come all over my hand."

My muscles began to contract.

"Come, baby. Come," Atticus urged.

When my climax erupted, I felt it in every nerve ending of my body. Just before I came down, Atticus removed his fingers. He grunted, and I felt the heat of his orgasm against my backside. We were both clothed, but it was the hottest freaking thing I could remember.

Chapter 21

ATTICUS

Later that morning, I left the bedroom before Nicole did and went to make coffee.

When she finally appeared in the kitchen, she didn't say a word to me while she drank it. She fumbled with the utensils in the drawer, seeming anxious. "Is Mimi up?" she asked.

"Not yet," I answered. "Last I checked she was still out."

All I wanted to do was drag her back to the bedroom and fuck her properly. But alas, that was the fantasy, and this awkwardness in the kitchen was the reality.

"We don't have to talk about it, Nicole. We got off. There's nothing wrong with a release. We both needed it."

"Right." She stopped messing with the silverware. "It didn't mean anything."

"I didn't say that. It sure as fuck meant something to me. But we don't have to *talk* about it."

Our eyes met.

"It can't happen again," she whispered.

I'd figured she'd say that. "Whatever you want," I said softly. "I'll sleep on the floor from now on."

"I can't let you do that." She frowned. "I'm the one who started it."

"I'll turn around and face the other way, then. That way I'm never up against you. That'll make it easier for me, too."

She looked down at the floor but said nothing.

"What's wrong? You don't trust me?"

"It's not that." She sighed. "I don't know if I like you turning away from me, either."

"You *like* sleeping next to me, that's why..."

Nicole nodded. "I like feeling you close at night, yeah."

My heart filled with hope. "Well, it's mutual."

"But it's been confusing," she added.

"I think we can agree on that. You don't feel like it's okay to want me anymore."

She shook her head. "I have never *not* wanted you, Atticus. Not a single second this entire time. But it's stronger when I'm in your presence. Wanting you has been the worst torture I've ever experienced. But I can't go backwards. I've worked so damn hard to get over you."

"How's that going, though?" I raised a brow. "Maybe trying so hard is having the opposite effect."

Nicole's phone rang, and she practically dove to answer it.

I listened as she spoke to someone. She kept nodding and jotting down a bunch of information.

After she hung up, I asked, "What's going on?"

"They found someone for Mimi. She can start any time. I guess her previous client recently passed away. She lives here in town and would even be willing to do what Louise did, popping in and out during the day and sleeping here at night."

"Wow. I'm surprised they found someone so soon." My heart felt heavy. I wasn't ready to leave her. And I wasn't talking about Mimi. "This almost sounds too good to be true."

"I know."

"Well, she can't just start," I said quickly, feeling panic rise. "We have to meet her. She has to meet Mimi. I want your grandmother to like her." *Anything to extend our time here.*

"Yeah, of course. They gave me her number and said we can contact her to arrange that."

"Okay, uh, I guess this is good news." I sighed. "Will you go back to the city right away if it turns out she's a good fit?"

"Yeah. That was always the plan, right?"

I nodded.

"You gonna stay in town or go straight back to L.A.?"

"I'll spend a couple more days with my sister, but eventually I have to get back to L.A. Recording is gonna start soon."

"That's right." Nicole slipped her hands into her pockets.

I heard rustling from down the hall. "She's up," I said, gesturing toward Mimi's room. "Should we give her a heads up about this woman?"

"Might as well."

We walked in together and Nicole sat by the bedside. "Mimi, we have great news."

Her eyes fluttered fully open. "Oh?"

"The agency found a nice lady who's local to work with you. She can do the same type of schedule as Louise did and sleep here overnight."

"Who has that kind of time?"

I laughed. "Well, it's not like she'd be doing it for free."

"Who is this person?"

"Her name is Fiona," Nicole said. "I'm gonna give her a call to come by and meet you."

I patted Mimi's leg. "If you don't get a good feeling, you let me know. I'll get you someone else you like better."

"Don't promise anything you can't deliver," Nicole warned.

Mimi reached a shaky hand toward her granddaughter. "Well, I suppose it's time you lovebirds got back to your own life. You've been here long enough, and I've hated to inconvenience you."

"Are you kidding?" I said. "This has been the best time I've had in a long while. And I'm sorry I went so long without seeing you. I won't let it happen ever again."

I meant that. I flew back and forth between New York and L.A. a lot and vowed to see Mimi whenever I was on the East Coast.

She shook her head. "You don't worry about anything except taking care of my beautiful granddaughter."

I smiled at Nicole. Mimi had no idea how much I wished that were still my responsibility.

〜

That afternoon, a woman named Fiona Baumgartner came by to meet Mimi. Fiona was a widow who'd grown up here in Monksville. She definitely had the experience for the job, having had two elderly clients in a row over the past decade.

After showing Fiona around and describing Mimi's routine in detail, Nicole and I left her alone with Mimi for a bit. We'd told her we'd return in an hour.

In the meantime, we walked around the neighborhood, circling the block a couple of times before I decided to broach the subject on my mind.

"Even though this trip ran longer than expected, things are coming to an end faster than I'm ready for," I said. "I want to make sure you know how much this time has meant to me. Even fighting with you is better than not communicating, never seeing you. This time has broken the ice between us, and I never want to go back to the way things were when we weren't speaking. Even if I can't have you as my wife, Nicole, you mean so much to me. I want to be your friend, at the very least."

She stopped walking and turned to me. "I don't know *how* to be friends with you, though, Atticus. I don't know how to be around you and not feel *everything*—the good and the bad."

A wave of panic hit. Did *she* want things to go back to the way they were? "So what's the alternative?" I asked. "Never seeing me again because you feel *too much*?" I shook my head. "Not an option for me. I'm willing to feel it all, Nicole, even if it kills me. I don't want to live in a world where the mention of my name makes you sad. I don't want to live in a world where one of the guys mentions you, and I can't perform well for the rest of the night. We've been through too much together to remain strangers like we've been for the past few years," I pleaded. "I need you in my life."

"What does that life look like if we're not together? You can't handle the idea of me moving on any more than I could handle the same."

That was exactly right. Deep down, I knew my version of staying in touch was different from hers. Mine meant working toward ultimately being together again. But if she didn't see it that way, she was right. Staying in touch *wouldn't* be easy. I'd never handle being around her if she was with another man. *Never.*

Still, I warned myself to slow my roll.

"I don't have the exact answer, Nicole, but maybe it starts with a promise to call each other once in a while. To check in."

After a pause that felt like a lifetime, Nicole nodded. "I can do that."

A rush of relief washed over me, and we resumed walking. At one point, we passed the house she'd always said was her dream home here in town. I didn't say anything, but I could tell by the look on her face that she was thinking about it, too.

When we returned to Mimi's, we found her and Fiona laughing together in the bedroom.

"You two getting along?" Nicole asked.

Fiona smiled. "I have to say, Miss Mimi here is a hoot. I think I hit the jackpot."

"Aw, well, we're glad you see what we see," Nicole said.

"I can start any time if you two need to get on with your lives."

"Like how soon?" I asked.

Fiona stood. "How about tomorrow?"

My pulse raced. "Tomorrow?"

"That would be fantastic," Nicole answered faster than I could process this.

That night before bed, I called Ronan to update him on the latest situation.

"Dude! When are you coming back to L.A.?" he asked in greeting.

"Sooner than I thought." I ran my hand through my hair. "And I'm not thrilled about it."

"You found someone for Mimi?"

"Yeah. A local widow. She seems great. And she's supposed to start tomorrow, which means I have to get out of here. I'll spend at least a few days at Tina's, then book my flight back to L.A."

"I know it sucks leaving Nicole, but I'll sure as hell be happy to have you home."

"Thanks, man." But L.A. wasn't *home. This* felt like my home.

"You okay?" he asked after a moment.

"I think I had this deluded thought that if I had more time, I could somehow win her back. I could find a way to make things so great that she'd forget everything. Or maybe she'd just finally be willing to work through things we never have. It was a fantasy, though."

"I get it, man."

"We messed around a little in bed this morning," I confessed.

"Whoa, what?"

"We didn't have sex...but it surprised me that she was willing to go where we did. I can't stop thinking about it. I can't stop thinking about *her*, and I haven't even left yet."

"She cheated on her boyfriend?"

My blood pressure rose. "No." I shook my head. "I didn't tell you they broke up?"

"No! Really?"

"Yeah."

"That's huge."

"It happened before she came out here. But he showed up once, and I almost fucked him up. I don't trust that he's out of the picture."

"You need to call me for backup for shit like that. I thought I told you to let me know if you needed me."

I chuckled. "I didn't know he was coming. But getting you into trouble isn't going to make anything easier. If two of us are out of commission, there's most definitely no Delirious Jones."

"There's no Delirious Jones without any one of us."

"That's true, I guess."

"Well, I'm glad you're coming back. But I wish you'd gotten the outcome you hoped for."

"I'm still better off than I was before I came. Nicole and I are on speaking terms at least."

Ronan snorted. "Sounds like you've been doing more than speaking."

"I wish that had changed something, but it didn't."

"At least she kicked Julian to the curb, though. Or is trying to. That's a win, if you ask me. It could've been so much worse. She could've married the dude or had his kid. Then she'd be trapped with him."

"That would've been a disaster." I shuddered. I wasn't sure how Nicole felt about having kids these days, but we'd once had a pregnancy scare of our own. Although, the only one *scared* had been Nicole.

Chapter 22

ATTICUS - PAST

I rushed back from the recording studio the moment Nicole told me she'd bought a pregnancy test. We had always used protection—with the exception of one time. Hence our current situation. She'd been meaning to go on the pill but had been reluctant to start it, fearing how her body might handle it. And we'd slipped and had sex without a condom.

We'd just moved to a one-bedroom apartment in Brooklyn to be closer to where the guys and I had been recording. Nicole had started her first official hairstyling gig, and I was waiting tables. We could barely pay the rent, so it seemed impossible to fathom how we'd afford a baby.

My beautiful girlfriend met me at the door, and I followed her back to the bedroom. "Have you checked the test yet?"

"No." She shook her head, rubbing her arms vigorously. "I'm too scared."

"I know." I enveloped her in a hug. "Don't be scared, baby. I'm here. No matter what happens, we'll be okay. We have each other, and we'll get through it."

She stepped back to look at me. "This is not a good time for us to bring a child into the world. I'm only twenty-two and just getting started at the salon. And you're finally getting some traction on the music front."

I shrugged. "It's not ideal, but is anyone ever truly ready for such a huge thing to happen in their life?"

"We don't have any money," she said, looking so discouraged.

I stared into her eyes. "I'll quit the band if I have to and get a full-time job."

I'd recently hooked up with two musicians, Tristan Daltrey and Ronan Barber. We'd started a band called Delirious Jones and were currently recording our first demo album.

"That would be horrible if you had to quit now. You shouldn't even consider that."

"Well, I'll do what I have to. It'll be okay."

Nicole closed her eyes and took a deep breath. "If I have to go through this with anyone, I'm happy it's with you."

"Same, beautiful." I exhaled. "We should really check the stick, though, so we know what we're dealing with. But before we do, I want you to know something."

"What?" She blew out a nervous breath.

"From the moment you and I met, I haven't wanted anything more than *you*—to be your boyfriend. You might think my music is everything to me, based on how much time I devote to it, but it's not. *You* are. And if that test is positive, you should know that there is nothing more important to me than you and this baby."

She smiled, and it brought me comfort to know I'd given her a little bit of peace. I'd meant every word.

"Okay." She took my hand. "Come with me."

We walked together to the bathroom. The stick lay on the corner of the sink.

My heart raced as she reached for it, looked down, and let out a huge breath. "Oh my God! It's negative!" A burst of air left her body. "I'm so happy." She beamed, a look of true relief on her face.

I exhaled slowly as a strange feeling came over me. It definitely wasn't relief. It felt a lot like...disappointment.

She wrapped her arms around me and tilted her head. "Why do you look sad?"

I blinked, unsure how to explain it. "I don't know how to feel."

Nicole searched my face. "You were hoping it was positive?"

"I would've been happy if it was, yeah," I admitted.

She ran her fingers through my hair. "Really?"

I swallowed. "Yes."

"I didn't think a baby was something you'd want in your life right now."

"Just because the timing isn't ideal doesn't mean I wouldn't want it. It's something I've always dreamed of."

"You've never said that before."

"Well, didn't a certain someone once tell me to keep my dreams to myself?" I leaned my forehead against hers. "If I went around telling people I wanted a baby right now, they'd call me crazy and tell me I had no business considering that. So I kept it to myself. But, yeah, nothing would make me happier, even if it would be tough. But *you* have to be ready."

She smiled. "I will be someday."

"I can't wait to share that with you."

"Wow," she murmured.

"What?"

"You really do love me, don't you?"

I ran my hand down her back. "Why would you doubt that?"

"I don't. But seeing how you would've been okay with being bound to me for life really brings it home."

"I'd like to be bound to you for life whether we have a kid or not."

My hands shook as I considered whether I should go with my original plan. The moment she'd told me she was taking a test, I'd wanted to do the right thing and ask her to marry me. She didn't realize it, but I'd come *prepared* to do the right thing—tonight. But as I stood before her now, I realized asking Nicole to marry me wasn't just the right thing, it was what I wanted regardless of whether or not there was a baby in the picture.

"I need to confess something..." I told her.

She licked her lips. "Okay..."

"I was sure you were pregnant—after the time we didn't use protection. I was so certain you were carrying my child...that I'd planned to ask you to marry me to-night."

Her mouth dropped. "Tonight?"

I nodded. "I have a ring in my pocket right now. It's not a great ring. But it was going to have to do."

"You bought a ring?" She blinked. "When?"

"Earlier today."

"That fast? Where did you get it?"

"I went to a pawn shop. Tina gave me some gold to sell to help cover the cost. It's small, but it's real." Shaking my head, I looked down at the ground and laughed. "I'm a little embarrassed to show it to you."

She covered her mouth. "Oh my God. I can't believe you were about to propose to me!"

"The thing is...I was pumped to ask you. I *do* want us to get married."

Her mouth curved into a smile. "So do I."

"You want to, then?" An impulsive urge came over me. "Get married?" Excitement rushed through me. "I'm talking about, like, *now*. Tonight or tomorrow. Let's just do it."

"Are you serious?" Her mouth fell open. "You mean go to a courthouse?"

I shook my head. "Let's do something crazy, like go to Vegas for a couple of nights. Tomorrow, maybe."

Her cheeks turned red. "Our families will kill us."

"We don't need to tell them until we're ready. That'll be the beauty of it—our little secret."

She bounced up and down. "I can't believe I'm saying this, but I think I want to do it. Am I insane for loving you so much that I want to skip the wedding altogether? Are *we* insane?"

"I should probably propose for real, then."

Nicole covered her mouth. "Oh my God. What is happening right now?"

I got down on one knee and sighed. "I just feel like you deserve a better ring."

She looked down at me. "Is the ring from you?"

"Yes."

"Then it's the only ring I want. It doesn't matter what it looks like."

It felt like that was my cue. I paused a moment to gather my thoughts and took both her hands in mine.

"Nicole, today was one of the most stressful yet beautiful days of my life. It's made me realize even more how much I love you. We might not be having a baby, but it's clearer to me than ever that I want a future with you, whether we're blessed with a child or not." I took the velvet pouch out of my pocket and held out the small solitaire. It was only about a quarter of a carat, but the diamond sparkled brightly. "Know that someday, if I ever make it big, the first thing I'm gonna buy you is the ring of your dreams. But for now, I hope you'll wear this one."

I placed it on her finger, and it fit like a glove.

"I don't need the ring of my dreams if I have the *man* of my dreams," she told me. "From the moment I laid eyes on you, that's who you've been to me. But honestly..." She looked down at her hand. "It's perfect. And I'm not just saying that. This is the *only* ring I ever want to wear." She paused. "I love you so much."

"I love you, too, baby." I stood and wrapped my arms around her, lifting her into the air. "I promise to make you happy."

"You already do, more than anything in the world."

The following night, we flew to Vegas and got married in secret. I promised to always protect her, to never let her down.

Little did I know at the time, that was a huge lie.

Chapter 23

NICOLE

Departure day had come before I was ready.

I was picking up the living room before Atticus and I were set to leave when I overheard him having a conversation with my grandmother.

I stood behind the door, listening.

"What's wrong, sweetheart?" he asked. "You look down. Is it because we're leaving?"

"It's hard sometimes," Mimi said.

"What's hard?"

"Feeling like you serve no purpose anymore. Like you can't help anyone. My life has gone from participant to observer. There's so much I want to do but can't."

"You do serve a purpose, Mimi," Atticus assured her after a moment. "Before I came here, I felt very lost in my life. I was consumed by my career when that shouldn't be my priority. Being in your presence has reminded me how important it is to be a good example and to put family first always—like you've done. You are my biggest inspiration.

And Nicole and I wouldn't be who we are without you. You're serving your purpose every day just by being here."

"Well, that's very sweet, Atticus."

"Will you promise me something?"

"What?"

"I programmed my phone number into your cordless phone here. I know you have other numbers on speed dial, but now I'm number seven. Will you promise to call me whenever you're having moments like this one, when you're feeling sad? I'd love to be able to talk to you and remind you how amazing you are."

"What if you're performing?"

"If I see your call, and I can get away, I'll drop everything. And if I miss it, I'll call you right back."

"What did I ever do to deserve such a kind grandson-in-law?"

"You gave me Nicole. She's the kind, wonderful person she is because of the example you set and the love you always showed her."

My heart melted. How could he possibly still feel that after the way I'd treated him? Then again, this was all a show for my grandmother. Did he truly feel that way?

"I'm sad that I won't be around to see your beautiful children," Mimi cried.

I shut my eyes. That hurt my heart and soul. Atticus remained silent.

"I'll never forget what you've done for me these past two weeks," my grandmother added.

My heart couldn't take any more of this, so I stepped into the room.

"Oh." Atticus turned toward me. "Hey."

"Hi." I offered a weak smile.

"Hi, dear." My grandmother held out a shaky hand. I took it.

Atticus's eyes met mine. "Is it time to say goodbye?"

I nodded. "Yeah, I think so. I should probably try to beat rush-hour traffic."

His mouth curved into a frown.

Wrapping my arms around my grandmother, I whispered in her ear, "I love you, Mimi. I'll come visit you soon. I promise."

"I'll be counting the days, my sweet granddaughter. Please take care of yourself and be careful driving."

The plan was for Atticus to stay with her until Fiona arrived in about an hour.

He walked me to my car in the driveway. "So this is really it, huh?"

I wrapped my arms around myself. "Thank you again. I couldn't have done this without you."

"Yes, you could've. You're stronger than you realize. But I'm damn glad you didn't have to do it alone."

"Are you going to Tina's after Fiona gets here?"

"Yeah. I'm gonna hang out with her and the kids—I mean, the adults—and spend the night."

I smiled. "Then you head back to L.A.?"

He nodded. "Tomorrow night. The guys are waiting on me to get started in the studio." He looked down for a moment then back up at me. "When will I see you again?"

I took a deep breath. "Actually... I've been in touch with Emily a few times since that night we all hung out. We were talking about hairstyle ideas for her wedding, and she asked if I'd be willing to fly out and do her hair. And then stay for the ceremony."

"Really?" His eyes widened. "That's a couple months from now, right? What did you tell her?"

"Yeah, it's in two months, and I told her I'd think about it. But I need to let her know by the end of the week so she can book someone else, if needed."

"I *really* hope you do it."

"Noted," I said, still not a hundred-percent sure I was on board. I hated weddings. They reminded me of a lot of things I didn't want to remember. "If I don't end up going, maybe we could grab coffee the next time you're in New York."

"I would love that." He smiled. "That'd be the best coffee ever."

"Okay." I grinned. "Well, have a safe trip back."

"Careful driving, Nicole."

As we hugged goodbye, I could feel his heart thundering against mine.

"I don't want to let you go," he whispered.

I closed my eyes for a moment, relishing the feel of being in his arms. Forcing myself away, I rubbed my hands together, trying to distract myself from the fact that I already missed being held by him.

Atticus reached into his pocket. "Hey, I want to give you something before you go." He handed me a small box.

"What's this?"

"Open it."

I opened the box to find a white gold charm attached to a thin rope necklace. It was a figure-eight infinity symbol.

I rubbed my thumb over the metal. "It's beautiful."

"You refused to take anything from me when we split, but I'm hoping you won't refuse this."

"When did you have the time to get this?"

"I had Clemson's make it for me."

Clemson's was a local jewelry store.

"It represents who you are to me," he explained. "And maybe the new normal of our relationship. Even if we're not married or together, you're a part of me forever. And I'll always be here for you."

Feeling my eyes water, I nodded. "I'm proud of us." I stared down at the necklace. "Of how we came together these past couple weeks."

"Me, too, baby."

I looked up at him. "Will you put it on me?"

"Of course."

The feel of his hands at the back of my neck sent shivers down my spine. I cherished every second. Turning around, I hadn't accounted for how close he'd be. His gorgeous lips were *right* there.

"I hate this," he said. "I don't want to leave you."

As his eyes flickered between my eyes and lips, I gripped his shirt as if to say *I don't want to leave you, either*. He leaned in and touched my lips with his. As my heart nearly leaped through my chest, I opened my mouth slightly, expecting his tongue, but his kiss simply grew firmer—intense yet controlled. *Closed*. Then he pulled back.

He placed his fingers over his lips. "Be careful driving."

I fondled the charm. "Thank you again."

"Of course." He smiled sadly.

I wasn't sure how to interpret that kiss, but without saying anything further, I forced myself to walk away. As

I started my car, Atticus stayed put. I looked over at him one more time before backing out. He waved and blew me a kiss.

I pulled out, and he walked to the end of the driveway, watching me drive down the road until he disappeared in my rearview mirror.

On the way out of town, I drove by the house we'd passed on our walk, the one I'd always envisioned as my future forever home here in Monksville. It was white with window boxes filled with purple flowers. I slowed down to get a better look at it, trying to ignore the pangs of sadness in my chest as I clutched the infinity charm around my neck.

Chapter 24

NICOLE

Billy Idol's "White Wedding" had been stuck in my head since I'd heard it in the car on the way here. That was fitting since I was in California for Tristan and Emily's wedding.

The happy couple had rented out an entire hotel in Malibu for the reception and also for their guests' accommodations this weekend, sparing no expense. The ceremony itself would be held at a nearby church.

I'd just finished doing Emily's hair, and she looked fantastic. I'd braided small sections in a half-up, half-down style. She'd recently put in some caramel highlights, which added contrast, and we'd pinned the tiniest white flowers in her hair to complement the design, especially since she wouldn't be wearing a veil.

Emily smiled at herself in the mirror. "It came out exactly the way I'd imagined. I can't thank you enough for coming all the way out here."

Standing behind her, I grinned proudly. "I'm glad I was able to."

She wore a white-silk robe that had *Bride* stitched on the back.

"Is today the first time you're going to see Atticus since you guys left New Jersey?"

The mention of his name made the butterflies in my stomach go wild. It had been two months since we'd left each other back at Mimi's, since that chaste kiss I hadn't been able to get out of my head. I knew he'd been mostly in the recording studio since then, and we'd only spoken a few times—when he'd initiated it. I'd continued my old habit of keeping my distance so as not to fall in love with him again. Although, technically that's impossible when you've never fallen *out of* love with someone.

"Yeah. This is the first time since then," I answered.

"How do you feel about that?"

"I guess I'll find out." I didn't know how to feel. My emotions were all over the place.

Now that my face had gone from pink to red, as evidenced by my reflection in the mirror, it was time to change the subject. "Are you going to see Tristan before the ceremony, or is it a surprise?" I asked.

"We're doing a first look. So we'll have our private moment, but he will have seen me before I walk down the aisle. I wanted to get the photos out of the way so we can enjoy the party."

"Makes total sense."

Emily had three bridesmaids, all of whom were friends she'd met out here in L.A. And her childhood friend, Leah, was her maid of honor. Their dresses were a beautiful sky blue silk, each one a different style.

Emily hadn't put on her gown yet, but I could see it hanging. It was gorgeous—strapless, in a mermaid style, with lace from top to bottom and delicate sequins strategically placed throughout.

"There are still a few hours until the ceremony," she told me. "You're welcome to hang out here and have mimosas and food with us. Someone will be delivering breakfast soon."

"Oh. Thank you so much. But I think I'd like to get a walk in and explore the area around here before I have to come back and get dressed."

"Okay. Well, I hope you'll come find me later?"

"Of course." I bent to hug her, careful not to mess up her hair.

After leaving Emily's suite, I walked to a smoothie shop I'd looked up online. I got myself some breakfast, and I'd just gotten back to the hotel grounds when I spotted the male members of the wedding party gathered in a grassy area near the beach to get their photos taken. The sight stopped me in my tracks.

I hid behind a tree and watched as the men lined up. My heart beat rapidly at my first glimpse of Atticus, dressed in a maroon jacket and matching pants. The suit had satin lapels and was perfectly tailored to his muscular body. His hair was styled differently, the tresses that normally fell over his forehead parted slightly to the side, showing off a bit more of his handsome face. He looked stunning.

I watched for several minutes as Kenzie snapped away. Tristan was flanked by Atticus and Ronan, along with two other men I didn't recognize. Tristan looked so incredibly happy, and I truly wished him and Emily the best. They had been through so much to get to where they were, and despite their fifteen-year age difference, they were perfect for each other.

I looked down at my phone to check the time. I was running late but couldn't take my eyes off of them, particularly Atticus. My heart longed to be standing next to him. Having eloped, we'd never experienced a traditional wedding like this. And even though I hadn't wanted one at the time, since then, I'd often dreamed of what our wedding might've been like, how he might've looked all dressed up like this. Now I didn't have to imagine it. I could basically taste it. And it was certainly easy to envision Atticus as the groom, to imagine for a moment that this was *our* wedding day. I took a long, deep breath of the salty ocean air.

As I watched, Atticus separated from the group, walking over to a tree several yards from the one I was currently hiding behind. He took out his phone.

A few seconds later, my phone chimed, causing me to jump. I looked down to find a text.

Atticus: Are you here?

Goose bumps peppered my skin.

The last time Atticus had asked me if I'd be attending Tristan and Emily's wedding, I was noncommittal. While I'd agreed to do her hair, I wasn't sure if I wanted to stay for the actual wedding. But Emily had insisted, and I'd decided that since I was coming all the way out here, I might as well.

Nicole: Yes. I'm here for the wedding.
Atticus: Cool. I've been looking forward to seeing you.
Nicole: You look great.
Atticus: How do you know what I look like?

Shit. Shit. Shit. I'd lost my damn mind. How the hell would I know what he looked like if I weren't stalking him from behind a tree?

Nicole: I saw you taking photos.
Atticus: I sensed you.
Nicole: What do you mean?
Atticus: I can't explain it. But I sensed you. That's why I asked if you were here. Where are you?
Nicole: Hiding behind a tree, hoping you don't spot me in my workout clothes and baseball cap.

He immediately turned and looked around until he found me. His mouth curved into the most adorable smile. Then he ran over and pulled me into the biggest hug. I had no time to warn my heart to stop beating so fast. He squeezed me tightly, and I took a long whiff of his spicy scent. He smelled just as delicious as he looked.

"Holy shit. I can't believe you're here."

"I look like crap," I said, surveying my workout attire. "I didn't want you to see me like this."

"You're fucking beautiful, Nicole. It doesn't matter what you're wearing." He wrapped his hands around my cheeks. "It's so good to see you right now."

"You look very handsome." I smiled. "I don't think I've ever seen you in a suit before."

"That's pretty sad considering how long we've known each other. But yeah, I can't remember the last time I wore a suit. Maybe my first communion as a kid."

"Well, it was worth the wait." I reached out to straighten his jacket. "You ready for the big event?"

He sighed. "I have to give the best man's speech. Not really looking forward to that."

I tilted my head. "Really? You're anxious?"

"Yeah. I wish he'd asked Ronan."

"He was probably afraid Ronan would roast him hard."

He laughed. "Well, little does he know that Ronan helped me with my speech."

"Well, that backfired, then. But you'll do fine."

"If you say so."

It was kind of cute to see Atticus nervous. I guess speaking in front of an audience was a lot different than hiding behind a drum set.

He moved a piece of my hair off my face. "I was worried you weren't gonna make it. I've been afraid to ask because I didn't want you to think I was pressuring you. Didn't want to jinx it." He winked. "You know, keep your dreams to yourself and maybe they'll come true."

I shrugged. "Well, I promised Emily, so..." Sure. *Emily*. That's why I was here. I could've found her someone great to do her hair. But I *wanted* to be here. It was my excuse to see Atticus again.

I realized my hand was still lingering on his lapel. How long had it been there? When I looked up, he was staring intently. My legs felt ready to collapse.

Clearing my throat, I patted his chest and placed my hand by my side. "You'd better go in case they need you for more photos. I have to get dressed anyway."

"Yeah. Okay." His eyes lingered, and he didn't move.

I had no desire to move, either. Why would I, when I was looking into the eyes of the most beautiful man I'd ever seen while a gentle California breeze caressed my skin?

But then Kenzie called him over, and Atticus was forced to return to the wedding party.

As I watched him walk away, I knew tonight was going to be one *very* long evening.

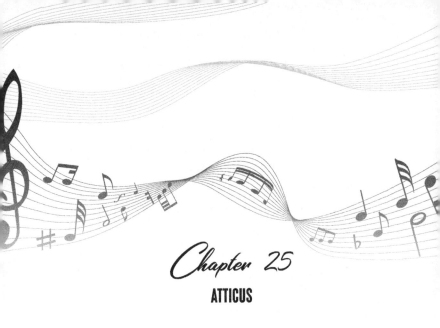

Chapter 25

ATTICUS

The moment I spotted her, everything else had faded away.

The church was now packed with people as the organist played the Wedding March. But all I could focus on was Nicole, sitting five rows back to my left.

She wore a light pink dress that was off the shoulder on one side. Her hair fell down her back in loose, black tendrils. When had her hair gotten so long? She'd had it up in a ponytail earlier so I hadn't noticed. It had only been a couple of months, but it felt like forever since I'd seen her. Stuck in the recording studio and missing her more than ever, it had been the longest two months of my life.

I couldn't get over how damn gorgeous she looked in that dress. The shoulder that was bare had a small beauty mark that I'd always loved circling with my tongue. And she'd pinned a silk flower in her hair. She'd never looked more beautiful, and my chest ached with longing.

Ronan leaned in to whisper in my ear. "Hey, the bride's over here, you know."

I hadn't even realized Emily was walking down the freaking aisle.

That's not *my* bride. *My bride is in the fifth row.*

"You okay?" Ronan mouthed, seemingly amused.

I nodded and forced my eyes to where Tristan now faced *his* bride. I tried my best to pay attention to the ceremony. But it was damn hard not to look over at Nicole.

While I was so happy for my friends, my eyes inevitably wandered back to her as the ceremony continued. But she kept her gaze on the happy couple.

The priest started a sermon about the covenant of marriage, citing a verse from the Bible and talking about how marriage is a commitment through all seasons of life. *I should've fought harder against the divorce when she filed.* Yet despite all we'd been through, she was here. We'd be together today, and I couldn't complain about that. I needed to trust that there was a reason for everything that had happened, and the man upstairs had it handled. At least I hoped he didn't hate me enough to make me endure watching Nicole marry another man someday.

I glanced over at Ronan to find him smirking. He'd noticed me daydreaming again. I felt like the kid in class who's constantly getting caught goofing off.

When the ceremony ended, I winked at Nicole as I passed her on my way down the aisle and out of the church. When she smiled, I felt my heart come alive. The last thing I wanted was to continue walking away from her, but alas, it was a procession that couldn't exactly be stopped.

Once I made it to the exit, I hoped to wait for her there. But Kenzie and her team led the wedding party aside for a group photo outside the church. By the time that was finished, Nicole was nowhere to be found. I assumed she'd already left for the reception. I hoped she wasn't skipping it altogether. She'd only said she was coming to the wedding...

When we got to the venue, the wedding party was kept from entering until the DJ was ready to formally announce us. To make matters worse, the wedding planner told me that after we made our grand entrance, the very first thing on the agenda was my best-man speech and toast.

At least I'd get it over with. I had it memorized for the most part but was still pretty nervous. Public performing was a cinch. But public speaking? That was uncharted territory for me. Especially with Nicole in the audience. If I so much as looked at her, I'd lose my damn train of thought.

When the time came for the grand entrance, each member of the wedding party was announced individually. Fucking Ronan decided to do a backflip after his name was called, which made the crowd go absolutely wild. *Way to one-up my speech.* It was likely dull as it was, but now it would be overshadowed by a circus act.

Just as we were seated at the head table, the wedding planner prompted me to stand.

My pulse raced as I made my way to the podium and tapped the mic, which didn't seem to be on. "This thing working?"

As I spoke, the mic let out feedback like a high-pitched squeal.

Excellent way to start things off.

Tristan gave me a thumbs up.

I forced myself to start. "Hey, everyone. Thanks for being here today. For those of you who don't know me, I'm

Atticus Marchetti, one of Tristan's best friends. I love him to death, but clearly he hates me for making me come up here and speak."

Tristan blew me a kiss.

"I can perform in front of thousands, but for some reason, public speaking gets me. I'd rather grab some silverware and start drumming like an idiot right now. So bear with me."

I took a deep breath. "Anyway, I hope you've been enjoying Tristan and Emily's wedding thus far. I'm sure when most of you saw Emily walking down the aisle you thought..." I paused for effect. "What a beautiful flower girl. But where's the bride?"

Laughter rang out.

"But alas, no, Emily was indeed the bride, marrying this lucky old fuck over here. There's only fifteen years between them, which isn't a big deal, right? I mean, when Emily was born, Tristan was in high school and shit." I chuckled. "Nothing a little Viagra can't help now, right, man?" Lifting my chin, I cracked, "Congratulations in advance on staying awake past nine PM tonight."

Tristan gave me the finger, although he was laughing, as was Emily right alongside him.

"Anyway, age is just a number, right?" My eyes darted over to him. "Sort of like Tristan's AARP membership."

The audience seemed to really like that one, as the laughter was even louder this time. At least I wasn't getting dead silence from them. The more they laughed, the more I felt myself relax.

"In all seriousness," I said as the room faded to silence and I turned toward Tristan and Emily. "A love story like yours is something most people dream of. I'm sure some of those here don't realize all of the obstacles you've over-come to get to where you are right now. I'd tell everyone the details, but no one has time for a scandal tonight…" I chuckled. "They're hungry and want to start drinking."

I exhaled, feeling a bit of relief, knowing this was about to come to an end. "All this ball busting to say, I'm so happy that the two of you found the loves of your lives." My chest filled with regret and sadness as that sentence exited my mouth, and my speech lurched off on an un-scripted trajectory. "Not everyone is lucky enough to be married to the person they love most in the world, and there's no greater pain than knowing that person is out there without you. But you have inspired me to keep go-ing, keep hoping, and to reprioritize what really matters."

My eyes began to water. *Fuck.* I took a deep breath in, refusing to let a single tear fall. "At the end of our lives, it won't be about how many albums we sold or the accolades we have. It will be about the people we got to love and the memories we have of them." I raised my glass. "Please join me in raising a toast to Tristan and Emily, two of the best people I know."

As everyone lifted their glasses, I snuck in one more jab. "By the way, Emily, the bartender is asking to see your ID, please, before you drink that…" I winked and stepped down from the podium.

The audience cheered, and I didn't even return to my seat, wasting no time before going in search of Nicole. It felt like someone had taken my shackles off.

I walked around and scoped out each table. But she was nowhere to be found. A sinking feeling developed in the pit of my stomach.

She's not here.

Chapter 26

NICOLE

The bathroom was my refuge. After Atticus' speech, I needed a moment.

His niece found me staring at myself in the restroom mirror.

"Hey, Nicole. You okay?"

I turned, forcing a smile. "Yeah."

Kenzie narrowed her eyes. "If you say so..."

I smoothed out the wrinkles in my dress. "You've been working hard."

"It's been nonstop craziness." She sighed. "Since everyone's eating, this was my first opportunity to use the bathroom." Kenzie entered one of the stalls. "You sure you're okay?"

I could hear her peeing. "I'm fine. I just needed a breather..."

"After my uncle's speech, you mean?"

I stilled. "That didn't help."

"I nearly died when he mentioned you. Well, not directly, but you know what I mean."

Yeah, that hadn't been on my bingo card, either. I exhaled. "I think my coming here might have been a mistake, Kenzie."

She exited the stall and came over to the sink. "Why?"

"Seeing him here today...under these circumstances... it's just been a lot."

She pumped some foamy soap. "Seeing him makes you realize how much you still love him?"

"It's never been about not loving him."

"The feeling is clearly mutual." She smiled. "And gosh, Nicole, can I just say... You look beautiful. No wonder he couldn't take his eyes off you during the ceremony."

I smiled. While that didn't surprise me, I hadn't noticed because I'd kept my eyes fixed on Tristan and Emily to avoid feeling too much when it came to Atticus standing at the altar.

She dried her hands. "Gotta run." Kenzie sped out the door.

I lingered for a few more minutes before forcing myself to leave the bathroom. Except instead of returning to my assigned seat at a table filled with strangers, I walked out another doorway, which led to a balcony. A set of stairs there led to the beach below. I took off my shoes and walked down to the shore.

Staring out at the ocean, I let the wind blow through my hair. I knew I couldn't hide all night, but I wasn't ready to face him.

A deep voice came from behind me. "If I didn't know better, I would think you were avoiding me."

I turned to find Atticus looking even more handsome than before, the ocean breeze tousling his previously coiffed hair. The sadness in his eyes brought down my guard a bit.

"I think I have been avoiding you," I admitted.

"Why?"

"Because being here is overwhelming. And every time I look at you, I'm reminded of what I threw away."

He took a step toward me. "You know damn well that *I'm* the reason we're not together. Not the other way around."

"Not entirely. If I hadn't given up on us in the first place, we *would* still be together."

"You had your reasons at the time."

"Well, none of them make sense to me anymore. How the hell could I have let you go like that?" I shook my head. "Anyway, this wedding is just bringing out a lot of emotions in me."

He sighed. "I'm glad you didn't skip the reception. I was about to text you, thinking you went back to the hotel, or maybe you were already at the airport, headed back to New York. How long have you been out here?"

"Not long."

"Where were you before then? I looked everywhere for you."

"I was hiding in the bathroom after your speech."

He nodded slowly. "So you *did* hear it?"

"Yeah. I did."

"I wasn't planning on going off the rails like that. It wasn't part of the script or anything."

"We've never really stuck to the script, have we?" I smiled sadly. "Nothing turned out the way it was supposed to."

PENELOPE WARD

"Well, I *do* feel like you were supposed to be here with me at this wedding. I've felt it from the moment I first sensed your presence earlier." His eyes traveled the length of my body. "You look incredibly beautiful, Nicole. I wasn't prepared for how it was gonna feel to see you in the church. I couldn't take my eyes off you."

"I came because of you," I admitted. "Sure, it was nice to do Emily a favor. But she could've gotten another stylist. This was an excuse. I've missed you so much."

Atticus reached for me, pulling me to him. The smell of the ocean was quickly replaced by his woodsy scent. I let myself melt into the warmth of his arms as the waves crashed around us. "Please stop running from me tonight," he whispered against my neck. His breath heated my entire body. "Feel however you need to, say whatever you need to, even if it hurts me—just stop running."

"Okay, definitely not sneaking a smoke out here like I thought," someone said.

I pulled away from Atticus, and we both turned to find Ronan standing there.

"Uh..." I muttered. "We were just—"

He held up his palms. "No explanation needed. I was only checking to make sure my dude was okay after his... *demure* speech and all." He turned to Atticus. "Saw you leave, so figured I'd see what you were up to. Now I know."

Atticus nodded. "I'm good."

"I can see that." Ronan smirked. "I'll let you two be."

As he walked away, I turned back to Atticus. "We should go inside. I don't want them to think you're being rude. It doesn't matter if I'm not in there, but you're a member of the wedding party."

"Trust me, no one but Ronan is paying attention to my whereabouts. I'm happy to go back in, but I'm not going anywhere without you."

I rubbed my arms. "It's getting kind of chilly anyway."

Atticus reached for my hand. "Let's go inside."

He led me up the stairs and back into the venue.

Rather than return to where the wedding party was seated, Atticus joined me at my assigned table of strangers. Thankfully, some of the tension had lifted, and we both enjoyed the food that had been served. We just ate it a bit late, thanks to me.

People were already dancing as we had our meal, and just as Atticus and I finished, the DJ played a slow song.

Atticus stood and held out his hand. "May I have this dance?"

Without overthinking it, I got up and let him lead me to the dance floor.

Atticus pulled me close as we began to sway to the music. As always, being in his arms felt all-consuming. With each second, the space between us narrowed until I fully surrendered and let myself relax into him. The heat of his body penetrated mine. His hands lowered to the small of my back as he brought us even closer, his breath caressing the back of my neck as he rested his head on my shoulder. A rush of warmth moved through my entire body.

After a few minutes, my heart stopped racing. Time slowed down, and even though I was vulnerable in his arms, being in them was like home to me. As we moved with the music, I wished we could stay in this safe place forever—locked here with no decisions to be made, nothing to forgive, just holding each other and dancing for all eternity.

When the song ended, the DJ transitioned to something faster, and Atticus led me to the edge of the dance floor. As we faced each other, his eyes fell to my neck. He reached out to touch the infinity charm he'd given me. I hadn't taken it off since the day we'd left each other in New Jersey, not even to shower.

"You're still wearing it…"

"Yeah, ever since you gave it to me."

He let go of it. "It's my wedding ring."

"What?" My eyes widened. "What do you mean?"

"I gave the jeweler my ring and asked if they could melt the gold and make it into that pendant."

Wow. As we headed back to the table together, I was speechless.

Chapter 27

NICOLE

Atticus asked me if I'd go back to his suite after the reception, but I declined, instead practically fleeing to my own room before I could change my mind.

We'd planned to get together in the morning, though, for breakfast before I had to catch my flight. *That seems safe enough*, I told myself.

Yet despite successfully breaking away from him, every second since I'd returned to my room, I regretted not spending the night with him. He'd promised "*not to try anything*," saying he just wanted to lie with me. And I would've been fine with that—but after today, I didn't trust *myself*. I didn't want to sleep with him. I wanted to *sleep* with him, and that was the problem. Taking that step with him wasn't fair when there were still things about his current life I wasn't sure I could ever accept.

As I lay on my hotel bed, staring at the ceiling, I realized I still had the two pieces of cake I'd wrapped in napkins and stuffed into my purse earlier. When they'd served it, neither Atticus nor I had an appetite for cake.

Something had kept me from getting out of my dress and taking a shower. Intuitively, I knew I wasn't done for the day. It was the middle of the night now, but all I could think about were those two pieces of cake burning a hole in my purse—not because I was hungry, but because they were my excuse to see him again. Because as much as I'd already decided it was a bad idea, Atticus was all I could think about.

I didn't want to leave California tomorrow, either. Didn't want to leave him. And I couldn't believe I was wasting this precious time alone in my room.

Reaching for my bag, I headed out the door. He'd given me his room number in case I changed my mind, and I hoped I remembered it correctly.

When I got to his door, I took a deep breath before knocking.

A few seconds later, Atticus opened, and his mouth curved into a smile. "Hi, beautiful. This is a surprise." Though he didn't seem that surprised at all.

I raised an eyebrow. "It almost seems like you were waiting for me."

"I'm always waiting for you, baby. Always."

He still wore his suit, though he'd loosened his tie, and his hair was beautifully disheveled, as if he'd been running his hand through it since we parted.

I entered the room, reaching into my bag. "I, uh, forgot to give you this."

He took the cake. "Thank you." It was mostly just a lump inside the napkin. "You came here to give me a smashed-up piece of cake?"

I felt myself blush. "I know how much you love... cake."

He set it on an end table. "Not as much as I love *you*."

My heart felt ready to explode. The words *I love you, too* were at the tip of my tongue, but I didn't feel brave enough to unleash them yet.

"I've been staring at the ceiling, wishing you'd come, but not wanting to cross the line by calling and begging you. I guess wishes do come true sometimes." He inched forward. "I've had that happen more than once today. Anyway, you're right. I did have a feeling you'd show."

As he stared down at me, he placed his hand on my chin. Then he took my mouth in his, the long-lost yet familiar taste consuming me. I moaned. *My Atticus*. It had been too damn long since he'd kissed me like this. It was different from our chaste kiss back in New Jersey. That had been controlled. *This* was completely unbridled, wild, and ravenous. His tongue searched desperately for mine as our bodies pressed together. I knew there was no turning back.

"Don't fucking leave me tonight," he rasped. "Stay with me. Be with me. I can't handle being apart from you." He moved back to look at me. "It's what you want, right? That's why you really came?" His eyes glistened, as if he might cry.

Any potential response was squelched as his lips returned to mine, devouring me before he lowered his mouth to my neck.

I whimpered as he sucked on my skin, my head bending back in sweet surrender. "Atticus..."

"Let me make love to you, Nicole. I need to release this tension inside of me, everything I've been bottling up for more than three fucking years. I need to give it back to you tonight."

I panted, clawing at his back. "Yes..." I managed to say.

Atticus groaned as he kissed me harder. My panties were already completely wet. I could feel how much he wanted me as his erection pressed against me. My knees quivered as the muscles between my legs contracted.

My chest rose and fell as I pulled back for a moment of air and looked up to meet his incendiary stare. I was going to give all of myself to him tonight. I was going to let myself have something I'd wanted for so long and love every minute of it. I wasn't going to worry about the reper-cussions. Not until tomorrow, at least.

My husband.

For one night, I'd have my husband back.

My body filled with heat as the space once again closed between us, his lips on mine. Never in my life had I been more ready to be consumed by someone—craving not just sex, but the unmatched connection he and I shared, the way it had always felt like we were one, body and soul, whenever we made love. An experience only possible with him, no one else.

"You're so fucking beautiful," he mumbled over my mouth. "You're so fucking *mine*." He hissed. "But you know that, don't you?" He kissed down my neck to my col-larbone as his warm hand slid over my spine.

Atticus worked to unbutton his shirt, but not fast enough for me. I moved his jacket off his shoulders and slid it down to fall to the floor. He unzipped my dress, and it too fell, followed by the remainder of our clothes in quick succession. I'd lost awareness of who was removing what until suddenly we were both almost completely naked.

Atticus shook his head slowly. "So fucking perfect, baby. Fucking hotter than ever."

His glistening dick bobbed as he removed his boxer briefs, and it was hard not to gawk at his beautiful, thick cock. My mouth watered. I pried my gaze upward, only to find him exploring me with his eyes. As his gaze traveled down from my breasts to my legs, I took in the beautiful ridges of his abs, the ink on his tattooed chest. Not a blemish on his golden skin.

Atticus lifted me and walked us over to the wall. With my back against it, I wrapped my legs around him, ready to accept anything he'd give me.

His eyes lingered on mine for a moment before he took my mouth again. My fingers threaded through his hair, both of us breathless and crazed. I couldn't explore him fast enough and struggled to control my frenzied need for him.

He flipped us around, carrying me over to the bed before we tumbled to the mattress. With the weight of his body on top of me, I fully surrendered, spreading my legs wide. He looked into my eyes as he thrust into me for the first time. I kept my eyes on him, making an unintelligible sound at the sweet burn of him entering me. I'd been unprepared for the intensity of that first push, having nearly forgotten how he filled me, how amazing it felt to have him inside of me.

What started out slow and easy quickly grew faster. Atticus groaned as he fucked me harder, my worries fading away as we fell into a beautiful rhythm. "You're mine," he said as he plowed into me. "I hope this helps you remember you're still my wife." Atticus kissed down to my breasts, taking a nipple in his mouth. "God, I've missed these tits." He sucked harder before letting it go. "Missed every inch of you, baby."

I dug my nails into his back as he pumped in and out, his lips eventually finding mine again.

"Never forget who you belong to," he growled, pulling out slowly and thrusting hard.

I bucked my hips to meet his while he lowered his mouth to my neck, sucking on the skin there. He eventually kissed his way back up to look me in the eyes. I studied his every expression as I squeezed his muscular back.

"I love the way you look at me when you take my cock," he breathed. "Like you know I belong to you."

My mouth opened, but no sound came out—just the most intense orgasm I'd ever felt roll through my body. "Atticus..." I panted.

My muscles clamped down around him as I came. He pumped into me one last time as he shrieked, the force of his own orgasm shattering me as his hot cum filled my core.

We rocked back and forth for several minutes until there was nothing left in either of us.

"I'm afraid to let you go," he whispered over me. "I don't want to pull out. *Ever*. My beautiful wife."

~

The following morning, I woke with Atticus spooning me, his arms wrapped tight. His cock was fully erect as it pressed against my ass. It felt just like old times at Mimi's, except that *everything* had changed since last night. It had felt right to make love to him, yet where would we go from here?

I tried not to give in to my fears right away. When I turned to face him, he was wide awake, just looking at me.

"Good morning," I mewled.

"Good morning," he said softly. "I never wanted morning to come, though."

"Me neither. How long have you been up?"

"A while. I've been wired since last night and didn't want to waste these moments with you by sleeping." He buried his face in my chest. "I have an idea."

Immediately turned on again by his scent, I dug my fingers into his hair. "What's that?"

"Cancel your flight and come back to my house and never leave."

"You're not even joking, are you?"

He lifted his eyes to mine, flashing an adorable grin. "Nope. Not in the least."

"I wish it were that easy."

"Is there anything I could say or do that would convince you to stay here for at least a little while longer?"

It was tempting to just say *screw everything* and stay in Cali for the week. But as the haze of last night lifted, I realized there was much more I had to work through before I'd be able to consider building a life with him again.

"I'm fully booked this week, so I have to get back."

While that wasn't a lie, it was a cop out.

Atticus nodded. "I understand." He rested his chin on his hand. "For now. I understand *for now*, Nicole. But I can't accept being apart from you forever. I need you to tell me what I have to do to get you back. I'll do anything."

Getting us back to a place where we could be together wasn't just his responsibility.

"It's not just what *you* need to do, Atticus. It's what *I* need to do, too. I need to come to terms with the biggest part of your life now. Don't you see? Until I can do that, we'll *never* be able to make it work."

"Don't say never." His face filled with fear. "I can't handle never. How can I give you what you need to come to terms with it?" His eyes watered and a tear fell. I hadn't seen him cry in a long time.

My voice shook. "I never imagined that the biggest part of your life wouldn't be me. And though I know it's not a competition, if I'm not absolutely certain I can learn to accept it, I can't lead you on. Because it's not just *us* who stand to get hurt here."

He sniffled. "I get it."

I caught his next tear with my fingertip. "I've tried so hard to stop loving you, but I can't. It's not about that. I couldn't love you any more than I do. You know that, right?"

He nodded. "I won't ever stop fighting for us. But you're right. We have to be willing to face everything. To feel the pain. I need to resign myself to the fact that you were with Julian and find a way to stop wanting to physically hurt him every time I think about it. And you..." He paused. "You need to face the person you fear the most, the person who happens to own the other part of my heart."

Tears blinded my eyes as I nodded. "I need to meet him."

Chapter 28

ATTICUS

A couple of weeks later, with Nicole back in New York, I had my first appointment with Dr. Jensen in a while. I took a one-hour break from recording and brought my laptop out to the parking lot of the studio where we'd been working.

One by one, I'd conveniently canceled all of my appointments with her since New Jersey. My schedule while we were in the studio had made fitting her in difficult, but mostly I was hesitant to continue from where we'd last left off.

But I finally felt ready. As I'd told Nicole, we needed to face everything in order to move forward.

"Atticus!" she greeted when our video chat connected. "It's been a while."

I nodded. "It has. Things have been really busy with the band."

"My husband was listening to *The Rocker's Muse* the other day. That's such a great album. I was tempted to tell him you were my client, but I wouldn't dare violate confidentiality."

"You should've. I don't care."

She grinned. "Do you have something new you'd like to discuss today, or shall we take up where we ended last time we spoke?"

Feeling rusty when it came to talking about my feelings, I sucked in some air. "We can continue where we left off."

She scribbled something down. "The last time we met, you were recalling for me the time after Nicole and you got divorced. You indicated that the two of you were falling in love all over again from across the miles. There was hope for a reconciliation, and she was considering moving to California. She'd been talking to you more about some of the reasons she walked away. And then you alluded to something happening that changed everything..."

Swallowing, I nodded. "Yeah."

She nodded.

I cleared my throat. "Nicole had booked a flight to come out to L.A. It would've been the first time we saw each other since the papers were signed. I had a couple of weeks before the band had to start touring, and I made all these plans for us." I paused. "But then a week before she was set to fly out, I got a phone call."

Dr. Jensen tilted her head. "Okay..."

I shook my head. "So—I need to back up."

"Alright."

"The night the divorce was finalized was the darkest of my life. Everything seemed over, like all hope was gone. All I wanted to do was forget. So, I made it my mission to get fucked up. I went to this bar by myself and drank so much that I blacked out."

"I believe you mentioned that in passing the last time we spoke."

"I took pills, too, and I have no recollection of anything that happened that night." I grimaced. "Including sleeping with someone while I was drunk and high."

Dr. Jensen shut her eyes momentarily and nodded.

"Some time later, after Nicole and I were talking again, this woman named Giselle called me. I had no idea who she was. None. She told me she was pregnant, and that I was the father." I took a deep breath. "I couldn't remember her from that night, but she knew exactly who I was because of the band. She'd gotten my contact information through my manager, told him it was an urgent situation. I hung up on her, thinking it was some kind of joke."

A troubled look crossed my therapist's face. "Oh my."

"I tried to forget about it, but it kept gnawing at me..."

"Understandable."

I sighed. "I talked to Tristan and Ronan about it, and they convinced me I was being stupid. They were right. I couldn't remember anything about that night, so it was quite plausible that I'd had sex with someone."

"Right..." She nodded.

"I still had Giselle's number in my phone, so I called her back. She lives in New York, where I'd been that night. I flew her out to L.A., and we met in person. Once I saw her, I did vaguely remember her. I soon realized she seemed pretty level-headed and honest, as much as I'd wanted to deem her a liar. It was clear she didn't want the situation any more than I did. But she wasn't going to have an abortion…"

"How did you feel about that?"

"Well, I didn't allow myself to feel anything until I knew the truth. She agreed to let me pay for an in-utero paternity test." I exhaled. "All the while, Nicole was calling me every night and still planning to come out to L.A. While I waited for the results, I pretended nothing was happening, as much as it killed me. I prayed so hard that it wasn't mine." I shook my head. "The results came in about a week later."

"And you were the father?"

I nodded.

"Wow. Okay." She jotted something down. Probably, *holy fuck*.

"I realized then and there that life as I knew it was over. I knew Nicole, and I *knew* she wouldn't be able to handle this." I shook my head slowly. "Not because she didn't love me enough, but just the opposite. She loved me too much to stand by and watch *our* dream unfold… with me and someone else. And I hated the thought of her experiencing that."

"Oh, Atticus… What a tough situation. How did you tell her?"

My chest constricted. This was the hardest part for some reason. "I told her there'd been a change of plans, and instead of her coming to L.A., I flew to New York. I didn't want to give her that kind of news away from home, where she didn't have a support system." I closed my eyes and breathed for a moment. "When I got to her apartment, she opened the door with the most beautiful smile on her face. She took one look at me, though, and knew something was very wrong." I cringed at the horrible memory and had to stop.

"Then what happened?" Dr. Jensen prompted a few seconds later.

"Then I had to have the most difficult conversation of my life." I paused. "I told her everything. She cried. I cried. And exactly what I knew would happen did. I hurt her so badly, and there was nothing I could do about it. I couldn't fathom how I was supposed to be a father to that child when it felt like I'd lost everything—lost my soul, lost my entire life as I knew it."

"But somehow, here you are, still standing."

I laughed angrily. "Barely, but yeah."

Dr. Jensen's eyes widened. "You have a child now..."

"A son." I smiled. "Christian."

She leaned back in her seat and crossed her arms. "All this time you've kept that from me."

"Well, I would've had to tell the whole story, and I wasn't ready."

"When we first started working together, that had to have been around the time you found out about him. I remember you would refer to things you couldn't talk about, and we focused on your general anxiety, but it's no wonder we weren't able to make much progress if you were holding back something so major."

I looked away. "It's not that I was ashamed of him. I was mainly ashamed of my own actions, and I couldn't talk about how badly I'd let down the person who means everything to me. In order to talk about him, I would've had to talk about *that*."

"So, after you told Nicole you were going to be a father...what happened?"

"She didn't want to see me for a while. I went back to L.A., feeling as horrible as you might imagine. When she was finally willing to talk to me again, we had a couple of long conversations where the conclusion was basically what I already knew—that she couldn't handle it, and it was better if we went our separate ways—for good this time." I felt my eyes water. *Fuck.* "And if you thought things couldn't get worse after that, you'd be wrong."

Her brows drew together. "What happened?"

"Months later, I found out Nicole had reconnected with a guy we'd both been friends with years before. Julian had grown up in our town in New Jersey but had moved to the city for work. That sent me spiraling—acting out on tour, sleeping with women. I hadn't been with anyone sexually since Giselle, until I found out Nicole was dating Julian. It felt like my life was over and I'd lost her forever. But then I had a new baby, and I had to find a way to focus on that, despite still being a mess."

She nodded and wrote a few things down. "Tell me about when Christian was born."

"When Giselle went into labor, I flew to New York. It was hard being close to Nicole geographically yet feeling worlds away. I wasn't in the room when he was born. I didn't want to be. But they called me in after he arrived, and the moment I held him, I fell in love. It was the first time in months that I'd felt like I had a reason to live. I was still heartbroken and messed up, but he gave me a little bit of strength back."

"And you and Giselle...did anything ever happen there?"

I shook my head. "Not at all. She's a nice person, but I never had feelings for her like that."

"How old is Christian now?"

"He's two. He still lives with his mother in New York. She's engaged to a great guy now, David. We all get along and do our best to make this work. I go back to the city whenever I can to visit my son. Obviously with my schedule, *whenever I can* is not really enough. But I'm pretty much bicoastal when I'm not traveling or recording. I have an apartment not far from where he lives."

She just looked at me for a few seconds. "I can't believe I never knew you're a father."

"While my son is a blessing, I still have a lot of trauma about everything I lost in the process."

"Nicole, you mean..."

"She *is* everything, yeah."

"When was the last time you saw her?"

"That's the thing... One of the reasons I called you for this session is because she and I reconnected—yet again—when she came out here for Tristan's wedding a couple of weeks ago. That was the first time I'd seen her since we left each other in New Jersey. Without getting into too much detail...one thing led to another."

Her eyes widened. "Really?"

"It was the first time we'd taken things that far, and before she left L.A., she said she wanted to meet Christian. That's a huge step for her."

"I should say. And a huge step for *you*. When do you think she'll meet him?"

"Well, I'm stuck out here recording for a while. So, hopefully when I'm able to get back to New York, if she hasn't changed her mind."

"You must be ecstatic." She smiled. "That she's open to it."

"No." I shook my head. "Just the opposite. Because now that she's facing everything head on, she might decide she really can't handle it. And then what?"

Chapter 29

NICOLE

Atticus had told me Christian had a sitter on Tuesdays and Thursdays who took him to a small playground around the corner from Giselle's house in Queens. He said they went religiously, even in the middle of winter. It was the only way Christian could get out all of his energy. According to him, they usually went around three PM, after Christian woke up from his nap.

It had been almost three months now since the wedding in California. Atticus and I had talked a lot over the phone, and he kept suggesting that when I was ready, I could go to that park and see his son without having to meet Giselle, if I preferred, as a way to ease myself into the situation. Meeting Giselle right away definitely wasn't something I wanted, but thus far I hadn't been brave enough to visit the playground, either.

I wasn't sure what possessed me to choose this particular Tuesday in the middle of January. But I'd been at the salon when I suddenly felt the urge to get it over with—as if that's a possibility when it comes to meeting a little human who's also the thing I fear most in this world.

But I canceled my appointments for the rest of the day and headed to Queens.

The train ride over felt like one big blur. As I walked down the residential street, following the directions on my phone, I became more nervous with each step. I passed a café filled with people, for a moment considering whether I should just go inside, have a cup of coffee and a croissant, and forget the reason I came here. It was a bit crazy to be stalking an innocent toddler, wasn't it? Or was I just trying to convince myself of that because I was scared?

When I arrived, there were only a few children at the playground. Two of them were older, more like ten. Then I saw one little boy running around while a woman watched.

I couldn't be sure it was Christian until I moved a bit closer. Atticus had shown me a photo of him back in L.A. My heart clenched at the sight of the little boy with beautiful, big eyes, full lips, and thick, caramel-brown curls. His cheeks were rosy from the cold air. I'd seen photos of Atticus when he was around the same age. He'd had the same hair. This little boy *was* Atticus. There was no mistaking that this was his son.

After several minutes of watching him, I turned to find the woman watching me. She had obviously noticed my staring, which made me nervous. I didn't want her to think I was a weirdo. While my original plan had been to not say anything at all, I opted to try to explain what I imagined seemed like very odd behavior.

I took a few steps toward her and fumbled with my words. "Hi. I'm—"

"I know who you are," she interrupted.

My eyes widened. "You do?"

"Yes, of course. I've seen photos of you."

"You have?" My heart raced.

"Yes."

It took a minute for me to realize this was *not* the babysitter.

This was Christian's mother.

Giselle.

The woman Atticus had slept with.

And while he'd been with several other women since, this was the one responsible for the permanent demise of our relationship.

"You're Giselle..." I finally said.

She nodded.

Giselle was pretty, much to my dismay. Her red hair framed her heart-shaped face. She had bright blue eyes that were full of expression. She wore a black Patagonia jacket and seemed like a ghost who'd come to life. It had been my goal *never* to cross paths with this woman. But here she was in broad daylight. I'd never be able to go back now.

My throat felt ready to close. "I'm sorry. I thought you were the sitter."

"She had the day off today." Giselle smiled as she looked over at her son in the sandbox. "Did Atticus tell you to come here because he figured I wasn't with Christian at this time?" She shook her head. "You know, I've told him multiple times that you're welcome to come to the house anytime to meet my son..."

"Yes. He did mention that, but I was hesitant and thought this might be more convenient. I'm sorry if it's awkward. I was just trying to take baby steps." I exhaled. "And I'm sorry I didn't know who you were. I've never seen photos of you."

"What do you think?" She chuckled.

I narrowed my eyes. "You could stand to be a whole lot less attractive..."

"Well, thank you. Not bad for someone hardly getting any sleep, right?" She sighed. "I can see why he's so obsessed with you, though. You're drop-dead gorgeous."

Before I could respond to that, Christian came running over, interrupting our conversation. He handed Giselle a stem of some sort that he'd picked up off the ground. In his other hand was a red lollipop.

I knelt down to be closer to Christian's eye level, but looked up at her. "Can I?"

"Of course." She nodded encouragingly.

"Hi," I said, awkwardly.

The little boy waved at me then promptly ran away.

"He's beautiful," I told her, still kneeling.

We watched as Christian began to climb up a little blue slide.

I stood slowly. "I should've had the balls to come to your house or to call first for a formal introduction. I'm sorry for showing up like this."

"Look..." she said, her expression turning serious. "I get it. You have your reasons for being apprehensive." She kept her gaze on Christian. "The night I met Atticus, I had no idea how complicated his personal life was. I didn't know much about him, except that he was the drummer for Delirious Jones—certainly not that he'd been married and the ink wasn't even dry on his divorce papers. If it makes you feel any better, I barely remember that night myself. Although I remember more than he does, which is apparently nothing." She turned to look me in the eye. "Anyway, I never thought I'd see him again. I didn't want a child any more than he did, Nicole. I'd just come out of a breakup myself. But there's nothing now that I would change, because Christian is the single most important thing that's ever happened to me."

"Of course. I can only imagine how much you love him."

"My fiancé, David, loves him, too. He's really embraced the role of father. Christian is lucky to have two dads in his life who love him. Atticus can't be here every day, but he does the best he can and has been very generous in his support. I couldn't ask for anything more, given the situation."

This knowledge settled over me. I'd really been blind when it came to everything Atticus had been through since becoming a father. Even in his absence, he'd been a major part of my world, and yet *his* current world was unfamiliar to me: Atticus, Giselle, and David coparenting. While I'd been wallowing in everything I'd lost, Atticus had been growing up fast, figuring out how to make this situation work for Christian. It made me incredibly proud of him.

"What made you come today of all days?" Giselle asked.

"It just felt like I'd been running away long enough. For some reason, it had to be today. I don't really understand it."

She nodded. "I can relate to that. Once I make up my mind that I'm gonna do something, I just want it done."

She sighed. "Well, I hope you can see there's not anything to be afraid of."

"Yeah. I can see that," I murmured, turning my attention back to Christian, who was digging his hand into the pebbles that covered the playground.

"Does Atticus know you're here?"

I shook my head. "I didn't tell him in case I chickened out. And it was sort of a spur-of-the-moment decision. But he was the one who suggested I come see Christian first before meeting you."

"That plan backfired." She laughed.

"It did." I shrugged.

"Well, I won't say anything," she assured me. "I'll let you tell him."

"I appreciate that."

I spent the next half-hour getting to know Giselle a little while Christian played. Ironically, she used to do hair like I did, but had switched plans and decided to go to nursing school. She was halfway finished with that now. This whole afternoon in the park felt surreal, like I could've been dreaming it. For so long, she and Christian had been the people on this Earth I'd feared the most. Now that I'd met them, I'd faced my biggest fear. That's not to say I didn't still have some jealousy and bitterness. It's hard to totally squelch old habits. But those feelings were no longer overpowering. They no longer made it impossible to open my eyes and accept the situation as it was.

"Thank you for making this much easier than it could've been," I said as I stood, readying to leave.

"I don't have time for awkward." She laughed.

I looked down at my phone. "I'd better get back to the city."

"Okay...well, it was nice meeting you."

"You, too," I said, looking over my shoulder at Christian. "Is it okay if I say goodbye to him?"

"Of course." She nodded.

Giselle stayed behind on the bench while I walked over to where Christian was playing.

I knelt. "Bye, little guy. I know you don't know who the heck I am, but thank you for being sweet to me today. I promise not to be afraid of you anymore."

He stuck his sticky lollipop hand out and placed it on my mouth. He kept it there for several seconds. My heart soared and crumbled all at once.

Beautiful little Atticus.

Christian had never deserved the fear I'd projected toward him. My instant love for this tiny human only proved yet again just how much I loved his father.

⌣

After I returned from Queens, I decided to capitalize on my bravery and read the last of Atticus's emails. There was only one I hadn't opened because I knew it had been written after Christian was born.

Nicole,

I debated not writing this email. But this is my last one, because I don't even know if you're reading them, since you haven't responded.

I can't stop thinking about you tonight. I wish I could talk to you because I'm in the middle of one of the biggest moments of my life, and it doesn't seem right that you're not a part of it, as crazy as that might seem. This is an experience I was supposed to be having with you. But for reasons I may never truly understand, someone up there chose a different path for me.

My son was born today at 2:53 AM. MY son. I have a son. I wasn't in the room when he came into the world. I didn't want to be, partly because every second of this process has felt like a betrayal of you, and I've wanted no part of it.

But Nicole, the moment his grandmother brought him out to meet me, I looked into my son's eyes and saw my own freaking eyes staring back at me. I realized that I owe him so much more than resenting his existence. He did nothing to deserve that. The other thing I realized is that my love for him was not only instant, it was innate. It wasn't a choice. I just loved him from the moment I first held him. It doesn't matter how he came to be. My son deserves my whole heart, and he has it—well, he has as much a part of it as you still do. I now realize it's possible to give your heart equally to two people without diminishing an ounce of love for either one.

It's my greatest wish that someday you can meet him and see what I see. That may be a pipe dream, but I'll always hope for it.

His name is Christian Michael Marchetti. Six pounds, nine ounces. Ten fingers, ten toes. One broken dad.

Always lost without you,

Atticus

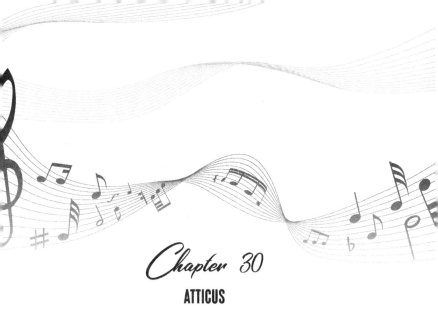

Chapter 30

ATTICUS

Delirious Jones had continued working on our upcoming album in the desert. There was a hidden studio here that we'd used to record our last few albums. It was the perfect remote location. We had probably a couple of weeks left before we'd have it done.

During our final break of the day, Tristan sat down beside me. "Hey, man. You seem distracted. Everything okay?"

"I *am* distracted," I admitted.

"Why?"

"Nicole just called. She met Christian and Giselle today."

His eyes went wide. "Are you kidding? How did that come about?"

"Long story, but she met up with them at a park while he was playing." I exhaled.

"Well, I can see why your mind was elsewhere. That's huge."

I shook my head. "I should've been there."

"Yeah, but she clearly didn't want you to be."

"I think it was more that she couldn't wait. It was eating away at her, and she needed to do it, with or without me."

"Why don't you go to New York, if that's where your heart is right now?"

"How is that an option in the middle of recording?"

He shrugged. "If I say we need a break, we need a break. Are you forgetting that *I* make the rules around here?"

"Fuck you, Tristan," Ronan said as he waltzed in. "*I* make the rules." He looked between us. "What rule am I enforcing right now?"

"Nicole just met Christian back in New York. I think Atticus should go be with her."

Ronan smacked my arm. "Holy crap, man."

"I know." I ran a hand through my hair. "I can't concentrate for shit today."

"Well, you're no good to us here if you're not at the top of your game," Tristan said. "It's almost the weekend anyway. Go for a few days. See your son. See Nicole. We can reconvene next week. We've stayed on schedule all this time. A few days isn't gonna make or break us."

"*I* give you permission to do that," Ronan added.

Tristan rolled his eyes. "Anyway, I don't think my wife will complain about having my full attention for the weekend."

Ronan sighed. "What the hell am I gonna do while you two are all up in your love fests?"

"I'm sure you'll figure it out." I couldn't get out of the desert fast enough. "Let's finish for today so I can book my flight."

~

The following afternoon, I arrived in New York. I'd nearly forgotten how damn cold it was here in January. Due to our hectic recording schedule, I'd only been back to the city once in the past few months. That was the longest I'd ever gone without seeing Christian. And Nicole had ironically been back in Monksville that weekend, so we hadn't crossed paths.

Originally, I'd thought my first stop today was going to be Nicole's. But she was still working, so as soon as I landed, I called Giselle to see what my son was up to. Apparently, Christian had a playdate with another toddler this afternoon, but I arranged to pick him up this evening and keep him with me overnight. He had his own room in the apartment I kept in the city. I tried to spend as much time as possible with him when I was in town, and I could give Giselle and David a break, too. That was the least I could do and yet not *nearly* enough.

Only having a few days here, I didn't want to waste a second. There was something I knew I had to do if I was going to move on. Just like I imagined Nicole had felt yesterday when she went to meet Christian, I didn't think this could wait much longer, either. If Nicole could put aside her fear and meet my son and Giselle, I needed to confront the thing I knew I had to get past if she and I were going to have a second chance.

Julian worked at a financial company in Midtown on East 53rd Street. I hopped the subway and went to his building, taking the elevator up to his office. No one seemed to care as I walked straight past reception. *Great security they have here.* I marched through the busy office until I finally spotted him. Julian was working in his cubicle when he noticed me.

He flinched as he looked up. "What the fuck?"

"Don't worry. I'm not going to shoot up the office."

He looked around. "What are you doing here?"

"You and I need to talk."

He lowered his voice. "You have some balls barging into my office like this."

"Yeah, well, it can't wait."

"There's nothing to say. Nicole and I aren't together anymore. So why don't you just leave me alone?"

"There's a lot left to say. There's a lot I still don't understand." I paused, willing myself to stay calm if I wanted any chance of him agreeing to talk to me. "Look, I know you don't owe me anything. You don't *have* to talk to me. But I would greatly appreciate it if you could give me a half-hour of your time."

"You know that I'm in the middle of my workday and can't just leave, right? Some of us have traditional jobs where we have to answer to people."

I nodded. "You have a point. I'll wait for you to get off work then. When's a good time to meet you out front?"

He sighed and looked at his phone. "I can be down there at four."

That was an hour from now. I could kill some time in this area. I hadn't eaten since I landed. "Thank you. I'll see you then."

THE *Drummer's* HEART

I didn't have much of an appetite, but I visited a deli down the street and forced myself to eat a pastrami sandwich. At ten minutes before four, I went back to Julian's building and waited not so patiently for him to walk through the revolving glass doors. In the meantime, someone recognized me, so I put on my best fake smile and posed for a photo. Nothing like having to seem happy when you felt miserable and anxious.

When I spotted Julian coming out, I straightened.

He noticed me right away. "Where do you want to talk?" he asked.

"There's a park about a block away with some benches."

He nodded, and we walked in tense silence until we arrived at the park. I took a seat on one of the benches, and he followed suit.

He fidgeted as a couple of pigeons landed by our feet. They quickly flew away as if sensing some shit was about to go down that they wanted no part of. When Julian finally looked at me, I could see the fear in his eyes. He thought I was going to try to kick his ass again.

"Relax. I'm not gonna hit you or go ballistic."

"And why should I believe that, based on your history?"

"You're just gonna have to trust me this time."

He crossed his arms and huffed. "What do you want to talk about?"

I rubbed my palms on my pants. "I need to know what happened between you and Nicole. How it came about. Who initiated things. I need to know the whole story," I explained. *Am I actually asking for this?* But the only way

245

past my trauma was through the fire. If I couldn't hear this story, I was never going to move on. Nicole had inspired me to grow some balls.

"Why would you want to torture yourself with that information?"

"Because if I can't face the things that haunt me, they'll never go away. And I'm at a point now where I really want my life back. I can't get my life back without getting my *wife* back. I can't be the man she needs until I've faced the hard stuff." I swallowed hard. "And there's nothing harder for me than the idea that you and she were together."

After a few seconds, he nodded. "You want me to tell you everything?"

"Start from the beginning," I said, taking a page out of Dr. Jensen's book.

"The beginning was that I didn't even know you guys weren't together when I ran into her one night in the city. It was never some premeditated vendetta like you seem to think. I'd just moved here from New Jersey for my job, and it was really nice to see Nicole after such a long time— like a slice of home in an unfamiliar place." He shook his head. "But the moment I asked her about you, she broke down. I didn't know it at the time, but it was right after you'd told her you were having a child with someone else."

I blew out a breath and nodded. "Alright..."

"To my surprise, she told me everything. And honestly...I just felt so bad for her. I wasn't thinking about taking advantage of the situation. It wasn't like that at all, even if you think I'm full of shit. She was clearly messed up and in no way ready for me to make a move on her. But what I *could* do was be a friend. I've always really liked Nicole.

You know that. And I'm not talking about just physical attraction. I'm not freaking blind, but she was always smart and really cool. I still cared about her when I ran into her that night in the city. It sucked to see her so hurt. She needed a friend."

I narrowed my eyes as the weight of all that washed over me. "You're saying you were just friends when it started?"

He nodded.

"For how long?"

"I don't remember exactly, but we were friends for a long while after that first meeting—several months, maybe. She wasn't ready for anything more. And I wasn't too keen on being someone's rebound, believe it or not. I liked her, but I wasn't stupid. I knew she hadn't gotten over you, and I wasn't sure she ever would." He exhaled. "But over time, we did grow closer and things evolved. She at least knew she could trust me because she'd known me for so long. After we started dating, I definitely fell in love with her, and she..." He laughed angrily. "Well, she fell a little bit *less* in love with you. Maybe that's the best way to put it. She was never over you, just learning to forget a little. I was never completely sure I could get her to want me for me. But that didn't stop me from trying."

I clamped down on the intense jealousy brewing inside of me. "You're still in love with her?"

He nodded. "I think I'm the better person for her. But it doesn't matter what I think, does it?"

I looked up at the sky. His relationship with Nicole had always seemed hard to believe, but hearing him explain how it had evolved—more slowly than my imagination had led me to believe—did make some sense. He'd been there to pick up the pieces of her heart that *I* had shattered. And I couldn't entirely fault him for that.

"I didn't set out to hurt you or take advantage like you seem to think," he continued after a moment. "It was never about *you*. Nicole turned to me to keep from going off the deep end. And you? You slept with random women and dove deeper into the rockstar life. At least with me she was safe. She was protected." He looked over at me. "I don't know what else you want me to say."

He had a point. There wasn't much left to say. I needed to stop digging while I was ahead. "Thank you for talking to me."

"That's it? You'll let me go now?"

"What else did you think I was going to do?"

"With you I have no fucking idea what to expect. The last couple of times I've seen you, you tried to attack me."

"I'm done with that."

"Well, that's good, at least." He cracked a slight smile and stood. "Have a good rest of the night."

I watched as he walked away but felt compelled to call after him. "Julian..."

He turned back around. "What?"

"Thank you for looking after her when I couldn't."

Chapter 31

NICOLE

Today was a big deal. It felt like I was being paid a visit by royalty, so I had to make my apartment perfect.

Atticus was bringing Christian by this afternoon, and I had no idea what to do to entertain a toddler. Atticus had come into town yesterday, but I'd told him to spend the evening with his son and we'd get together today.

My place wasn't set up for kids. I was also a little worried that Christian would recognize me as the weird lady from the park. Or worse, that he wouldn't recognize me at all, and I'd have to start all over again. And what if he didn't like me this time?

When the bell rang, I rubbed my sweaty palms on my shirt and rushed to the door. I opened it, swiping a hand down my hair. "Hey."

"Hi." Atticus smiled, holding Christian in his arms.

The sight nearly broke me in half.

"Hi." Christian mimicked his father, waving his little hand.

I tugged on his striped shirt. "Well, hello there."

Atticus leaned in to kiss me on the cheek. "Can we come in?"

"Of course." I moved aside.

As they stepped into the living room, I took a good look at them. It had been surreal seeing Christian for the first time the other day, but it was even more surreal seeing the two of them together: the love of my life and his mini-me.

"I don't know which of you is more handsome. You both have the same face."

Atticus put Christian down. The toddler's eyes sparkled, his cheeks rosy and big as he began to run around my living room excitedly.

Atticus stepped into gear, chasing after him. "Slow down, Bubba."

"It's okay. He can roam around," I said.

Giggles escaped the boy as he ran down the hall.

"Yeah, but he'll get into stuff he's not supposed to."

Apparently, I knew nothing about the potential dangers here. It made me feel like a kid in this situation myself. I followed the chase. "He's fast on his feet, huh?"

"You have no idea." Atticus caught him, lifting Christian and tilting him upside down as the boy giggled harder.

A child's laughter certainly had a way of soothing even a bitter soul like mine.

The second Atticus put him down, Christian took off again, running into my kitchen. He began opening all of the bottom-cabinet doors.

I chuckled. "He's a little explorer."

"He's loving that you don't have anything child-proofed. He's not used to being able to open everything like this. He'd ransack my place, if I let him get away with it. I've got locks on everything."

I winced as Christian slammed one of the cabinet doors. "I guess I live in a danger zone."

He took out one of my pots, turned it bottom up and began banging the top of it. I found a wooden spoon in the drawer and handed it to him. He flashed an adorable grin as he whacked it against the stainless steel.

"He understood the assignment." Atticus laughed.

"He's a little drummer boy like his daddy, huh?"

"Let's hope." Atticus shrugged. "Or maybe not. His life will be a lot simpler if he stays away from that scene."

I gestured over to the counter. "I ordered pizza for us. I hope he likes pizza."

"Are you kidding? It's his favorite thing to eat."

I smiled. "Oh good."

I'd gotten two large pies, which might've been too much. I set one of the boxes on the kitchen table, along with some plates.

"What does he like to drink?"

"Water's fine."

That seemed so boring. "Are you sure? I bought lemonade, too."

"Water's good. He had some candy earlier. He doesn't need the extra sugar. He'll be up all night."

I nodded, impressed.

Atticus sat, placing Christian on his lap.

He opened the box and took out a slice of pizza, taking a bite to test whether or not it was too hot. I watched as he used a napkin to dab some of the grease off the top. Finally, he held the slice up to Christian's mouth and fed it to him. Every bit of it made my heart squeeze and ache at the same time. He was much more experienced at this than I'd ever imagined. Perhaps it shouldn't have come as a surprise, given that he'd been a dad for two years now.

"This is surreal," I confessed. "Both seeing Christian and watching you as a dad. You take care of him very well."

He smiled. "Thank you. That means a lot." Atticus kissed the top of Christian's head. "I love being his father. But the truth is, I'm not here for him enough. I live with a lot of regret about that."

I nodded. There was so much that Atticus had never been able to share with me until now. I'd shut him down at every turn. I smiled down at the boy as he chomped his pizza. "He doesn't seem to be holding it against you."

"He definitely doesn't. He's always happy to see me. That makes me even sadder sometimes. One day when he's old enough to realize I'm essentially choosing to live away from him, he might start to resent it. I worry he'll wake up one morning and be like, 'Wait a minute, that asshole should've been here every day.'"

"Actually, maybe one day he'll wake up and realize who his famous father is and be proud to tell everyone."

"I want him to be proud of me for reasons other than my fame, though, you know? And I still have a lot of work to do where that's concerned. David is the one who's there for him more, so I worry Christian will end up closer to him than he is me. He's too young to play favorites now, but when it comes time to get involved in sports and all that...who's gonna be the one tossing the ball around with him day in and day out, you know?"

"You're doing the best you can right now," I assured him. "That's very evident to me."

He took a slice of pizza for himself and bit into it. "I'm banking on Tristan having a kid, and then he'll want to slow down a bit. Delirious Jones can't continue at our current pace forever."

"You think Tristan and Emily will have kids soon? They just got married."

"Well, Emily still has plenty of time, but hopefully they won't wait too long, because Tristan is getting old as fuck." Atticus cringed when he realized what he'd just said. "Sorry, Christian. You didn't hear that word."

"Fuck!" the little boy repeated.

"No, no, no. Don't say that." Atticus sighed. "I've been scolded more than once for teaching him bad words. It's my area of weakness."

I chuckled. "What is Ronan gonna do if you guys scale back to spend more time with your kids?"

"Same thing he always does—smoke weed and eat out of our refrigerators, at least until he meets someone and settles down."

"What are the chances of that happening?"

Atticus shrugged. "Ronan's very picky, so I'm not sure. He says he *wants* to settle down *someday*, but I'm not sure I believe him."

Atticus wiped Christian's hands and mouth every so often so they never got too greasy. He was talking to me, yet his mind was still on his child. His life had really changed in the past couple of years. And in turn, *he* had really changed, yet his feelings toward me hadn't.

"So..." Atticus cleared his throat. "I have a confession."

I suspected I knew what this was about. "You went to see Julian."

Atticus nodded. "He told you?"

"He did."

"I figured he might."

"What possessed you to go see him when you're only in town for a few days?"

"You inspired me to be brave. I'd never allowed him to explain himself, never opened myself to the truth. And while I don't think I'll ever feel good about the idea of you and him, I can better understand how it happened now."

"He's not a bad person. He was good to me."

"I realize that. Even if I still want to kill him. I don't think that itch will ever go away. But I probably won't actually do it."

"Well, that's good at least—for him."

He winked. "Wouldn't want to set a bad example for my son."

"More!" Christian cried as he pointed to request another slice.

"You got it, buddy." Atticus reached for another piece of pizza, repeating the process of soaking up the grease with a napkin.

I smiled. "Is the pizza good, Christian?"

He nodded happily.

"Good."

Atticus again kissed the top of his head. "Thank you for having us."

"It's my pleasure."

His eyes lingered on mine, and I sensed a hunger in them. Good thing Christian was here as a buffer. I'd missed Atticus so much and wouldn't mind a repeat of California one bit.

"You look so beautiful," he said. "I missed you tremendously."

"I missed you, too."

After Christian finished eating, we brought him into the living room and put on a kid's show Atticus was able to find with my basic cable. Christian chose a spot on the floor as his gaze locked on the television.

"Giselle limits his TV watching, so whenever he comes to my place, he's glued to the screen like this. He'll be good here in this spot for a while." I felt Atticus's hand on my waist. "Come here for a minute. I want to ask you something."

Atticus led me around the couch, which blocked Christian's view from the floor. Before I could blink, Atticus pulled me in for a kiss. I whimpered at the shock, gradually melting into his arms. He groaned into my mouth, causing a rush of desire to travel from my head to my toes.

"Fuck. I've been dying to do that since the moment I walked in the door," he muttered, kissing me harder.

He pulled back, glanced over the couch, and wrapped his hands around my face as he returned his mouth to mine.

Feeling a bit too turned on, considering the circumstances, I stepped away. "We'd better stop before he sees us."

"Him seeing me kiss the woman I love wouldn't be the worst thing in the world." Atticus rubbed his thumb along my cheek. "I want him to get to know you as the most important woman in my life. But it's not gonna happen overnight." He exhaled. "Listen, I need to clarify something in case it's not completely clear..."

I swallowed. "Okay."

"Delirious Jones goes on tour soon, and I'm afraid that's gonna create a huge divide between you and me again. But I need you to know that the days of me being stupid and messing around on tours are over. That was only ever a vain attempt to get over you. Now that you're back in my life, I don't ever want to be with anyone else, and I'm not going to be." He looked into my eyes. "I need you to believe me. I know we're taking things slow, but I want you to understand me when I say I have no plans to undo any of the progress we've made." He looked at me a moment, but I said nothing. "What are you thinking right now?" he asked.

I sighed. "If it were easy for us to pick up where we left off before everything happened, that would be too good to be true. I do think we need to take some time before we jump back into anything. While you're away, I need to continue working on my own stuff." I looked over the couch at Christian. "Meeting this beautiful boy was only part of the process. Just like you've been seeking therapy, I need to do the same. I've talked about it, but never actually went. I owe it to you to work out any lingering fears because I would never want to become a part of *his* life only to disappear."

Atticus nodded, seeming relieved at my answer. "I think that's a good idea. I'm convinced everyone should be in therapy."

"Well, especially people as fucked up as us." I winked.

"Yeah." He chuckled. "Hey, how's Mimi? I've spoken to her on the phone, but obviously that's different than being there."

"She's okay. Her health and mobility aren't getting any better, but things are stable. She really likes Fiona, so that's been a blessing."

He shook his head. "When I left Monksville, I promised myself I would visit her the next time I came to New York. But this trip, I'm on borrowed time, so getting out to New Jersey before I have to head back to L.A. would be impossible."

"Next time." I smiled. "She doesn't know you're here. And it's more important that you spend time with Christian. Anyway, Mimi's showed me the videos you've been sending to Fiona's phone for her. She loves getting to see your face every week."

"Well, I regret those years of no contact with her so much. An occasional phone call and those videos are the least I can do."

Christian suddenly appeared at our side. He handed Atticus a piece of candy. "Open, please."

Atticus's eyes widened. "Where did you get that?"

Shit. "I forgot I have those mint lifesavers in a jar on the end table."

"You can't have this, buddy. It's a choking hazard."

I frowned. "I have a lot to learn about babyproofing, huh?"

"Well, by the time you figure it out, he probably won't need it anymore. So don't kill yourself."

I sighed. "What are you guys up to tonight?"

"I'm taking him back to my apartment, giving him a bath, reading him a story, and putting him to bed. A wild and crazy evening." He lifted his son. "You wouldn't want to come with us, would you?"

Despite the hopeful look in his eyes, that didn't feel right. "I think you should have some alone time with your baby boy tonight. But what time is your flight tomorrow?"

"Noon."

"Maybe we can meet for breakfast before you have to go?"

"That's not as nice as sleeping next to you would be, but I'll take what I can get. I'm in no rush as long as we're moving forward." Atticus caressed my cheek with the back of his fingers. "You gave me everything I ever dreamed of back in California. I'll never forget that night. But I'd rather go slow and steady than risk losing you again."

"Daddy, who dat?" Christian asked, pointing at me.

I couldn't help but laugh. "He's finally trying to figure that out. Great question, buddy."

Atticus hugged him close. "That's Nicole. You guys share Daddy's heart."

Chapter 32

ATTICUS

It was finally the last day of recording the new album, and since returning from New York, it had felt damn near impossible to reach this finish line.

Those couple of days away had been much needed, but it wasn't enough. My time in New York had reminded me that the two people I cared most about in this world were too far from me. As long as I continued with this career, there was no easy way to put them first.

I returned to my empty house after a long day of work and imagined how much fuller my life would be if Christian had come running toward me when I got home. How amazing would it be to hear his little laugh echo through this big house? And what a dream to have Nicole to come home to, sleeping next to her every night.

I took a shower and was about to make myself something to eat when my phone rang. I recognized the number as security for my private, gated community. They called me to vet anyone trying to enter the grounds.

"Hello?"

"Hi, Mr. Marchetti. It's Chuck at the booth. We have a woman here who claims you know her, but we don't have record of any preapproval."

If I had a nickel for every time some random woman found out where I lived and tried to get in by pretending to know me. I'd had to move more than once due to lack of security at my previous residences.

"Yeah, I'm not expecting anyone," I told him.

"So sorry, sir. She claims to have the same last name as you. So that was a little suspicious."

I froze. "What are you talking about?"

"She says her name is Nicole Marchetti."

Nicole? "Can you put her on the phone, please?"

"Of course."

The sound of her voice followed a few seconds later. "Hey."

Oh my God.

"It's really you…"

"So much for surprises. Not sure how I didn't know I'd have to get through security."

My heart practically leaped out of my chest. "Put him back on the phone."

The guard returned to the line. "Yes, sir?"

"That's my wife. Let her through, please."

"Your…*wife*, sir?"

"Yes."

"Uh. Okay. Will do."

I'd have to explain the situation to Chuck later. I bolted for the door and waited.

Nicole parked in my circular driveway, and when she emerged from the car, I felt alive for the first time since I'd come back from New York.

"Oh my God. This is the best freaking surprise." I took her into my arms and squeezed her tightly. "You have no idea how badly I was missing you tonight. I came home from recording to this empty house, so depressed." I wrapped my hands around her face. "But why didn't you tell me you were coming?"

"It was a spur-of-the-moment thing, and I wanted to surprise you. Although I botched that."

I took her hand and led her into my house. "You couldn't have timed it any better. I was ready to lose my mind tonight."

Nicole's shoes clicked against the black marble floor. This was the first time she'd ever set foot into one of my California residences. Her mouth was agape as she looked up at the crystal chandelier.

I followed her as she explored. The entryway was lined with framed platinum records, an homage to a life consumed by a career.

"Your ceilings are so...high."

"It's a bit much, I know. Stupid when I'm the only one who lives here."

"It's not stupid if you can afford it. You earned it. It's beautiful."

When she turned around to face me, I rubbed my thumb along her cheek. "It is now." I'd give up all of it if it meant erasing the pain of the past and having her full trust back.

"Today was your last day of recording, right?"

"Yep."

Her expression turned melancholy. "And you leave for the tour in a few days…"

I hung my head. "Unfortunately."

I hated this. There was barely any time for us to enjoy each other's company before I had to take off. But why the sadness in her eyes? Was she upset that I was leaving, or was there something more?

"Baby, talk to me. What's going on? It's the tour, right? You're afraid of things going back to the way they were? I knew this was gonna happen. That's why I've tried to assure you that—"

"No. That's not it, Atticus. This is not about a lack of trust. That's not why I'm here."

My stomach sank. Something had compelled her to come all the way out here, and I was starting to freak out. Maybe I'd misinterpreted the reason for her trip, especially given the continued serious look on her face. A flash of panic hit. Back in New York, she'd said she needed time to work through things. Maybe she'd decided she could never accept my life. Maybe she'd come to break the news to me in person.

Moving in to cradle her face again, I looked deeply into her eyes. "I need you to tell me what's wrong."

"I'm not sure *how* to tell you…"

Dread filled me. "You need to just say it, Nicole…"

"I think I had too much seafood," she blurted.

My eyes narrowed. "That's code for you love me…"

"Not this time." She stuttered, "I mean, I *do* love you. But that's not what I meant."

I drew in my brows. "I'm not following…"

Nicole unzipped her coat. Then she took my hands in hers and slipped them under her shirt and over her stomach. "The seafood part was a lie. But my stomach *is* upset."

Running my hand along her stomach, I noticed it was…protruding a little. My mouth slowly opened. "What's happening?"

"I'm pregnant, Atticus."

Pregnant? My first instinct was to panic. "With *my* baby?"

"Of course it's yours."

"How?"

"You got me pregnant the night of Tristan's wedding. I didn't know until this past week. My periods have been wonky for a while, so I hadn't questioned missing them. I'm almost four months along."

My mouth dropped. "*Four* months? Is this for real?"

"It is."

"We made a baby? Together?"

"That's how it works." She laughed.

"This isn't a dream…"

She shook her head. "No."

My hands trembled as I lifted them to her face. "Holy shit."

"I know."

I kissed her forehead. "Are you okay?"

"Yeah. I mean, I've been in shock since I took the test. Well, *tests*. All twelve of them."

"This is really happening?"

"I think so. I haven't seen a doctor yet. And I know that's bad considering I'm already showing."

I lowered my hands to her belly again, placing my palms against it. "My God. Look at you with my baby inside of you."

"It's bad timing. You're about to go on tour and—"

"Fuck the tour! This is the *best* thing that's ever happened to me."

"I don't feel ready. I don't know anything about babies. You saw what a fish out of water I was around Christian. I don't know what I'm doing. I might've killed him if you weren't—"

"Don't worry. You're gonna do amazing. And I have a little experience I can share when it comes to kids. How long are you here with me?"

She shrugged. "I have no plan. I just booked a flight here as soon as I found out. I wanted to tell you in person."

"How can I leave you like this?" I shook my head. "I can't go. I can't go on tour."

"What choice do you have?"

"Come with me. Come with me on tour," I begged. "Please."

"I can't do that, Atticus."

"I don't want you to be pregnant and alone. I want you with me, where I can take care of you when we're not performing."

"You think being pregnant on a rock tour is going to be a positive experience?"

That made me realize how ridiculous it was to expect that. "Okay, maybe that doesn't make much sense. But selfishly...I want to see your belly grow. I want to experience every moment of this." Closing my eyes, I pressed my forehead to hers. "But shit, I know it's not ideal. I can't force you. You have to do what feels right for you." My skin tingled with excitement. "We should go see a doctor while you're here."

"I don't think I'd be able to get an appointment that fast."

"Doug's wife just had a baby. I can find out who she sees. Maybe they can get us in."

"Okay. I mean, if you think that's doable."

"You should have a doctor out here anyway." Not wanting to sound presumptuous, I added, "It'll be good for you to have a doctor on *both* coasts for when you're... visiting." I knelt and placed my cheek against her stomach. "I didn't want to go on tour before this. But now? The last thing I want to do is leave you." I looked up at her. "Tell me I'm not dreaming. It still feels like I'm about to wake up any second."

She ran her fingers through my hair. "It's real, Atticus."

"How the hell am I gonna concentrate on my performances, knowing you're out there with my baby inside you?"

She shrugged. "I guess we'll find out."

～

The following day, we were able to get an appointment at an OBGYN's office in Beverly Hills. While I generally tried not to abuse my celebrity status, I had no problem throwing my name around to get Nicole seen before I had to leave.

After seeing the doctor, who confirmed she was, in fact, pregnant, we were taken to an ultrasound room. I'd never attended a prenatal doctor's appointment, so this was the first time I'd see my child on a screen.

"Nicole is far enough along to determine the gender," the tech said. "Is that something you both want?"

"Definitely not," Nicole said at almost the same moment I said, "Yes!"

My eyes widened as we looked at each other. "You don't want to know?"

"No, I don't. I like the idea of being surprised for my first one. You *want* to know?"

"Yeah. I mean, I would *love* to know. But if you don't want to, I'm good with waiting."

"Well, let's get started," the woman interrupted. "And unless one of you tells me you want to know, I won't reveal anything."

A grainy image appeared on the screen as the tech moved the wand around Nicole's stomach. A moment later, I saw the tiny flickering heartbeat. A little hand, the gentle curve of its head.

Emotion rushed through me as I realized everything that had happened to us in the past few years had brought us right here. To this moment. To this heartbeat. A part of Nicole and a part of me and the personification of our love. I'd been given a second lease on life. I just hoped Nicole felt the same. I squeezed her hand. "That's our baby."

She whispered, "I can't believe it."

The tech confirmed that Nicole was indeed past her first trimester and printed us out some pictures. I could've stayed in this room watching our child all day.

Exiting the ultrasound room, I felt like I was walking on air. Yet today was also a bittersweet reminder of the work I still had to do rebuilding Nicole's trust. That mattered now more than ever. Our child's life depended on it.

As we left the building, I wrapped my arm around her. "Let's get ice cream."

She laughed. "That's random."

"We should celebrate."

"Okay. I'm not gonna refuse. Ice cream sounds really good."

I took Nicole to a little ice cream place off the beaten path about thirty minutes outside L.A. No one recognized me, which was freaking glorious.

She and I took our cones out to a bench under a tree. There was a warm breeze. It still felt like I could wake up at any moment and realize this was all a dream. She glided her tongue along the side of her cone and moaned as if eating it rivaled the best sex of her life. I chuckled.

"Why are you not eating?" she asked.

My cone was basically just sitting in my hand, melting. "Sorry. I was busy watching you."

"Watching the hungry pregnant lady eat ice cream is a spectacle?"

"A blessing is what it is." I finally took a bite of my cone. "Tell me how you're feeling right now—besides ravenous."

Nicole licked ice cream off the corner of her mouth. "I'm happy, but also overwhelmed."

"I can sense the latter. Don't forget I know you. While I want you to be as happy as I am right now, I'm not naïve enough to think everything that we've been working through is just magically fixed because you're pregnant. In many ways, I'm more scared than ever to lose you now."

"Why?"

"I'd never want you to feel stuck with me."

She nodded, but stayed silent, taking another bite of her cone before she finally spoke. "When I imagined having kids, I never saw myself raising them alone while their dad was on the road much of the year."

I nodded. "I've felt guilty not being the type of father Christian deserves, and now that guilt is about to double. Maybe I need to reassess my priorities."

"There's no perfect situation here. If you leave your career, *I'll* be the one feeling guilty. I don't think that's the answer. But you know what?"

"What?"

"You're this baby's daddy, Atticus. Nothing will change that, no matter what you're doing with your career or otherwise."

I smiled, but her support didn't change the truth. "I have some decisions to make. Christian is still young enough that I can change the trajectory of his memories of me. And he's about to have a sibling. Our baby needs me. Both my kids need me."

In the midst of my mini panic attack, Nicole's phone rang. She held one finger up as she answered. Within a few seconds, her face changed. She covered her mouth.

What's happening?

"Oh my God," she murmured. Then she started to cry.

Fuck. Did they find something wrong with the baby after the fact on the ultrasound? "What's wrong?" I pleaded.

She looked white as a ghost. "Mimi died."

Chapter 33

NICOLE

Delirious Jones canceled the first three shows of their tour so Atticus could accompany me to New Jersey. They rescheduled those cities on the back end.

I'd told Atticus he didn't have to come for Mimi's services, but he wouldn't hear of it. He insisted that there was nothing more important than being there for me, and he'd indeed stood by my side throughout Mimi's wake and funeral.

My mother, who'd flown in from Florida, was understandably surprised to see Atticus with me. She knew he'd come to stay with me and Mimi here, but I hadn't told her he and I had remained in touch since then. And I'd also told her nothing about the pregnancy because I only knew myself right before I flew out to California, and I'd wanted Atticus to be the first one I told.

After a whirlwind three days, it was now the morning after the funeral, and Atticus, my mother, and I were cleaning out Mimi's little house, getting it ready to put on the market. Mom was eager to get as much done as possible while she was still in town. She said she needed my opinion on what I wanted to keep versus what should be donated.

Atticus was out getting coffee when my mother accosted me in Mimi's kitchen. "So what's the deal with Atticus?" she asked. "You two seemed very affectionate at the service."

"What do you mean?" My cheeks burned.

"What do I mean? He had his hand on your back. I saw him kiss you multiple times on the top of your head…"

It had been a long few days, and I didn't feel like explaining everything right now. But this was likely the last time I'd see my mother for a while. I needed to tell her about the pregnancy. My loose black dress had done its job not giving anything away, but might as well just rip the Band-Aid off.

"I'm pregnant," I blurted.

My mother jumped back a little. "What?"

Unfortunately, Atticus walked in with our coffees at that very moment. Horrible timing.

"I got some donuts, too, if you—" He paused, likely sensing tension in the air.

"I just told my mother about the baby."

"Oh." He put the tray of coffees down. "Should I leave so you can talk?"

My mother held out her hand. "No, you need to stay, Atticus. I'm assuming you're the father?"

He turned to me. "You haven't gotten very far in the conversation, I take it."

"He is, Mom."

She placed her hand on her chest. "When did this happen?"

"Atticus and I have stayed in touch since we visited Mimi, and we...reconnected when I went out to California for that wedding."

My mother turned to him. "I wanted better for her than to get back with you."

My stomach sank. That wasn't fair. Atticus looked like she'd just stabbed him in the heart. "Mom..." I scolded.

After a brief moment of shock, he straightened. I recognized the fighting look in his eyes. He wouldn't back down easily. Atticus looked over at me. "It's okay, baby. I can take it." He turned to my mother. "I get why you're apprehensive, Maria. But I'll earn your trust back."

"Do you know how long it took her to get over what happened with you? What she deserves after all that is a fresh start. But obviously, with a child in the picture—or I should say *another* child for you—that won't be happening."

My mother's reaction was harsher than I'd expected. She was even more scarred by what happened to me, and likely how it related to her past with my father, than I'd realized.

"Your daughter and I have been through a lot, but I think even you can agree there's never been a doubt about how much I love her," Atticus said calmly. "This baby is a blessing, and I hope you'll see it that way eventually. But I never want Nicole to feel stuck with me, and I've expressed that to her. While I will always be here for this child, I only want her to give me her heart if that's what *she* truly wants for herself. She will always have a choice."

Mom crossed her arms over her chest. "I can see the baby as a blessing, but that doesn't mean I believe Nicole should take you back after everything—"

"Mom, please stop!" I yelled.

But my mother refused to calm down. "Your grandmother would be rolling in her grave if she knew what really happened between you two. Not sure why I ever went along with your ruse to keep it from her."

"That's precisely why we worked hard to make sure she never found out. We didn't want to hurt her," Atticus insisted.

"Well..." My mother sighed. "Nicole is a grown woman. She can make her own decisions. And while I can accept and love this baby, because it's my grandchild, I will *not* accept her being left alone to raise it while you do God knows what on the road."

I closed my eyes a moment. My mother's attitude was partially the result of my own attitude for so long; I knew that. She'd fed off of what I'd told her, so I couldn't completely blame her. I'd used her as a sounding board, and that had backfired. I'd now have to work to get her to come around. It was likely something only time could fix.

Atticus continued to be resilient. "I can understand why you're wary, Maria. And by all means, take the time you need to get used to this, but I'm not going anywhere. Never again—unless *she* tells me to." He walked over and wrapped his arm around me. "And for the record, if it were a matter of giving up my career or your daughter, I would choose her in a heartbeat. She hasn't told me to make that choice, but it's one I'm prepared for at any given moment."

My eyes widened. I would never ask that of him, but it warmed me to hear him say it.

My mother's shoulders relaxed a bit, and she walked over to me. "I'm sorry for not congratulating you. Obviously I'm thrilled to be having a grandchild. I just feel very protective of you."

I smiled as I hugged her. "You don't need to protect me. Atticus and I have both made mistakes in the past several years. We both played a hand in our breakup. But with this baby inside of me, I'm in a vulnerable place. Stress is not good for me right now. So while I've always valued your feedback, I need to kindly ask that you keep further negative opinions about Atticus to yourself." I placed my hand on my stomach. "I know for certain that he's going to be a damn good father to this baby, just like he's a good father to his son."

My mother nodded. "I won't say anything else except congratulations again and I love you. And I hope to come visit you, wherever that may be, and help you when the time comes."

"Thank you." I nodded. "I appreciate that."

"It's a shame that Mimi passed before you could tell her," she added. "She would've been so happy to be having a great-grandchild." She grabbed a donut and one of the coffees Atticus had brought. "I'll be out in the yard for a bit."

As she slipped out, Atticus took me in his arms. "I had no idea your mother harbored so much resentment toward me. But I shouldn't be surprised."

I shook my head. "It's my fault for the way I handled things for so long. I turned her against you, and I'm sorry. Both of us have had our share of fucking up. I started it. You finished it. But we're both still here. And I love you."

I placed my hand on his face. "All Mimi wanted was the best for us. The least I can do to honor her memory is start being honest with myself. I love you. I never stopped, and I want this baby with you so much. You don't need to give anything up. I wouldn't let you do that. We'll figure it out, okay?"

His eyes glistened. "Nicole...my love. I don't know what I did to deserve this, but I'll take it. The only opinion that matters to me is yours. And to hear those words come out of your mouth again?" He held me in his arms. "I love you so much, baby."

After a moment, Atticus picked up the remaining coffees and offered me one. "Let's take our coffees for a walk."

"Now? We still have so much work to do."

"It can wait. We need to clear our heads and get caffeinated—well, half-caf for you. The fresh air will do us good."

My head was pounding, so I wasn't going to argue. "Okay." I pulled back the lid and took the first glorious sip as we headed out the door.

A couple of blocks down the road, we passed my dream house, the white one that had purple flower baskets out front in the spring and summer.

I sighed. "There she is..."

"You still love that house, huh?"

"I do."

"You know, you've only ever seen the outside. How do you know you'll like the inside?"

"I can't imagine it's not nice on the inside if they take such good care of the exterior."

Atticus slowed his pace. "I wonder if the owner would let us see it."

"What good would that do? It would just make me want it even more."

"I still think we should ask."

I shook my head. "That's totally weird and rude, Atticus. I could never do that."

"Seriously...ask him."

"How do you know it's a man? You know him?"

"He's standing right here." Atticus stopped suddenly and gestured toward himself. "Ask him."

My jaw dropped. "Are you trying to tell me something?"

"Ask me to see the house, and I'll let you know." He smirked.

"Can we...see the house?" I asked, my heart pounding.

Beaming, he reached into his pocket and took out a key. He tossed it in the air and caught it. "Sure. Let's go."

What is happening? I followed Atticus as he led me into the house.

Wandering around a bit, I realized the inside *was* just as beautiful as I'd imagined—a combination of dark, rustic wood and weathered pieces, vintage-looking but not old. The furniture was beautifully upholstered, and the place was impeccably clean.

"I don't understand," I told him. "Explain this to me."

"Okay. Well, when we were here taking care of Mimi, I made the owner an offer he couldn't refuse. He agreed to sell it to me. The guy and his wife were thinking of downsizing anyway. So it was perfect timing."

"You've owned this house since then?"

"Yeah. I've been holding onto it and having work done."

"Was the inside already decorated like this? Because this is exactly how I pictured it."

"Not entirely. Some of the stuff is theirs. But I know your taste, and well, I have access to your Pinterest boards. Tina has a key and has been coming over the past few months to help set it up. I gave her my credit card and told her to go to town."

"Oh my God." My mouth fell open. "When were you planning to tell me? This trip wasn't even planned."

He shrugged. "I wasn't sure when I was gonna tell you. It's not completely ready yet. I wanted it to be a surprise, and I was going to give it to you whether you wanted to be with me or not. You've never taken anything from me, but I wanted you to have your Monksville dream house. The way you looked at it last time we were here, I knew it still meant a lot to you. The only thing that would make it a dream for *me* would be to share it with you. But that part's up to you. Ultimately, this will be your house."

I continued to walk around in shock. The same beautiful purple violets that filled the baskets out front were arranged in various vases throughout the place. "Tina put these flowers here, too?"

"Well, you always talked about the purple flowers out front more than anything, so I told her to add more inside. They're silk, though, so they won't die."

"I don't know what to say…"

"I'm not gonna lie. I've worried about your reaction a little. I never want you to think I'm trying to buy you or buy my way into your life. That's not what this is about. But honestly, the way you stood up for me with your mother today? This felt like the right time to let you know about it.

For the first time, I'm feeling encouraged that I might get to enjoy this house *with* you."

"I wouldn't let you gift me a house unless you were living in it, too."

He took my hand and smiled. "Let's tour the rest of the place."

Atticus led me upstairs. There were three bedrooms, one primary and two others.

"I was surprised there were only three bedrooms, given the size of the house," he said. "But we can always put on an addition someday."

"Well, I guess they're all accounted for, then," I said.

"They are?"

"Our room, Christian's, and the baby's."

Atticus's eyes filled with emotion.

"I know you've doubted whether I could accept Christian into my life, and with good reason," I told him. "But there's no way I can be with you without accepting Christian as my son, too. The old me could never have fathomed that. She had way too much ego to consider such radical acceptance. But I've grown and learned so much about forgiveness in the past several months. Letting go of the jealousy and animosity over how Christian came to be gives me the freedom to love both of you."

Atticus exhaled as he wrapped his arms around me. "Thank you," he whispered.

We returned downstairs, and I noticed a set of built-in shelves just outside the kitchen. They had recessed lighting and displayed dozens of Starbucks mugs, each from a different location around the world. Atticus knew I liked to collect those, but because I didn't travel all that much,

I'd only ever had a handful from various states—nothing from outside of the US.

"What's this?" I asked.

"Took you long enough to notice." He smiled. "Whenever the band and I were in a new city, I'd try to get you one or I'd ask whoever was going to fetch coffee to get me one. A few times they got broken or lost in transit, but these are all the ones I saved. I brought them home after every tour. I never knew if I'd have the chance to give them to you, but collecting them was my way of hanging on to hope. I recently came up with the idea for this shelf, so I wrapped them all up, put them in a box, and asked Tina to set them up for me here. As you can see, no matter where I was in the world, I was always thinking of you."

Chapter 34

ATTICUS

The last song we performed each night on tour featured my drum solo. Tristan would look over at me, and I'd nod before launching into the thunderous rhythm that evolved into an explosion of beats mixed with crashes of cymbals. The crowd always went wild—talk about an ego boost.

This performance in Philly had been probably one of the best of my career. It was only the second stop of this tour, and I should've been totally revved up since we hadn't had time yet to tire of traveling.

But instead, I felt empty when the show was over, no longer thrilled by the excitement I'd once felt at the start of a tour or at the end of my drum solo. It was disheartening and troubling. There was just a lot on my mind. I was still in a funk after Mimi's passing, sad that she'd never know her great-grandchild and that I hadn't gotten to say goodbye.

Tristan caught up with me in the dressing room. "Hey, man. Freaking amazing performance tonight."

"Thanks." I hung my head—not exactly the reaction you should give when you've just been given a compliment.

"What's up?" he asked. "Everything okay?"

"I'm pretty miserable, actually, if you want to know the truth. I miss Nicole. I feel like I should be there for her. And I don't see an end to these absences with our music still blowing up the way it is. I don't want you to think I don't appreciate how lucky we are. But some days, I just want a normal life. And today is one of those days."

He nodded. "You remember when I used to talk about craving a normal life and you'd tell me I was crazy? This was back when you were using our success as an escape from your problems. I think you're finally at the point where you see where I was coming from. It's not that we don't appreciate success, but moving at this pace can't continue forever."

"I think I would've been fine with it if not for getting Nicole back."

"I get it," Tristan said. "And I'm about to ask you a serious question. I don't want you to think I'm bullshitting you."

"Alright..."

"You want to call off the tour?" His expression *was* dead serious.

My eyes went wide. "Why would you even say that? You *know* we can't do that."

"Says who? You're forgetting I'm the boss."

"Ronan would beg to differ. He'd also freak out if he knew you were suggesting this."

Tristan put his hand on my shoulder. "You've given up everything for us. We got famous overnight, and it literally ruined your marriage. You went through hell after that, and yet you showed up every single freaking night. Every single damn show. Even *I* canceled a show once for a mental-health break, remember? But you have never once not shown up. Even tonight, you were amazing out there, and yet you're telling me you're suffocating. If you hadn't said something, I would never know. You need a break before *you* break. And I'm gonna give it to you, whether you like it or not."

I shook my head. "I can't let you do that."

"You don't need to *let* me do anything, I'm just gonna do it."

"I don't need you to cancel the tour. I just need a little time to see her. Then I can come back reenergized."

Tristan scratched his chin. "Okay. How about we cancel the next three shows due to undisclosed illness? And we'll play it by ear after that. When you're ready to come back, we'll take this thing on the road again, but not a second sooner."

"You're serious about this?"

Tristan nodded. "Go home for a week. Be with your woman. I'll go home and be with mine. And we'll reconvene when you're ready."

It was hard to turn down the opportunity. "Thank you. I'm gonna take you up on this."

He slapped me on the back. "I'm not gonna say anything to anyone until tomorrow, including Ronan. Everyone worked hard tonight. Let them decompress before I break it to them in the morning. I don't need their anxiety when I just want to crash tonight myself. But get the hell out of here, and I'll make an excuse for your absence if anyone asks."

A huge wave of joy washed over me.

I'm gonna see my baby.

My babies.

All three of them.

~

I was able to get a flight out to New York that night. But as I stood in line at the airport, my phone lit up with a text.

Tristan: You need to get back here.

My stomach dropped.

Atticus: What's wrong? I was just about to board.

Almost immediately after, I got a text from Nicole.

Nicole: Where are you?

Atticus: About to board a plane to New York.

Nicole: Don't! I'm here in Philly!

I looked around.

Atticus: What? Where?

Nicole: On your bus.

What the hell?

Atticus: Stay there. I'm headed back!

My heart raced as I weaved through the airport crowd. I called a car and sweated every second of the hour-long ride back to where our tour bus was parked.

Out of breath, I rushed onto the bus to find my beautiful woman lying back on one of the seats with her feet up. "Why didn't you tell me you were coming?"

She sat up. "I wanted to surprise you. My flight got delayed, which is why I'm here so late. I can't believe you were gonna leave the tour."

Caressing her cheek with my thumb, I knelt. "I couldn't take being away from you anymore."

"I guess we're on the same wavelength, because that's exactly how I felt."

"How long are you here?"

She shrugged. "You tell me."

I blinked. "I don't understand."

"I'm here for as long as you need me. Honestly, being in the salon with all the chemicals was making me sick. It's not good for the baby. But that's just the official excuse to do what my heart has wanted from the beginning. I want to be here with you. I've just been scared to go on tour. But I need to get over it."

My heart felt ready to explode. "You're staying on tour with me?"

"If you can make room for us." She smiled and patted her stomach.

"You have no idea what this means to me."

"It's not just for you. It's for me, too. If we're really gonna do this, Atticus, I have to get used to this life—your life. I have to stop being afraid of it. I have to stop thinking it's the enemy and embrace it. It's a part of you."

I took her face in my hands and planted a long kiss on her lips. "I promise you won't regret being here. We'll spend every moment together that I'm not performing."

"You don't have to go that far…"

"You're gonna be so fucking sick of me!" I yelled to the back of the bus. "Hey, Tristan! I'm gonna need the bedroom for my pregnant wife."

"Already on it. Clearing out my shit. I think you've finally earned it. Although if Emily comes to visit, we may need to cave and get a second bus with a bedroom."

Ronan groaned. "Talk about feeling like the odd man out. I'd better get a woman soon so I can secure my own bedroom in the back of the bus. Apparently, you have to be a lead singer or a whipped man to avoid sleeping on the bunks."

"When your ass gets into a real relationship, I'll be happy to give up my room for you, too," Tristan assured him.

"If you'll excuse me, I need to spend some time with my wife." I took Nicole's hand and led her to the bedroom at the back of the bus.

She lay down on the bed. "You keep calling me your wife."

I closed the door and locked it. "You *are* my wife."

"Technically I'm not anymore."

I crawled onto the bed and faced her. "You're the love of my wife..." I shook my head. "I mean my *life*. God, I'm still so shocked you're here... I can't think straight and don't know how to talk. But the bottom line is, you *are* my wife. You always will be. A piece of paper means shit." I kissed her nose. "Not only can I not believe you're here, I can't believe you're actually gonna see me perform in an arena for the first time."

Nicole and I had split before my first major tour.

She got a funny look on her face.

"What?"

"I actually *have* seen you perform in a larger venue..."

I squinted. "What are you talking about?"

Nicole looked away. "I was never gonna admit this..." She paused. "But a couple years back, I bought a ticket to see you guys. I went to one of your shows here in Philly, actually."

"You did?" My chest constricted. "How the hell did I not know this?"

"The seats were horrible." She chuckled.

"Well, I certainly could've done better if you'd just told me."

She shook her head. "It was a last-minute decision. We weren't exactly talking. As sad as I was, I missed you so damn much. I just wanted to be near you for one night, to be in the same slice of the world for a couple of hours—without you knowing, of course." Her voice shook. "I was with Julian at the time. I lied and told him I was going on a girls' weekend with some friends. I drove to Philly by myself, stayed in a hotel, waited in line with my shitty ticket, and sat in the nosebleeds."

"Jesus. It fucking breaks my heart that you were in the audience, and I didn't know you were there."

"That was the point, though. And it's probably better that you didn't. It would've affected your performance."

"Absolutely, it would've. Especially back then." I exhaled. "But I can guarantee that while you were up in the nosebleeds, I was thinking of you. Because I've never played a song when you haven't crossed my mind at some point. Even when I was most hurt over us, nothing ignited the passion inside of me like you. At my best and at my worst, I play for you. Just like those days in the basement when you watching from that couch made me feel like the king of the world."

She threaded her fingers through my hair. "Well, now you know my little secret."

I buried my head in the crook of her neck, taking in a long, slow breath. Knowing this woman was pregnant with my baby made me absolutely feral for her.

I tugged at her shirt. "Can you take this off? I want to see you."

She slipped the shirt over her head. Tossing it aside, she unsnapped her bra, displaying her gorgeous breasts. Her nipples were three shades darker than the last time I'd seen them.

I ran my tongue over my bottom lip. "These nipples..."

"I know. They're huge and darker."

"I love it." I circled my fingers over one of them before tracing the line on the skin of her stomach. "Look at you with this baby inside of you. I've never seen you so beautiful, and I still can't believe this is real. I'll never deserve this." I ran my tongue along her nipple, then kissed down to her stomach. "This is why I needed to leave the tour. Look at everything I was missing."

"Well, now you don't have to leave." She massaged my scalp.

I looked up at her. "What changed? I know it wasn't just the chemicals in the salon..."

Nicole sat up on her elbows. "I'm fortunate that I have a job I can always go back to, clients who have stuck with me through the years. It hit me that I'll never get this time with you again. I have no way of knowing whether this is the only pregnancy I'll have. We're not guaranteed anything in life. I just felt like I needed to come. *Wanted* to. And that means putting aside my fears about tour life." She grinned. "I never imagined you were on your way to me."

I rested my head on her chest and placed my hand on her stomach.

"Oh my God." She jumped.

"What?" I lifted my head, afraid I'd hurt her.

"I think I felt our baby move."

"Really?"

"It's too early for you to see it move, I think. But I definitely felt something."

"Our kid is happy we're finally together, maybe?"

She giggled. "He just did it again. Your baby likes to kick."

I rubbed my hand over her skin. "Maybe he's drumming..."

Chapter 35

NICOLE

A couple of days later, when everyone went down to the arena for a sound check before the show, I let Atticus know I'd be heading back to the bus to take a nap. Being pregnant made me tired.

The bus was empty when I got there. It was probably the only time I'd ever been on it all by myself. I was just about to get under the covers in the back bedroom when I realized the door was still open a crack. But after I got up to lock it, I heard voices.

There was a peephole on the bedroom door, which I'd always found odd, but it was very convenient at the moment. I peeked through, and my pulse calmed when I realized it was Ronan.

His back was to me. "I only have a few minutes," he said to someone—I couldn't see who. "I told them I needed a break and I'd be right back."

"You lied and came to find me? Sounds pretty desperate," a female voice replied.

"I *am* desperate for you. You're right."

Then came the sound of lips smacking.

"Are you sure no one is coming back here?" she asked.

"Everyone is down at the sound check," he said. "The coast is clear."

Great. He'd brought a groupie here with him? I'd been lucky enough to make it through the tour thus far without walking into anything of that sort. *Oh well. It was good while it lasted.* I was just about to give them privacy and go to bed when Ronan shifted, allowing me a clear view of who he was talking to.

It was no groupie. It was Kenzie.

Kenzie.

"This is still risky," she said.

He wrapped his arms around her. "I know. But I miss you, and I don't have a lot of opportunities to be with you alone."

Then they were kissing.

Holy shit.

Kenzie and Ronan.

Atticus's *niece* and Ronan.

How long has this been going on?

She sighed. "It's really frustrating that we have to hide like this."

"I told you, I'm perfectly happy to tell him and deal with the aftermath," Ronan said.

"And have him beat the crap out of you while you're on tour? We can't let that happen. It has to be after everything is over."

My mouth dropped open.

"This is ridiculous," he said. "We're both fucking adults. We shouldn't have to sneak around."

"I know. But he doesn't see me that way because I'm like his kid."

"He's got enough kids at the moment."

She gasped. "That was bad."

"I know. Look, I love the guy like a brother. And I'm scared shitless of him finding out, too. But I love you more, and I don't want to have to hide it."

Love?

"It's just a few months," she insisted. "Trust me, he's going to need time to process. That can't happen in the middle of a tour."

Ronan sighed. "You're right."

"I know I am."

After a few minutes, she left first, and he followed shortly after.

Their stolen moment was over, but my jaw remained on the floor. I lay down in bed, but I didn't feel so sleepy now. How the hell was I supposed to keep this from Atticus?

~

A half hour after Kenzie and Ronan left, I heard footsteps on the bus again.

I went over to the peephole and immediately opened when I saw who it was.

"What are you doing here?" I opened my arms and ran to Emily.

She reached out to hug me. "I came to surprise Tristan." She stepped back to look at me. "Oh my gosh, you're showing already."

"I am...just a little." I rubbed my belly. "It's good to see you. I've been feeling out of place being the only wife here."

Seems I was now following Atticus's lead and referring to myself as his wife again.

She spoke low. "Can I tell you a secret?"

"Of course."

"Tristan and I haven't told anyone yet, but we're gonna be joining you guys soon."

My eyes went wide. "You're pregnant, too?"

"I am."

"I'm so thrilled for you!" I reached out to hug her again.

She spoke into my hair. "I'm happy to have someone to talk to about baby stuff."

"How far along?"

"Two months. We're not gonna tell anyone until I hit the three-month mark. No one else knows. He hasn't told the guys. But I had to tell you."

I squeezed her hand, and we sank into a couple of seats. "I'm only a couple of months ahead of you. I don't know what I'm doing, but I'll pass down everything I learn as I go along."

"Believe me, I appreciate that."

"Are you staying for the whole tour?"

"I wish. I took a week off from work, but then I have to go back. What about you? How long are you here?"

"I took a leave of absence. So, for now, indefinitely."

"That's huge!"

"I've always put my career first. But Atticus dropped everything when he came to help me with Mimi. I owe him this experience. I knew he didn't want to be apart from me right now, and I don't want to be apart from him, either." I shrugged. "I followed my heart for once."

She nodded. "That's amazing. But how are you handling it? I know from experience that it's not easy being in this environment. It's hard to see women throw themselves at the guys constantly during the shows and then stalk them after."

I lay back in the seat and kicked my feet up. "It's not fun, but strangely? It's easier than I thought—nothing I didn't anticipate or anything. I think I'd blown it so far out of proportion in my mind that the reality isn't as bad. I let fear ruin the best thing I ever had, Emily. I can't do that again. At some point, I have to trust what I know and stop letting fear dictate my life."

"Well, I'm proud of you. You're being very mature." She chuckled. "I still want to scratch a bitch's eyes out most days."

I laughed. "Don't get me wrong, I don't *love* that part of being here. But I can't allow it to get inside my head, you know? It's ruined too much of my life already."

The bus door opened, and Kenzie popped in.

Back so soon?

When she saw us, she put her camera down and came over. "Emily! I didn't know you were coming."

They hugged as I fidgeted awkwardly, trying to seem like I didn't know a huge secret.

"No one else knows I'm here yet," Emily told her. "I came to surprise my husband, but he's apparently still at the sound check. How's the tour photography going?"

Kenzie sat. "I absolutely love it. The tour has barely started, and it's already the best experience of my life."

I bet.

She turned to me. "And having Nicole here now has made it even better."

"Are you kidding? She has no time for me." I winked. "Every time I turn around, she's snapping away. I hardly have a chance to talk to her."

"Um, that's because you're holed up with my uncle every night when I'm off work."

"That's true, I guess."

"I get it, though." She grinned. "Making up for lost time."

Now felt like a good time to bring up something that had been on my mind. "Listen...I need both your input on something."

Kenzie leaned in. "Okay..."

"I sort of...found out what we're having by accident."

Emily gasped. "The gender?"

I nodded.

"Oh my God." Kenzie clapped. "What is it?"

"Atticus doesn't even know, so I'm keeping it a secret until I can tell him."

I was holding lots of secrets, apparently.

Emily covered her mouth and stomped her feet. "I can't believe you know what you're having! I'm so freaking excited to find out. You have no idea."

"I can't wait to meet my beautiful little cousin." Kenzie smiled. "But wait, how does one *accidentally* find out the gender?"

"Well..." I sighed. "I went to an OBGYN before we left Delaware for a check-in, and the tech somehow thought I knew and let it slip. I guess more and more people just agree to find out these days. I feel bad knowing if Atticus doesn't, especially since he was the one who wanted to find out in the first place. So I was thinking I could surprise him with a gender reveal on the tour."

"When do you want to tell him?" Emily asked.

"I have an idea!" Kenzie interjected.

She explained her thoughts, and we devised a plan to make the announcement during one of the performances later this week. I was nervous to do it, but excited at the same time.

Emily reached for Kenzie's camera. "Any good photos?"

Kenzie practically leaped out of her seat to take the camera back. "Not really in this set."

Emily narrowed her eyes. "What's that all about? You almost jumped out of your pants to snatch this camera back from me."

Kenzie blushed. "No, I didn't."

"Yeah, you did." I laughed.

Kenzie's face turned even more crimson.

Emily held out her hand. "Why can't I see them?"

"You can, but these are just photos of the guys practicing. Nothing exciting."

Playing dumb, I narrowed my eyes. "Is there something you don't want us to see?"

"No. They're just...not edited."

"Who cares?" Emily held her hand out again. "Let me see..."

Kenzie reluctantly handed over the camera.

I leaned over Emily's shoulder to see the photos in the viewfinder. Every single one of them was of Ronan. Mostly

candids. Nothing X-rated or anything, which made me relieved for her. There were some of him practicing, strum-
ming on his guitar when he didn't seem to notice he was
being photographed, and many closeups of his handsome
face. When I looked over at Kenzie, her face was beet red. I
knew *exactly* what was going on, and it seemed Emily now
suspected something too, based on the smirk on her face.

"You seem to have a favorite," Emily teased.

I smothered a grin.

Kenzie cleared her throat. "No, I was only messing
around. Those aren't even photos we're gonna use."

"My point exactly," Emily said. "They were for your
own entertainment. Why are you embarrassed to have a
crush? Ronan is hot, even if he's a bit nuts."

"Don't read into it. I don't have a crush on him." Kenzie grabbed the camera and nearly dropped it. "Anyway...I
have to go get back to work."

She exited the bus faster than a bat out of hell.

Emily and I looked at each other.

Emily cringed. "I feel bad now. I didn't mean to embarrass her, but she totally has a thing for Ronan." She
laughed. "Which is horrible for her, because Atticus would
kill him if he touched his niece."

"Yeah..." I muttered, feeling ready to explode.

"And knowing that, Ronan would *never* touch Kenzie," she added.

You'd be surprised.

"So she's probably out of luck, even if she's super
pretty. I could see Ronan liking her, if things were different. How old is she again?"

"Twenty-four, I think?" I gulped.

"Okay, so a decade younger than Ronan. That wouldn't be bad, I guess. Less of an age gap than Tristan and me. Anyway, Lord knows I've seen Ronan date all ages."

"It's not the age," I said. "It's the principle of the matter. Atticus is like a father to her, and Ronan is his best friend. So that would be awkward."

"That's true. But it's a long tour. She's gorgeous. And if she has the hots for him..." Emily shrugged. "Anything can happen, I guess."

I felt like the truth was ready to explode out of me.

"What's that look?"

"What look?" I felt myself burning up.

She squinted. "You look like you know something..."

I cleared my throat. "What makes you say that?"

"Nicole, what the fuck is going on?"

Crap!

I let out the air I'd been holding. "You have to promise not to say anything."

She nodded eagerly. "Okay..."

"I saw them together earlier. Ronan and Kenzie. They didn't know I was in the back bedroom when they snuck onto the bus to be together for a few minutes while everyone was at sound check."

She covered her mouth. "Holy crap."

"I saw them kiss and overheard them talking. They've been seeing each other. It's serious and sounded like it's been happening for a while. He used the L word. Ronan said he wants to tell Atticus during the tour. But Kenzie was freaking out about it. She's been the one holding back. She wants to wait until after the tour."

Emily leaned in and whispered, "No one knows but you?"

"Pretty sure it's just me." I started to panic. "You can't tell Tristan."

"It's not my place to say anything to anyone. But *you're* keeping this from Atticus?"

"I don't know what to do. Do you think that's wrong? I need your advice."

"Shit." She blew out a long breath. "I usually have an answer for everything, but I don't know what the right thing is here."

"I wasn't supposed to find out. I feel like I should just try to forget and move on, let them tell him the way they want to. It's their right."

"But at the same time, that's pretty big news to be keeping from your man."

I pulled on my hair. "You would tell Tristan if you were in my position?"

She chewed on her lip. "You know what? As you know, when I first went on tour with the band, I was hiding a pretty damn big secret. I'd made the decision that I wasn't going to say anything to Tristan until the tour was over. I've never regretted that because he was able to at least get through the North American leg without that interruption. I made the call I felt was best for *him* at the time, not me. I'm thinking you know Atticus best, and if you think finding out will throw him off for the rest of the tour, you should wait."

I nodded. That made sense and gave me the justification I needed to keep quiet. "Thank you. When you put it that way, I feel better about holding back, for *his* sake."

"I'm certain Ronan and Kenzie will thank you, too." She blew a breath up into her hair. "Gosh, I feel bad for taunting Kenzie now. The poor girl is stressed about sneaking around as it is. And there she was, thinking I was about to blow her cover."

"She'd freak if she knew I heard them talking."

Emily chuckled. "Let's start a prayer chain now for Ronan's well-being once Atticus finds out. Do you think he'll go ballistic?"

I shook my head. "I hope he doesn't. I hope he's smart enough to realize that when two people are determined to be together, no one can stand in their way."

Chapter 36

ATTICUS

We'd just arrived in Minnesota, and the guys and I were chilling on the bus while Nicole and Emily took the rental car to get lunch for everyone.

Ronan had left his phone behind while he went to the bathroom. When it lit up with a text, I thought I was seeing things.

Kenzie: Just wanted to tell you that I love you.

That doesn't say Kenzie, does it? I blinked to even out my vision.

It *did* say Kenzie.

What? *Love?*

My *niece* loves Ronan?

What the fuck is going on?

I willed myself to calm down. Maybe it was a different Kenzie.

What were the chances of that, though? My hand shook as I grabbed the phone and turned the screen toward Tristan. "What the hell is this?"

Based on his stoic expression, whatever fuckery this was didn't come as a surprise to him.

"What the fuck is going on with Kenzie and Ronan?" I demanded.

"Take a breath."

Not even a denial. "You knew about this?" I seethed.

"He had to tell someone who wouldn't kill him."

Adrenaline coursed through my veins. "How could you keep this from me?"

"You're proving how well you would've taken it. You really wanted to get news like this in the middle of a tour?" He shook his head. "But honestly, I have no guilt about it because they're not doing anything wrong."

Ronan emerged from the bathroom.

"What the fuck are you doing with my niece?" I roared.

His face turned white. He held his hands out. "Okay... calm down."

"I won't calm down." I felt like I was about to hyper-ventilate. "You can have any woman in the world—why my niece, you prick?"

"Why *not* her? Do you have any idea how special she is?"

"Does she know how many women you've fucked around with?"

"If that was relevant, then Nicole shouldn't be with *you*, should she? None of us would be worthy of a good woman if we were judged by our past actions."

I rose and began to pace. "I knew there was some-thing weird going on. You've been acting strange for a while now."

"What do you mean?"

"You've messed around with zero groupies this entire tour. And even before that, you weren't as talkative as you normally are. I knew you were keeping something from me."

"So *not* sleeping around makes me suspect? Think about what you're saying. I haven't been with any groupies because I've been *loyal* to Kenzie." He paused. "I love her."

"Love?"

He nodded. "It's been going on for a while. It's not new."

I drew in my brows. "Since when?"

"Since Tristan's wedding."

Spit flew out of my mouth as I shouted, "You've been seeing my niece for months behind my back?"

"I get that you're not happy with this. No one is ever gonna be good enough for her in your eyes. But I'm your best friend. Do you really think I'd do this to you intentionally? Out of malice? Are you crazy?"

"He's got a point," Tristan chimed in.

I ignored him, waving my index finger at Ronan. "You kept it from me. Friends don't do that."

"Really? Just like you told Mimi the truth about you and Nicole getting divorced? Sometimes we keep things from the people we love to protect them."

I opened my mouth, but then snapped it shut. His last point left me without a comeback. "I need some air," I said as I left the bus.

Thankfully, the guys let me be. About five minutes passed before I saw my niece approaching across the parking lot.

"Uncle Atticus..."

"Yeah," I muttered.

"We need to talk."

"I'd say so..."

She placed her hands on her hips. "You need to listen to me."

I nodded once, letting her continue.

You're *way* too quick to blame Ronan for us being together when in fact it's *my* doing."

Rolling my eyes, I huffed. "I highly doubt that."

"I need you to hear me out."

"Alright." I crossed my arms.

"I pursued him. I've had a crush on Ronan basically since you started performing with him. For *years* now. Obviously, I was way too young back then to be dating him, but the crush never waned."

"A crush is fine, but—"

"You said you were gonna let me talk." She glared.

"Okay..." I murmured.

"After Tristan's wedding, almost everyone had gone back to their rooms. I'd just finished breaking down all of my equipment when I noticed Ronan hanging out by the water. So I went to join him." She looked away. "We had a long talk that night—about his abusive upbringing, his parents' alcoholism, my pain over losing my dad, my career aspirations. We stayed up *all night*. And I realized my physical attraction to him all these years was just the tip of the iceberg." She paused for a moment. "I asked him out that night. And you know what?" She chuckled. "He turned me down."

"He did?"

"Yes. He said as much as he'd enjoyed talking to me that night—more than anyone he'd ever opened up to before—he couldn't do that to you. I was devastated because I *really* liked him."

"But clearly the story didn't end there," I said.

"I *thought* that was the end of it, but then the following morning, we walked out of the hotel at the same time. I told him I hadn't been able to stop thinking about him. And he confessed to having thought about me all night, too. I didn't want to leave him. I knew in my heart that he felt the same way about me, but he was scared to hurt you. I took another chance. I dared him to come to the airport with me and travel to the East Coast for a couple of days."

I sighed. "Ronan has never been one to turn down a dare."

"Right. He told me that even if he followed me back east, it wouldn't change anything. He still couldn't pursue me. Yet he accepted the dare, and when we landed in New York, we spent a few days exploring the city together. He put me up in a hotel near Times Square—separate rooms. I was supposed to go back to Monksville at the end of it, but yet again, didn't want to leave him."

In retrospect, I remembered Ronan disappearing for a few days... "Well, he came back to California, because I remember seeing him a few days after the wedding."

She nodded. "He did, and that trip was totally platonic. He didn't try anything. We just had fun." Kenzie paused. "In the weeks after, though, we stayed in touch every day, talked on the phone late into the night. We just fell for each other more and more. I flew out to L.A. for a few days about a month later, and that's when things changed. I promise we weren't gonna keep it from you forever. We just didn't want to ruin your tour." She raised her chin. "But Uncle Atticus, this is not something you can change. We love each other."

As I stood there in silence, I knew she was right. There was nothing I could do.

"He's not perfect, but you love him, right?" she added. "You trust him. Why shouldn't I?"

"I don't have a good answer for that." I breathed in and out. "I just need to let this sink in for a while."

"That's fine...but please don't let this ruin the tour, or more importantly, your friendship."

"I've never let anything stop me from performing. This won't be any different."

"Okay..." she mumbled. She looked like she wanted to say something else, but then she didn't.

Nicole and Emily approached with the takeout just as Kenzie was leaving. While Emily entered the bus with the food, Nicole got a look at my face and turned to watch Kenzie walking away. She looked back over at me. "You know..."

What the fuck? Was I the only one who didn't know? "*You* know?"

Nicole blushed. "I accidentally found out a couple of days ago when I came back to the bus to take a nap instead of going to sound check. They didn't know I was there, but I saw them together briefly."

I ran a hand through my hair. "Jesus."

"It wasn't my place to tell you. And I didn't want to ruin the tour..."

"Why does everyone think I'm so damn weak? I performed after losing *you*. If I could do *that*, I can get through anything."

She placed her hand on my chest. "We've never been happier, right? You and Tristan are with the loves of your lives. Ronan deserves the same."

Rubbing my temples, I tried to calm myself. "He's never even had a girlfriend for as long as I've known him."

"Well, maybe that's all the more reason to believe this is the real thing. He's picky, and he has amazing taste, because he's chosen the best girl I know."

As much as I wanted to be enraged, it was impossible to stop two adults from being together if they really wanted to. I had to figure out a way to accept it. "Make no mistake, I will absolutely kill him if he hurts her. I don't care how close he and I are."

"I think he knows you well enough to understand that." She reached up on her tippy toes to kiss me on the cheek. "Remember once we had a conversation about people we trusted with our lives who weren't family? You asked me if there was anyone else besides you I trusted. There wasn't, but do you remember who you said was your *one* person?"

I nodded. "Ronan."

"Think about that. If you could trust him with your life, why can't you trust him with Kenzie's?"

Ronan suddenly emerged from the bus. "Can I interrupt?"

"Of course." Nicole pinched Ronan's cheek as she went into the bus.

A staredown ensued before Ronan broke the ice. "Should I have worn a helmet?"

"You're lucky I'm surrounded by people who care about you. They've managed to talk me down."

His eyes were sincere. "I'm sorry I kept this from you."

"It's not a good feeling when people you love and trust are hiding things from you." I paused. "But I understand why you didn't say anything right away."

"I love you, Atticus. You know that. But nothing you can say or do will stop me from loving Kenzie, too. She told me she tried to explain to you how things happened. This wasn't an overnight thing. I knew from the very beginning that I was taking a huge risk. But you should know better than anyone that when you love someone, circumstances don't change how you feel. I could've tried harder to stay away to make you comfortable, but I'd still love her, and she'd feel the same about me. I don't think you want either one of us to be miserable for your sake."

I stared up at the sky. "You're right. I don't. But as that girl's only father figure, it's my job to protect her. That means scrutinizing you, even if it hurts me."

He opened his arms. "Scrutinize away. I can take it."

"Look, I know you wear your heart on your sleeve. I *know* you're a good person. But that doesn't mean you're ready for a serious relationship, the kind I know my niece has always wanted. She's a romantic. Having lost the man who meant everything at a very young age, she can't afford to have her heart broken."

"I have no plans to break her heart," he assured me.

I eyed him a moment. "Do you think you're ready for a relationship when you haven't ever been in one?"

He raised his voice. "Did you not hear me say earlier that I'm in love with her? It doesn't matter if I was ready or not when we met, it happened. I fell in love with someone who appreciates my flaws and loves me for me, not who

I am to the rest of the world. Kenzie is the one, Atticus. I know it sounds strange to hear me say it because she's your niece. But she's also *my* love. I promise never to hurt her. I give you full permission to annihilate me if I do."

"You can bet on that."

He let out a long breath that showed me just how much this had been weighing on him. "Where do we stand now?"

"I'm cautiously watching."

"So you won't make things difficult for us?"

"I don't plan to."

He shook my shoulders as he beamed. "I appreciate that, man."

"I want to be happy for you, but it's gonna take some getting used to."

"I understand. Just the fact that you haven't kicked my ass yet is a huge win. I'll take it."

"Don't jinx yourself."

"Okay, Uncle Atticus." He flashed a wicked grin.

"If you appreciate your teeth, you won't repeat that."

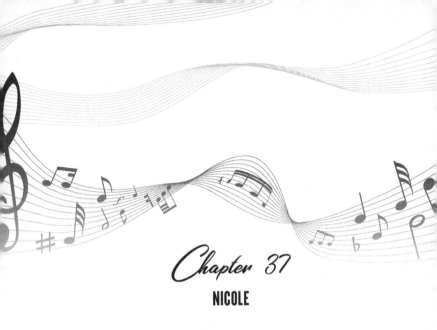

Chapter 37

NICOLE

The show went on as usual in Minnesota that night, with unsuspecting audience members blissfully unaware of the drama that had gone down earlier today. The fact that the guys were performing amazingly as ever together was a testament to their professionalism.

Now that I didn't have to hide their secret, I could feel fully thrilled about Ronan and Kenzie. It made me so happy that they no longer felt they had to hide. No one should have to live like that, especially since we're never guaranteed tomorrow.

To the audience, it might've seemed like just another concert, but little did they know how important this show was to *me*. This was the performance where I'd decided to set my gender-reveal plans in action.

Emily sat next to me in the front row.

"You know when you're doing it?" she asked.

"Yeah. At the point when they normally stop to talk to the audience."

She clapped excitedly.

I'd snuck in a rolled-up poster board with the gender announcement on it. I planned to hold it up so Atticus would see it. Most likely, he wouldn't notice at first, but I'd prepared Kenzie to take photos. There was also a videographer on staff tonight who'd be capturing the moment.

My anxiety grew as we got closer to the middle of the show. I was so tense, in fact, that I'd barely noticed all of the women screaming my husband's name. Normally I cringed every time. As always, there were women in the audience pulling the usual shit, like throwing their freaking bras and underwear toward the stage. But I'd vowed not to let any of it ruin my night. Instead, to calm myself, I swayed to the music and let it vibrate through my body, closing my eyes and enjoying every second. When the baby started kicking, it just added to the magic.

Rubbing my stomach, I spoke to our unborn child, "We've come a long way, baby."

When we finally got to the important time of the night, Atticus got up from his drum set. My stomach dropped. *Is he leaving?* Atticus went over to the front of the stage and said something to Tristan, who then handed him the mic and patted him on the back.

While the band often spoke to the audience during this middle part of the show, it was mostly Tristan and Ronan doing the talking while Atticus remained the elusive, mysterious drummer in the back. While he had a reputation for being the wildest one of the group, Atticus was usually the least vocal of the three. *Though not tonight, apparently.*

I sat on the edge of my seat, waiting to hear what he had to say.

As Atticus stood at the front of the stage, the crowd went wild.

Emily spoke in my ear, "What the hell is going on?"

"I have no idea."

He finally spoke into the mic. "Good evening."

Screams erupted again at the mere sound of his voice. It took several seconds for the noise to quiet enough for him to continue.

"I want to thank you all for coming out tonight. Minneapolis is always one of my favorite cities to perform in." He took a deep breath in. "There's someone in the audience tonight I want to tell you about." Atticus smiled before his eyes found mine. "You know me as Atticus Marchetti, the drummer for Delirious Jones. Because of you, I've had an amazing career, and I've felt the love, believe me."

He began to pace. "For years, I had a reputation as this wild, single, out-of-control rockstar. That's the part of me the tabloids have shown you. But that guy was never who I am." He paused. "Before I was famous, I was Nicole Marchetti's husband. She was the love of my life from a very young age. To this day, being her husband was the role I'm most proud of."

A series of *awws* rang out in the audience.

"Most of you are probably surprised to hear I was ever married. Nicole and I...we lost our way around the time my career started taking off. We made mistakes. Mostly me. I'd been in love with her since I was a teenager, but I let the best thing that ever happened to me go. And ever since that day, I've hoped the universe would somehow bring us back together."

He looked down at me again.

"In the time Nicole and I were apart, a lot happened in my life. I had a son." As a few audible gasps could be heard, Atticus continued. "This is the first time I've ever spoken publicly about being a dad. For my son's privacy, I've been okay with that. But tonight I feel like telling you about him because I'm so damn proud of my precious little boy who has to live a good chunk of his life away from his father. He's almost three years old and enjoys a private life with his mother in New York. Even though I don't deserve him, I have the sweetest, most forgiving soul for a child."

Atticus closed his eyes briefly. "Even with that gift, these past few years, I've still felt like a huge part of my life was missing. And that missing piece was my Nicole. She was, and is the love of my life. And thanks to an angel named Mimi, Nicole and I had the opportunity to reconnect again last year. Not only is Nicole in the audience right now, so is our baby she's carrying."

As the audience reacted to that news with mostly cheers, my heart pitter-pattered.

"I love them both more than words or music could ever express," Atticus went on to say. "I'm just so freaking happy, and I wanted you all to know about it. Because if you've been a fan of the band for any amount of time, you've seen me at my worst, even if you didn't realize it." He smiled. "This is me at my best. I can honestly say I've never been happier."

He climbed down from the stage, coming over to where I was standing in the front row. I covered my mouth in disbelief.

"I wasn't sure if I was gonna do this tonight, but I can't wait any longer." He breathed into the mic. "Nicole, being your husband was the greatest honor of my life. The only thing greater is getting to be the father of your baby. Of *our* baby. I love you so much. And even though I never stopped calling you my wife, I hope you'll give me the honor of making it official again." He got down on one knee and opened a ring box, revealing a diamond ring even bigger than the one he'd given me years back to replace the original. "Please say you'll marry me...again. *Forever*."

"Yes!" I jumped up and down and wrapped my arms around him. "I can't believe you did this."

As a continuous symphony of cheers erupted all around us, and amid the flashes of many cameras, he spoke into the mic again. "She said yes, by the way, for the people in the back!"

Then he put the microphone in front of me. "Anything you wanna say, baby?"

This wasn't how I'd envisioned it, but I couldn't pass up my chance. I spoke into the mic but looked straight at him. "It's a girl."

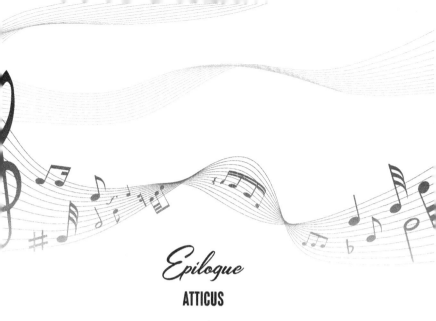

Epilogue

ATTICUS

The envelope had just arrived at our house in Monksville. Doug had overnighted us a copy of the magazine. We were the cover story this month for one of the biggest music periodicals, except by *we*, I don't mean just us guys. It was all six of us.

The title on the cover read, *Deliriously in Love: The women behind the men of Delirious Jones*

After my very public proposal during the tour last year, the press had gone crazy trying to learn more about Nicole. They also soon got wind of Kenzie's relationship with Ronan. And suddenly, the women in our lives became prime press targets.

We'd figured rather than deal with the press stalking us all the time, we'd beat them to the punch. Our manager had struck a deal with the magazine for this feature to set the record straight and hopefully give us some semblance of privacy after. Even if it didn't work, it was worth a shot.

I looked down at the cover photo, which had been taken by a world-famous photographer. It had been shot a year ago, and Nicole was eight months pregnant at the time, wearing a form-fitting white dress that showcased her navel popping out. We'd done a separate pregnancy shoot, but I'd always cherish this snapshot in time of one of the happiest periods of my life. In the photo, the three guys were seated, Tristan in the middle, with Ronan and me on either side of him. Off to the left, Nicole was lying on the ground by my feet, her long, raven hair wild and beautiful as she placed her hand above her stomach. Emily, who had also been visibly pregnant at the time, chose not to have her stomach on display, so she was standing behind Tristan with her arms around his neck, her long brown hair cascading over his chest. And to the right was Ronan with a laughing Kenzie on his lap.

I brought the magazine to the kitchen to show my wife. Well, she still wasn't *legally* my wife. The huge wedding we were planning was set to take place later this year. We wanted to be settled first and had just moved.

"Look what arrived this morning." I put the magazine on the counter.

"Oh my gosh." She smiled as she looked down at the cover. "I do *not* miss being that pregnant, but it came out so good. It seems like forever since we posed for that."

I kissed her neck. "You were the sexiest pregnant woman alive."

"I'd much rather have her on my back."

I kissed the top of our baby girl's head. Little Adele was asleep in the carrier Nicole had strapped to her back. Carrying her like this was the only way Nicole could get anything done on days that Adele wouldn't go down for her nap.

We had moved to Monksville at the end of May and planned to permanently relocate to New York City, keeping this house for occasional weekends and summers. We were in the process of closing on an Upper West Side brownstone.

Today was the first time we'd have everyone over at the Monksville house. It was a beautiful June day and our first official party here, not only to celebrate the article, but Tristan had said he had some sort of announcement. That had certainly piqued my curiosity; I had no clue what it could be about. Delirious Jones had already decided to take a year off, so I couldn't imagine that it had anything to do with the band. We were just beginning that much-needed break now, and I was loving every second of it.

Nicole cut up some vegetables. "Tristan and Emily flew in last night, right?"

"Yeah, they're at an Airbnb right down the street."

They'd taken their first flight from L.A. with their nine-month-old son, Levi. Ronan was also here, crashing at Tina's with Kenzie, who'd given up her apartment here a while ago to follow Ronan wherever he happened to be. She was mostly doing freelance photography now. Those two couldn't stand to be away from each other. I still couldn't quite grasp the thought of him sleeping in my niece's childhood bedroom with her tonight, but here we were. I'd try not to think about that too hard.

"You have any idea what Tristan's news could be?" Nicole asked as she arranged some olives on a charcuterie board.

"I have *no* freaking clue. Like, *none*."

"Should be interesting. It can't be that Emily's pregnant again. She had Levi less than a year ago. So I hope not, for her sake."

I popped a block of cheese into my mouth. "You don't think Tristan's trying to get his wife pregnant again like I am?"

She slapped my hand. "You'd better slow down, buddy."

"With the baby talk or the cheese?"

"Both." She laughed.

"You know I'm kidding," I said, stealing a second cube of cheese.

While I most definitely wanted another child with Nicole, we had our hands full for the time being with our almost-one-year-old, who only recently had started sleeping through the night. Our daughter was everything I'd dreamed she'd be: healthy, happy, and looking just like Nicole. Every time I saw her, I thought about how everything her mother and I had gone through had to have happened just as it did in order for Adele to be here now. I no longer had any regrets about the tough times Nicole and I had experienced. Adele made it all worth it.

The best part of today was that Giselle and David would be coming to the party with Christian and leaving him here while they went on vacation for a week. It would be my first time having my son at the Monksville house for any length of time. Since he'd last been here, I'd decorated his room with his favorite superheroes, and I couldn't wait to surprise him. At four years old, he was turning into such a little man.

When someone rang the doorbell, I went to let them in. I peeked through the peephole to find Ronan and Kenzie standing there. She held a platter of some kind.

Ronan wore a shit-eating grin. "Hope we're not too early," he said when I opened the door.

"Your ass is *always* early, so I'm used to it." He knew it annoyed me.

My niece reached up to kiss me on the cheek. "I want to help Nicole anyway." She walked past me toward the kitchen.

"What's Tristan's announcement all about?" I asked. If Ronan knew anything, he'd spill.

"I might have an idea, but I'm not allowed to say anything until he gets here."

I narrowed my eyes. "Shady."

He smirked. "You'll be happy with it."

"Well, I'll find out soon enough, I guess. He just texted that they're on their way. Their Airbnb is right down the road."

Ronan lowered his voice. "Hey, since things are gonna get a little chaotic here soon, you think I can talk to you alone really quick?"

I arched my brow. "What's the big secret?"

"Let's go out back for a second."

Oh my freaking word. Did he knock up my niece?

Technically, if they were going to stay together, that couldn't be avoided forever. And I had to say, Ronan had been a solid partner to her. He'd even cut down on smoking weed because she wasn't crazy about it. But mostly I saw how much he made her smile. I remembered a time, especially right after her dad died, that making Kenzie smile wasn't an easy feat. She'd never smiled more since getting together with Ronan.

"Follow me," I told him. I went to the kitchen, grabbing a couple of beers from the fridge. I kissed Nicole on the cheek. "Do you need me for anything yet?"

"Everything's under control until you have to start cooking the meat." She winked.

"Ronan and I are gonna take these out back. I'll fire up the grill in a bit."

He followed me to the backyard. We took seats across from each other at the outdoor table. Ronan chewed on his lip, seeming tense.

I narrowed my eyes. "What's up, man?"

He rubbed his palms on his pants. "You know how I feel about Kenzie. I've explained that to you in the past."

I nodded once. "Yes, I do."

"Well, my feelings for her have only gotten stronger since then."

I inhaled. "Okay..."

"I'm gonna ask her to marry me on our trip." He licked his lips. "And I want your permission. I've already cleared it with Tina, but your approval is just as important to me."

Wow. For some reason, I hadn't seen it coming. I wasn't sure whether to feel relief that she wasn't pregnant or surprise over this news. I stared at him blankly for a moment.

"Okay. Your silence is freaking me out." He laughed nervously and took a long sip of his beer.

"I'm just soaking in this moment," I assured him as I circled my finger over the top of my bottle. "For one thing, you're my best friend, and you're getting married.

That's huge in and of itself. But also my niece, who's like my daughter, is getting married...to you. So that's a lot to grasp in just a few seconds."

Ronan took another sip. "Getting married *assuming* she says yes."

I shook my head. "I can say for certain, Ronan, you're good where that's concerned. She's crazy about you." I smiled. "Mostly I'm speechless—and touched—that you asked for *my* permission. I'm honored to have that role in Kenzie's life. I know Brian is smiling down right now because I have his back. But he's especially happy because the man his daughter is going to marry is *you*. You're a good egg, Ronan. You're the real deal, truly the best and most genuine man I know. And you've proven over the last several months just how serious you are about *my* little princess." I sighed. "So the answer is yes. You have my permission. And congratulations, man."

We stood and hugged.

He spoke into my ear, "I promise not to call you *dad*."

"Do it if you want your balls cut off," I replied warmly.

"Ouch." He cackled.

I looked over my shoulder to make sure no one had crept up behind us. "When is this proposal gonna happen?"

"Well, like I said, we're going on a trip. So sometime while we're away. Not sure yet which day it's gonna be."

"Where are you guys going again?"

"I'm gonna wait until Kenzie's around to tell you because it's pretty exciting news."

"What the heck, man? All these freaking secrets today. My heart can't take it."

"*Your* heart? My nerves have been shot all morning over asking your permission."

I smiled and gripped his shoulder. We'd come a long way since his phone blew their cover on the tour. Given my initial reaction to them being together, I guessed I couldn't blame him for being nervous.

Ronan and I went inside to find that Tristan and Emily had arrived with baby Levi, who was asleep in his carrier.

Tristan looked us over. "What were you two up to?"

"Just outside talking shit about you," I taunted.

He chuckled. "Nothing new, then."

"Did you see the magazine?" I slid it in front of them on the counter.

Nicole chuckled. "You can't see much behind my eight-months-pregnant stomach."

"It came out amazing," Emily marveled. "This feels like so long ago now."

We skimmed through the article to make sure there were no surprises. They'd pretty much taken our answers word for word, which was rare. But of course, they'd chosen to emphasize the most salacious parts of our love stories. They'd focused on Tristan and Emily's age gap, Nicole's and my second-chance romance after me having a baby with another woman, and the fact that Kenzie was my niece. But if that gave people enough juice to lay off us for a while, it'd be worth it.

Someone else was at the door, so I went to answer it and found Christian lifting his arms toward me. "Daddy!"

I bent to lift him into the air and spun him around. "I missed you so much, Bubba."

Bubba had been my nickname for him ever since he was tiny, and it stuck. There was nothing like burying my nose in his hair and smelling him after we'd been apart.

"I missed you, too," he said in his sweet little voice.

"Thanks for having us." Giselle smiled, with David standing behind her.

"Of course. I'm so glad you have a little time to hang out before you leave for your trip."

I clasped hands with David. "Good to see you, man."

"Good to see you, too. Where can I get a beer?"

"Come right this way."

They followed me into the kitchen as I continued to carry my son.

"Where's my favorite?" David teased.

"I'm right here!" Nicole turned to hug him, careful not to get her food-covered hands on his clothes.

It was a running joke that Nicole and David would run away together someday. They got along so well. I was really proud of the dynamic we'd developed as coparents since Nicole and I had moved to New York. Nicole had gotten to know Giselle and David better, and while it wasn't a hundred-percent easy for her, she was finding her stride. I could honestly say the four of us were friends. Lord knows, getting along made Christian's life a hell of a lot easier. David and Giselle had gotten married in a small, civil ceremony recently. The trip they were taking was their delayed honeymoon to Puerto Rico.

"Nickel!" my son shouted at Nicole.

Christian used to mispronounce Nicole's name like the coin, and now he did it on purpose to be funny because we'd corrected him so much.

She kissed him on the cheek. "Penny! I'm so excited you're here."

Nickel and penny. Even if it seemed dumb, he got a kick out of it. It didn't take much to amuse my sweet kid.

"Who else are we waiting on?" Emily asked as she arranged some fruit.

Nicole poured Sprite into the punch bowl. "My mom is in town. She's coming in a few and then Tina and the boys. That's it."

"I'd better go start the grill now," I said. "By the time the rest of them get here, we can start eating." I put my son down. "Actually, I want to show my little guy something first. I have a surprise for you, Bubba."

He looked up at me and smiled. "A surprise?"

"Yup. Come on. Let's go."

Almost everyone followed us to Christian's room to see his reaction.

His eyes filled with wonder as he got a look at what I'd done. He squealed. "I love it, Daddy!"

Christian explored his newly decorated bedroom, taking in the life-sized superheroes-in-action poses stuck to his walls. Nicole had found a new Marvel comforter to match. Everyone laughed as Christian ran from wall to wall in excitement. It warmed my heart that my son wasn't spoiled. He had no idea his father was a millionaire, and he appreciated every little thing anyone gave him, big or small.

Giselle appeared by my side. "Thank you for doing this for him."

I turned to her. "Thank *you* for taking such good care of him. I want him to feel comfortable here. I can't compete with Mommy's place. It's not easy for him to be away from you. He misses you so much. Just hoping this takes the edge off a little."

After the novelty of Christian's room wore off, everyone dispersed, and I went outside to start grilling the food.

A little while later, Nicole's mom arrived, along with my sister and nephews.

After two straight hours of grilling, I was the last to enjoy a plate of food. Everyone else had moved on to dessert.

I'd just gotten up to serve myself a piece of the delicious coconut cake Nicole's mom had made when Tristan clanked a spoon against his beer bottle.

"Could I kindly have everyone's attention, please?"

About damn time for this announcement he'd been teasing. I put down the knife and opted to cut a slice after Tristan spoke.

He cleared his throat and repeated, "May I have your attention?"

When everything went quiet, he began to speak.

"We're at the beginning of an exciting year off for Delirious Jones, one that has been hard-earned and a long time coming. Now that our lives look a bit different, we have to prioritize what's important. This year will go by fast. And when the group reconvenes, things will be different than before. That might mean shorter tours or even no tours, depending on what we collectively decide. For the past several years, we've been busting our asses, and we deserve to slow down a bit and enjoy the most important parts of our lives: our families and loved ones."

He paused. I still had no idea where this was going.

"One of the biggest complications we've faced has been the bicoastal nature of our group. While Ronan and I have been firmly based in L.A. when we aren't touring, Atticus has had to divide his time between L.A. and New York to make things work for his family. He's recently made the smart move to relocate to New York, which means he'll have to travel out to L.A. a fair amount for recordings and other band business." He pointed his thumb over at Ronan. "This guy and I have discussed it, and we feel it will be in the band's best interest...if we also both relocate to New York."

I heard a collective series of gasps. One of them probably came from me.

Holy crap. Definitely hadn't seen this coming.

Tristan smiled. "Emily and I are not only here visiting, we're house hunting."

"Are you serious?" I finally managed to say.

He nodded. "Moving our operations to the East Coast will make things easier for everyone." He turned to Ronan. "I'll let Ronan speak for himself regarding his plans, though."

Ronan stood and cleared his throat as Kenzie blew him a kiss. "As you know, Kenzie and I will be taking a trip this year, but what we haven't told you is that we'll be traveling around the country in a van—and living in it. My girl has always wanted to experience more of America, and what better way to do that than together? We also plan to film a lot of it, documentary style." He smiled over at her. "Don't worry. It's a damn nice van with many amenities. But after we come back at the end of the year, we, too, will be moving to New York, not only to be closer to Tina and the boys, but to you guys."

My eyes met Tristan's. I knew him like the back of my hand, and I knew he loved L.A. He was making this sacrifice for *me*, even if he'd made it sound like an easy choice for the band. His doing this made it easy for Ronan to follow suit, which was a good move for him, especially since Kenzie didn't want to live in L.A., away from her family long term. My man was sacrificing his life as he knew it for his two best friends. And I loved him for it.

"Well, this was unexpected," I told him as I approached.

"I know. But it'll be great."

I put my hand on his shoulder. "You're really okay with this?"

He nodded.

I pulled him into a hug. "I love you, man."

"I love you, too." He patted my back. "Don't forget—it all started here on the East Coast. Why not end it here, too?"

～

After everyone left that night, I turned on the electric fireplace for Nicole and me so we could decompress after the party. Christian was snug like a bug in a rug in his new bedding, and Nicole had managed to get Adele down after a feeding.

It was one of those rare moments of peace that you never took for granted as a parent.

"Well, today was certainly chock full of excitement." She kicked her feet up on my knee.

Leaning my head back against the couch, I sighed. "I can't believe how well everything is coming together. I feel so damn blessed."

"Me, too. Emily is really excited about moving here. I was glad to hear that because I know she liked her marketing job. But apparently, she has some leads here that seem promising."

I shook my head. "I still can't believe he made that decision. He's making it seem easy, but I know it was a sacrifice."

"You're blessed to have true friends, you know. We both are."

"Yeah, they're family at this point."

She smiled. "I agree."

I noticed Nicole was holding an envelope. "What's that?"

"Well, you're never gonna believe this..." Her mouth curved into a smile. "It's a letter from Mimi."

My eyes widened. "What?"

She handed it to me. "Look at the front."

To be given to Nicole and Atticus after I pass away, was written in cursive.

"Where did this come from?"

"My mom gave it to me before she left tonight. You know how she stayed at Mimi's to clean up after the funeral, even after we left?"

"Yeah?"

"Well, Mimi left my mother all of her jewelry. Mom didn't actually open the jewelry box to go through it until the other day. And this letter was inside."

"What do you think it is?" I asked.

She shook her head. "I have no idea."

"Let's see. Open it," I urged.

Nicole took a deep breath and removed the letter from the envelope.

Dearest Nicole and Atticus,

If you're reading this letter, it's because I am no longer here. It's being dictated to Fiona, who is assisting me with writing it as my penmanship is not what it used to be. I've instructed her to leave it with my jewelry for safekeeping.

I want you both to know that I promise to watch over you, if that is at all possible from wherever I am now.

I am forever indebted to you both for coming together to spend those two weeks with me earlier this year. I know that wasn't easy for you.

You had your reasons for lying to me. I imagine you didn't want to hurt me by admitting the truth. But I am stronger than you think. Or I was while I was alive. (I keep forgetting I'm supposed to be dead as I write this. Ha!)

What does pain me, however, is knowing that two people I love very much had lost their way. I don't know what happened, but it had to have been something terrible to rip two people who were meant to be together apart.

My dears, I may have been old, but I wasn't completely deaf. The whispers. The not-so-quiet arguments. The strange people turning up at my door. If I didn't know better, I would've thought I'd died and woke up in an episode of As the World Turns. *(That show was before your time. But it was a soap opera I used to like to watch.) Both of you need to promise never to go into acting, because you're terrible at it.*

I never told you I knew because I wanted to hear it from you. After all, if you'd gone through all that trouble to hide your separation from me, I needed to give you some credit for that. As you know, I tried to hint at my suspicions, but you chose not to tell me what was going on. That's okay. It was none of my business.

Nicole, anytime you came to visit for the past few years, I could see something very wrong in your eyes. They'd lost the light they always had. Any time I asked about Atticus, you wouldn't even look at me. I worried that it had to do with your marriage, even if you insisted Atticus was merely on tour.

And, Atticus, my boy, it was so very unlike you not to visit me for so long. Not even on Christmas? I'd long suspected there was more to it than your career, which surely allowed more breaks than you let on. I hold none of this against you, as I imagine the pain of whatever you two have been going through superseded all feelings of obligation.

Despite not understanding everything, I felt in my heart that true love would always prevail. I wanted to see how you would handle it if I re-

quested that you both stay with me. I hope the time together helped you realize that not all was lost. That maybe someday you can find your way back to each other.

I'm sorry if it's jarring to realize you didn't hide things as well as you thought. Most of all, I'm sorry you two have experienced the misery of being apart from the person you love. I could very much see that you both still love each other.

All I can say is, you must have loved me very much to go through all of that just so I didn't have to feel a fraction of the hurt you did. Thank you for giving me the gift of getting to see two of my favorite people together again for what I believe was probably the last time.

I love you both so very much.

By the way, no one ever said love was easy. Just because you hit some roadblocks doesn't mean the road is closed forever. I hope it doesn't take you a lifetime to figure that out. When you get to be my age, all you have are the memories of the people you loved. Material things don't matter. Nothing else matters.

I will end this letter by telling you I had a very vivid dream last night. I've dreamed about your baby before, and it happened again. I mentioned this once to Atticus, who seemed uncomfortable when I brought it up. But it's been a recurring dream since then. In the past, I hadn't been able to make out whether it was a boy or a girl. But this time she told me she was a girl—black hair and looks just like my Nicole. But funny thing, she said her name was Adele, and I argued with her. "That's not your name. That's my name!" I told her.

Then she told me it was okay to come home, that she'd watch over you. I know it was just a dream, but it gave me some solace anyway.

Dreams are funny.

So is life.

Till we meet again, my darlings.

Love, Mimi

P.S.: Don't hate me. The chicken and dumplings were horrible.

Did you Miss Tristan and Emily's story?
The Rocker's Muse is Available Now!

Other Books by
PENELOPE WARD

The Rocker's Muse
The Drummer's Heart
The Rocker's Muse
The Surrogate
I Could Never
Toe the Line
RoomHate
Moody
The Assignment
The Aristocrat
The Crush
The Anti-Boyfriend
Just One Year
The Day He Came Back
When August Ends
Love Online
Gentleman Nine
Drunk Dial
Mack Daddy
Stepbrother Dearest
Neighbor Dearest
Sins of Sevin
Jake Undone (Jake #1)
My Skylar (Jake #2)
Jake Understood (Jake #3)
Gemini

Acknowledgements

I always have to first thank my amazing readers from all over the world who continue to read and talk about my books. Your support and encouragement through the years is my reason for continuing this journey. And to all of the book bloggers/bookstagrammers/influencers who work to support me book after book, please know how much I appreciate you.

To Vi – Where would I be without you? You're the best friend and partner in crime I could ask for. Until our brains give up on us, we will continue to make magic.

To Julie – Cheers to a decade-plus of friendship, great food conversations, and Fire Island memories.

To Luna – Thank you for your love and support every day and for our cherished Christmas get togethers. I'm lucky to have you as my earliest reader, but most of all as my friend.

To Erika – Thank you for your love, friendship, summer visit, and Great Wolf Lodge bar time—one of my favorite moments of the year. It will always be an E thing.

To Cheri –Thanks for being part of my tribe and for always looking out and never forgetting a Wednesday. I'm so happy to get to see you more than once this year!

To Darlene –You spoil me like no one else. I am very fortunate to have you as a friend—and sometimes signing assistant. Thanks for being literally the sweetest.

To my Facebook reader group, Penelope's Peeps – I adore you all. You are my home and favorite place to be.

To my agent Kimberly Brower –Thank you for working hard to get my books into the hands of readers around the world.

To my editor Jessica Royer Ocken – It's always a pleasure working with you. I look forward to many more partnerships to come.

To Elaine of Allusion Book Formatting and Publishing – Thank you for being the best proofreader, formatter, and friend a girl could ask for.

To Julia Griffis of The Romance Bibliophile – Your eagle eye is amazing. Thank you for being so wonderful to work with.

To my assistant Brooke – Thank you for hard work in handling all of the things Vi and I can't seem to ever get to. We appreciate you so much!

To Kylie and Jo at Give Me Books – You guys are truly the best out there! Thank you for your tireless promotional work. I would be lost without you.

To Letitia Hasser of RBA Designs – My awesome cover designer. Thank you for always working with me until the finished product exactly perfect.

To my husband – Thank you for always taking on so much more than you should have to so that I am able to write. I love you so much.

To the best parents in the world – I'm so lucky to have you! Thank you for everything you have ever done for me and for always being there.

Last but not least, to my daughter and son – Mommy loves you. You are my motivation and inspiration!

About the Author

Penelope Ward is a *New York Times, USA Today* and *#1 Wall Street Journal* bestselling author.

She grew up in Boston with five older brothers and spent most of her twenties as a television news anchor. Penelope resides in Rhode Island with her husband, son and beautiful daughter with autism.

With millions of books sold, she is a 21-time *New York Times* bestseller and the author of over forty novels.

Penelope's books have been translated into over a dozen languages and can be found in bookstores around the world.

Subscribe to Penelope's newsletter here.
http://bit.ly/1X725rj

SOCIAL MEDIA LINKS:

Facebook
www.facebook.com/penelopewardauthor

Facebook Private Fan Group
www.facebook.com/groups/PenelopesPeeps/

Instagram
@penelopewardauthor

TikTok
www.tiktok.com/@penelopewardofficial

Twitter
twitter.com/PenelopeAuthor